A NOSE *for* DEATH

To Maureen,

*So wonderful to
reconnect after so
many years!*

A NOSE *for* DEATH

GLYNIS WHITING

all the best,

Glynis

2013

thistledown press

Thistledown Press Ltd.
118 - 20th Street West
Saskatoon, Saskatchewan, S7M 0W6
www.thistledownpress.com

Library and Archives Canada Cataloguing in Publication

Whiting, Glynis
A nose for death / Glynis Whiting.

Issued also in electronic format.
ISBN 978-1-927068-40-3
I. Title.
PS8645.H5655N68 2013   C813'.6   C2013-900963-9

Cover photograph by Ken Hewlett
Cover and book design by Jackie Forrie
Printed and bound in Canada

All the characters in this book are fictitious, and any resemblance to actual persons, living or dead, is purely coincidental

Canada Council for the Arts   Conseil des Arts du Canada   SASKATCHEWAN ARTS BOARD   Canadian Heritage   Patrimoine canadien

Thistledown Press gratefully acknowledges the financial assistance of the Canada Council for the Arts, the Saskatchewan Arts Board, and the Government of Canada through the Canada Book Fund for its publishing program.

ACKNOWLEDGEMENTS

This novel is only publishable because of the support and encouragement of several dear and clever souls; if my friend and mentor Alan Twigg and his lovely wife Tara hadn't provided excellent feedback and convinced me to keep going and if that hadn't led to the Vancouver Mayor's Award for Emerging Literary Artist; if my daughter Amour Shukster hadn't eliminated the first thick layer of typos; if I hadn't had the camaraderie of the Cocktail Duck Writers with whom I regularly hole-up so that we can "retreat to move forward", as well as the enthusiastic feedback of librarian-with-a-passion and cousin Janine Jevne, and writer Andrew Campbell; and if not for the shelter of the Nicola River retreat provided by Randy and Jeff. My gratitude to all of you knows no end.

I also owe thanks to my editor Michael Kenyon, and the experts who tethered my imaginings to reality. Staff-Sergeant Kevin Morton provided feedback as both a member of the RCMP and an avid reader. Dr. John Butt confirmed that my chosen "cause of death" could be fatal and Provincial Court Judge Joe Galati gave me guidance about the judicial system in British Columbia circa 1979. Any errors, gaping or minor, are mine alone. My family, too, deserves my everlasting gratitude. My children, Amour, Shamus, and Kelsey, grew up to the sound of typewriter keys clicking, then my mutterings when computers wouldn't cooperate, and they never complained when dinner was delayed because I had one more page to finish. Then there is Ken Hewlett, my husband and best friend, who picks me up when I'm down, fills the house with soothing music, and was the very first to read *A Nose for Death*.

In memory of Glenys Nora Robb, my mom,
who believed in the powers of creativity, laughter, and books.

Smells detonate softly in our memory like poignant land mines, hidden under the weedy mass of many years and experiences. Hit a tripwire of smell, and memories explode all at once.
— Diane Ackerman, *A Natural History of the Senses*, 1990

The Impostor Syndrome, in which competent people find it impossible to believe in their own competence, can be viewed as complementary to the Dunning–Kruger effect, in which incompetent people find it impossible to believe in their own incompetence.
— Wikipedia, 2012

THE REUNION

Chapter One

THE DAY THE INVITATION ARRIVED JOAN chose to ignore it. Oh, she opened it all right. Felt the thick embossed letters on linen paper, read the greeting requesting her presence at the Madden High thirtieth reunion. Then she tossed it on the hall table among the real estate, pizza, and dry cleaning fliers. Whoever had sent it hadn't bothered to check the records. If they had, she wouldn't have been on the invitation list. She wouldn't tolerate that kind of carelessness in herself. Exhausted from too many nights at work, she had no patience for it in others.

It was several weeks before she could finally hang up her smock and emerge from the lab before dark. The front office was abuzz with news of the award. It wasn't everyday that Constellation Ltd. received the industry's highest honour for developing a new food flavour. Even the receptionist, Rosy, was giddy with pride, handing out cake and pouring champagne in the middle of the afternoon. Joan, though, just felt like going home and crawling under the covers. It was all too much. She was the one who had gone through a thousand compounds in the past year, testing and re-testing until she'd narrowed it down to just the right combination of flavours: a satisfying licorice, a subtle hint of spearmint with a whiff of peppermint, and a bare trace of wintergreen. She'd spent months consulting on texture and colour, insisting on rigorous international product testing of the "adults only" chewing gum. If they could nail a flavour that appealed to both the North American and Asian markets, they'd have a shot in the highly competitive world market.

Joan had two remarkable gifts. The first was a memory that helped her instantly identify over half of the six-thousand scents in the Constellation Ltd. inventory. The other was an ability to reach deep into the web of human emotions with her creations by engaging her keen senses. Smell was her most precious but each was a valuable tool: taste, for knowing how much sour would be too much or if another dash of salt would be perfect; touch to feel velvet on the lips, heat on the tongue; and sound, to hear a musical crunch or the delicate smacking of lips. She'd been on the ground in Japan, Korea, and Hong Kong to witness individual reactions, watching for the slightest tilt of the head, drop of an eyelid, shift in the body to tell her just what test subjects were feeling. Finally, after living in airports and out of suitcases for six months, she had presented Hint of Midnight gum. It was her baby. The award had her name on it. Dr. Joan Parker was an international celebrity in the cutthroat world of food flavour and aroma design.

Today she didn't feel like any sort of star. The dark service elevator was never her first choice of departure from the lab. It was infused with the sickly sweet smell of pineapple that had leaked from a cracked beaker months ago. But this route allowed her to bypass the Marketing Department. She couldn't face another "Way to go, girl!" Why did middle-aged women cling to Valley Girl lingo? It was like breathing stale summer air. The thought of being forced into water-cooler chat was more than she could stomach. Research chemists have never been hailed as social extroverts, and in Joan's case, it was true. The socializing that had been required to get the product launched had sapped her energy more than the actual work to develop Hint of Midnight.

Just when she thought she had escaped detection, Ted Harman caught up with her in the parking lot. Her boss was the high priest of the team approach.

"Not staying for champagne?"

She tucked her blunt-cut brown hair behind her ears and braced herself for an argument. "I have to get back here early tomorrow."

He studied her for several long seconds. "No, you don't." He wasn't smiling.

Joan waited.

"Take some time off. You deserve it. Tony can clean up the paperwork. I don't want to see your face around here for at least two weeks."

Anyone else would have been thrilled, but Ted had hit her most delicate nerve. She was afraid to go away. Deep in the marrow of her tired bones, she was afraid she'd lose everything, that she'd be found out. Despite her years of hard work and the accolades heaped upon her, she didn't believe she deserved success. She felt like an imposter.

"I'm fine, Ted. A good night's sleep, that's all I need." She unlocked her car door. Before she could slide in, though, he clasped her shoulder, turned her to face him, and solemnly looked her in the eye.

"No, Joan. Two weeks, minimum. Spring break." There was something else. Something she couldn't put her finger on. "I can't afford to have you crash and burn."

"And . . . ?" She knew that there was more. He paused then continued uncomfortably.

"Some of the staff interprets your distance as aloofness. It's affecting morale."

Her jaw dropped but she couldn't find words to protest.

Ted added, "I know that's not it. We all know you care, but it will help all around if you recharge." He held open the door to her Honda hybrid and she climbed in without a word.

When she arrived home, Mort was in the condo kitchen packing his gourmet-cooking utensils.

"Baby, you look like crap," he said with a smile.

"Thanks a lot." She poured herself a glass of red wine from the kitchen stash and studied him. "Why do you come in here when I'm out?"

"I have two forks and a spatula in my apartment. How am I supposed to cook anything?" He looked at her with those big, droopy eyes. He had aged handsomely.

"Take what you want. It's mostly yours. You bring anything to eat? I'm starving."

Mort could create a meal out of nothing. Necessity had been his mentor. When they had first moved in together a dozen years ago, they had both been struggling. They were thrilled to have snagged a little cottage with creaking floors and a stove with three functioning burners. Joan was finishing her dissertation and working as a lab assistant for a multi-national food supplier. She had no time to eat, let alone cook. Mort had just landed a job as produce manager with a local Grocery Cart food store and would haul home over-ripe fruits and vegetables at the end of the day, often exotic foods that the middle-class customers were wary of buying. Every evening their cottage welcomed her with the spicy aromas of a busy, happy kitchen. Now Mort was general manager for the western region and being groomed as V.P. of Human Resources for the entire Grocery Cart chain. Since he moved out four months ago, Joan had been busy with the Hint of Midnight project, and the kitchen now smelled of ripe garbage.

Mort's other preoccupation, besides food, was figuring out what made people tick. After a dozen weekend workshops, he fancied himself an amateur psychologist. "By the way, Joan. What's this?" He picked up the gold-trimmed reunion invitation from the kitchen counter and waved it at her. "Are you going?"

"Someone sent it by mistake. Or as a joke." As she spoke she grabbed it from him and nervously folded the invitation into a tiny square.

"You don't know that." He didn't take his eyes off her.

"If they wanted me there they would have invited me to the tenth reunion or the twentieth. No, someone's made a mistake. That or they want money for their alumni fund. They probably saw my name in the paper or they've got some new hotshot development officer who's turning over every rock to find cash." She dragged her sleeve across her eyes, mindless of the streak of mascara. "Madden's the distant past. I just need some sleep, is all."

Mort knew the tragedy that had been her final year in high school, why she'd left without graduating. Was he being cruel because she'd asked him to leave or was he just playing analyst? At that moment he put one of his big arms around her shoulder. She sank into his chest, quivering. She hated herself for crying.

"They want you there. Who wouldn't want you around?" He was fingering the top button on her blouse. "Sleep? You sure?"

"I'm sure, Mort." She moved his hand away firmly.

"Go, Joan. It would be good for you. There must be someone you'd like to see again. What about the geek and the dyke?"

She bristled at his flippant reference to Gabe and Hazel, her two best friends from high school, her only close friends. Mort could be so shallow, so insensitive, and he wasn't even aware of it. No wonder she kicked him out. Gabe and she had kept in touch for a couple of years after high school, then she'd lost track of him. He'd been a brilliant anarchist and was probably running a small Latin American revolution by now. She'd heard that Hazel had gone to San Francisco, the only place you could be out and happy thirty years ago.

Mort read her tight-lipped silence. "Sorry."

"They won't be there. They'd never go. I'd be all alone. Still shy, single, and plump."

"Demure, Rubenesque, and I'll go with you."

Her jaw dropped. "No! Absolutely not."

He raised one eyebrow and grinned.

Forty minutes later the light was fading and she was watching him sleep. Why did she do this to herself? Every time she let him stay it was harder to make him leave again. Shaking him gently, she whispered, "Did you mean it?"

"Huh?"

"Did you mean it when you said you'd come with me?"

He pulled her toward him. "Can't wait. Now go to sleep."

Joan lay awake watching the late-afternoon shadows on the spackled ceiling, imaging the contours of Madden as it had been thirty years ago. Thinking how the tradition of taking yearbook photos in the autumn sometimes misrepresents the truth. A lot can happen between September and June; yet on picture day, the record is set. On that crisp day thirty years earlier, Joan's greatest concern had been whether she should wear her hair in a ponytail, as she did most days, or down and straight, which was hipper. She couldn't ask Gabe Theissen, who was in line ahead of her. Her best friend had no patience for vanity. He'd only lecture her about all the cancer patients in the world who had no hair.

Joan wrinkled her nose. Someone was wearing too much candy-scented perfume and it mingled with the musk of three-hundred teens packed into the gym. As the line shuffled forward, she daydreamed, imagining the message she'd write in the yearbooks of her classmates when they were issued in the spring. Those words and that photograph would be how people remembered her for eternity. The flash of white light brought her back to the moment. Her photo had been snapped. There'd be no second chance.

As the spots cleared from in front of her eyes, the principal entered the gym. A teacher pointed in her direction. Her first thought was that one of her brothers had done something wrong. Anthony had started tenth grade that fall and she'd been waiting for embarrassing repercussions.

When she reached the office she saw her mom through the large glass window. Their eyes met and she knew that something had happened to her dad, and at that moment she became the caretaker of her mother. In her darkest hours she'd wondered if her dad's heart had given out because he could no longer cope with having a child for a wife.

Leo and Vi had both been twenty-two when they married and he had adored her wide-eyed wonderment at the world. She never lost that awe but it also meant she seldom bothered with the responsibility of adulthood. It had been Leo who had made sure that the three kids got off to school on time, that there were groceries in the house, and the utility bills were paid. Vi cooked dinner, occasionally did laundry, and never broke a fingernail over dishes or yard work. And she always, always looked beautiful when Leo arrived home. Despite the demands on the home front, he managed to build a successful roofing company. Vi never had a day of worry.

When Leo died, that all changed.

At eighteen Joan had planned her father's funeral. His brother, Uncle Nick, came from Waterloo for the service. Her mom's two sisters and their husbands arrived a day early from Vancouver to fuss over their youngest sibling. Neighbours left casseroles and cakes. Then, after a week, the circus was over and the bomb dropped. Vi had no idea whether or not Leo had insurance. It had been as irrelevant to her as gas bills and house payments. Joan turned the house upside down looking for a policy. She went through boxes, drawers, and his overstuffed, disorganized filing cabinet, but it soon became obvious that her father had made no provisions for this to happen. Leo didn't expect to die. And he had lived life large, spoiling Vi and the kids to the point where Joan had thought they were well off. When he had a big contract, he'd spend big. But in roofing there are slow times. None of them had known that the house had been mortgaged to their own roof to keep the business going. There was nothing in the bank and Leo owed salaries that would never be paid. Their life had been an illusion.

When the cupboards were down to cream corn and luncheon meat that smelled worse than dog food, Joan found a cashier gig at the gas bar owned by Dan Prychenko. His daughter, Marlena, was one of the popular girls at school. The job started as a part-time position at night, but the bills were mounting quickly. More hours became available, and by Christmas, Joan had stopped going to school altogether. She wasn't around to pick up her diploma the following June and had often wondered if her photograph had made it into the yearbook.

"I'm driving to Madden this weekend." Joan watched for her mother's response.

Vi lived in the basement suite of her sister Heather's house in East Vancouver. It had been her home for over twenty-seven years. Name-brand lemon cleaners didn't completely mask the underlying mildew and the apartment was in its usual state of colourful disarray, made worse by the ceramic knick-knacks and garage sale treasures. The dust collectors that gave her mother pleasure drove Joan crazy. The living situation had been a godsend for Vi, In the early days she had lived rent-free in exchange for babysitting Heather's children. It had been crowded back then, when Joan's brothers, Anthony and David, were still living at home. Now, though, the two elderly widows were good company for each other in the faded and aging split-level home.

"That's nice, dear. Do you have a safety kit in the car? I heard on the radio the other day that you should always carry one." Vi went off on a tangent about the recommended contents of an auto safety kit, avoiding asking why her daughter was returning to their old hometown for the first time in three decades.

"You were younger than I am now when we left Madden, Mom."

"Uh huh."

How many times had Joan felt that she was the one who had had to deal with the real world in her mother's place? She felt the energy sap from her body. Then, just as she was wondering why she'd even bothered to tell her mother, Vi veered back.

"You'll have to say hello for me."

"To who?" asked Joan.

"Well, to whoever you come across." Vi smiled. "After all, it was our home for nineteen years. Remember all the good times we had? Picking berries by the river, the outdoor skating rink, your dad barbequing steaks the size of tires. Oh, he was good on the barbeque, that man. Those long summer nights. Oh! And the northern lights."

Joan watched her mother stare wistfully. That had been Vi's time, so fleeting.

"I'm going to my thirtieth high school reunion," Joan stated flatly.

"Oh?" Vi's response left Joan hanging. She didn't know if her mother remembered that she hadn't graduated in Madden.

"I have no idea why they sent me an invitation."

Vi looked her straight in the eye and spoke with clarity and vehemence. "You're better than any one of them. You remember that."

That pointed insistence gave Joan an unexpected boost. As she was leaving, Vi gave her a list of people to see, including Joan's old English teacher, Mr. Fowler.

During the week she prepared for her trip. Months in the lab had left Joan looking as though she belonged in the morgue. She made her first trip to a tanning salon. As a fake 'n' bake virgin, she got the willies sitting in the waiting room, flipping through a *People* magazine. It reminded her of the dentist's office. She sniffed discreetly and was relieved not to smell burning flesh. After the tanning session she broke down and bought a rinse to hide the needles of grey in her hair. She grabbed a box of royal plum henna, later wondering if the choice had been bold or batty. How could a respected, upwardly mobile member of the science community do these things unless she was utterly deranged? A fraud? Those feelings gradually passed when she discovered that she hadn't been cooked alive on the tanning bed and that the hair colour had turned out quite well. A couple of visits to Tropic Tans and a decent haircut calmed the nagging feeling that the invitation was a ticket to disaster.

Before going to bed on Thursday, Joan called Mort and got his answering machine. It was probably his turn to work late. Or was he out seeing someone? Another woman? Joan dismissed the thought. If he was, he would have told her. Despite the mountain of differences between them, they'd never told lies. She fell into a comfortable sleep, a whisper of coconut tanning oil reminding her that she was actually going on a holiday. As she slept she dreamt. She was on a bicycle, not her own mountain bike, but the old-fashioned kind where the rider sits upright. She was barreling down the long hill leading into the river valley where Madden was situated. Her mother was perched on the handlebars and Joan had no control over how fast they were moving.

CHAPTER TWO

FIRST THING IN THE MORNING JOAN called Mort but, again, there was no answer. A few minutes later he rang her doorbell. When he stepped into her front hallway, he handed her a brown paper bag.

"Thank God. We have to leave by eight-thirty. It's an eight-hour drive."

"I can't go." He looked tired and rumpled, as though he hadn't been home all night.

"What do you mean you can't come? I'm not going without you."

"One of the stores had a fire last night. Nobody was hurt but there's no way I can leave town."

What a switch, she thought. It had always been her putting off their life because of work. "Just as well. I didn't want to go anyway. Sit down."

She ground coffee, and while the aromatic dark roast was brewing they argued. Mort insisted that she face her demons. Joan denied that she was avoiding anything. He was the one suffering a crisis. The harder she tried to divert the conversation to the fire, the more resolute Mort was that she make this trip. They lost track of time. It was almost ten when the phone rang.

"Hello?"

"I'm calling for Joan Parker."

"Speaking." She didn't recognize the girlish voice on the other end of the phone and braced herself for a charity pitch.

"Joannie! It's Peg. Peg Chalmers née Wong." She sang it out as though she'd been announcing herself that way a lot lately. "I'm just making sure you're going to be here in time for the welcome buffet and dancing tonight."

Joan suddenly felt trapped.

"Peg . . . " She hesitated then decided to face it head on. "I thought there had been a mistake. The invitation, I mean."

"Heavens no! I'm the reunion coordinator and head of the invite committee. I was in charge of the list. We were all thrilled, just thrilled, to get your RSVP . . . even though, technically, it was late."

Memories of Peg Wong came rushing back. In the days when fake fur and leather looked more 'fake' than anything else, Peg always wore pink in layers of nylon pile and shiny fabrics. As Joan listened to the sixty-second recap of Peg's life over the past thirty years — moved to Calgary, studied nursing, married, bred a couple of kids, divorced, then moved back to Madden sixteen years ago — she could see the Chinese-Canadian Marilyn Monroe wanna-be, too fluffy to be sultry. The constant gob of strawberry-flavoured gum hadn't helped. Peg had been one of the harmless ones. Although she had hung out with Marlena Prychenko and Candy Dirkson, she didn't have their mean streak.

"I've thought of you so much, Joannie, and wished I would have done something. You know, to make things easier."

Joan couldn't believe what she was hearing — that anyone had thought of her for a minute after she'd left Madden. Her throat tightened when Peg asked after Vi and the boys. She seemed sincerely glad that everyone had done okay.

"What time will you be here? The welcome desk closes at seven."

Joan listened to the silence. "I'll be there by then." She glanced at Mort. He was smiling. To her surprise, so was she. When she got off the phone, she opened the bag he had brought and laughed with gusto.

"If you're going to face your demons, you may as well do it all at once."

The bag contained a mickey of lemon gin, the poison she'd avoided since high school.

On the Labour Day weekend of her grade twelve year there'd been a bush party to outshine all others in its debauchery. Joan and Daphne Pyle, the prettiest girl in school and one of the nicest, had pitched for a forty-ouncer of lemon gin. Joan had become sicker than she'd ever been in her life. Now, to her surprise, the thought of that perfumed smell no longer nauseated her. Maybe she was more prepared for this journey than she'd believed.

Within half an hour she was on the highway. A small cooler sat in the passenger seat, filled with her travel favourites: fresh fruit, water, Cheezies, and licorice. A thermos of coffee was tucked behind the cooler and the invitation rested on the dash. The dread of going to Madden had been replaced by a tingling thrill. The sky was cloudy and the air signalled approaching rain. It would make the trip refreshing. Once past the stretching suburbs and pungent industrial areas, Joan cracked her window to welcome the spring air, sweet with the first scents of early clover. While the pounding beat of Credence Clearwater

Revival propelled her down the highway, she allowed herself to remember.

Those first few months after her dad had died were a blip now. At the time, the long days and nights had passed with aching slowness. Vi, having no skills, had finally taken a job as a chambermaid at the Twin Pines Motel. Despite her inability to deal with the world, her mom refused to go on welfare. Joan put in twelve-hour shifts at the gas bar. Dan Prychenko usually hired boys and had been wary of having her work by herself at night, but Joan hadn't been afraid for a second. What she found more hurtful was the change in the way she was treated by her peers, and the worst was Marlena, Dan's daughter.

Marlena was the main attraction anytime she walked into a room with Candy Dirkson, her shadow, and Peggy Wong. She had a firecracker wit with an atomic kick. While others laughed, someone was always the victim. Marlena sold nickel bags of pot, which she acquired on regular overnight shopping expeditions to Vancouver with her mother. This gave her a worldly caché in Madden. It was after one of those trips that Marlena targeted Joan for the first time. It was a Monday night. The aroma of muddy footwear blended with the stench of gasoline in the confined gas bar. Marlena and Candy pretended to be shoplifting. Joan played along with the joke. Then the bell above the door jingled and two young guys entered, Junior B hockey players who had been at Madden High a couple of years ahead of them. As often happened when Marlena had an audience, especially a male audience, she went for the jugular.

"Nice boots, Parker." Marlena smiled at the boys. "But I thought your grandmother was buried in that pair." The boys gave her an odd look and left. But Marlena didn't stop. "How are your new Pine Tree sheet sets fitting?"

Joan stiffened at the suggestion that her mom was stealing from the motel where she toiled as a chambermaid. "Is there anything I can do for you, Marlena?"

"Let me get this straight. Is your mom making beds or getting made?"

Candy laughed and made an obscene motion, poking her index finger through a circle formed with her other hand.

"She paying back all the men your dad screwed?" continued Marlena.

"Get out," Joan said quietly.

"Do you forget who owns this place?"

She wanted to wipe the sneer off Marlena's smug face but all she could do was stare. Her eyes watered and her throat tensed. The doorbell rang again. A local farmer came in, greeted Joan warmly, and asked after her mom. With a final contemptuous snort, Marlena left. Joan didn't know what had brought on the attack but she knew something for sure. Her family would have to leave Madden.

Joan slowed for the exit from the main highway. The last time she'd been through this way the secondary highway had been two lanes of bumpy pavement that had made the second half of the journey to Madden painstakingly slow. But that was the past. This road was a smooth slash of grey, four lanes of new highway headed north that would cut the travel time. Nothing looked familiar. The old farms that had squatted around this major turnoff were long gone. An industrial park had replaced them. Joan brightened at the thought that she might get into Madden earlier than expected and have time to get her bearings. She wasn't going to let the memory of Marlena ruin this trip. Her mom was right. There had been wonderful times and people.

She smiled as she remembered Gabe and Hazel. She'd admired Gabe who would fight for the underdog and stand up to any authority. Joan had had the desire to be an anarchist, but the courage of a dandelion gone to seed. One puff and her resolve disappeared on the breeze. Gabe was born for a fight; Joan was bred to follow the rules. And then there was Hazel, who embraced her sexuality in a town where adultery was a parlour game but lesbians were vilified. Joan had learned from both of them how to be brave, and they had sown part of who she was. She doubted that either Gabe or Hazel would be at the reunion. Gabe's family moved a year after hers and she'd heard that Hazel's mom and dad had passed away. They had no need to go back, but Joan had to go. She'd never said a proper goodbye. Maybe there'd be a bonus. Maybe someone would have news of her two high school friends. Maybe she'd find them again. Since she and Mort had officially separated, there had been a void, too many lonely nights. She filled her nostrils with the humid air then glanced up at the clouds. Rolling and black, they threatened to unleash a storm. She checked her odometer then sniffed again. If the weather held off another half hour she'd beat the rain.

After Vi Parker had left Madden with her three kids, things became easier. The real estate market was strong when they sold the house and that little bit of equity helped them to rent an East End apartment. They staggered to their feet in Vancouver. Joan still couldn't afford to return to school full-time, but eventually completed high school through correspondence courses. Life had given her a more serious outlook. When she wasn't working she was studying. She knew that university was her way out, her step up, but she was undecided about a major. In a Bachelor of Arts holding pattern, she enrolled in chemistry as a required science class. Proving herself a quick learner, she was offered a lackey job in the chem lab, which worked around her schedule much more readily than slinging burgers.

It was in the dim glow of lab lights that she first appreciated the beauty of chemicals and compounds. They were so simple, yet had the potential to alter the world. She switched faculties and threw herself into chemistry. Above-average grades entitled her to scholarships in her second and subsequent years of study. The first scholarship she received was an unexpected legacy from her father. He'd been a loyal Rotarian and offspring of members could apply to have part of their tuition paid. As time passed, the wound of their Madden exit became a faded scar. She was proud that she'd survived it and chided herself that it had ever bothered her that she had never worn a grad dress.

Her first reaction to the violent thumping from the rear of her Accord was the thought that her back wheel had hit the rumble strip. It took her another few seconds to realize that she had a flat. She veered to the shoulder to avoid traffic. Pulling on her jacket to protect herself from the drizzle that had started to fall, she got out to inspect the damage. Sure enough, the rear tire on the driver's side had blown. She couldn't be more than a couple of miles outside of Madden. Just her luck. It had been years since she had changed a flat and she considered calling the auto club, but she was already racing the clock. Scrounging the jack and spare from the trunk, she clumsily started the job, getting sprayed every time a vehicle drove past.

After giving the lug nuts a final hard twist, she heaved the blown tire into the trunk and threw the jack after it. Her coat and slacks were now splattered with mud. Her hair and skin looked as though she was testing some roadside spa treatment, a shrapnel mudpack. A gleaming champagne-coloured car, with an A-1 Rental sticker on the bumper, reduced its speed as it passed. The driver looked directly at her. There was something familiar about the woman with big, coal black hair, but before Joan could register anything further, the car sped up and was gone. Certainly the woman was too young to be one of her classmates. Joan groaned. What if she had aged worse than everyone there? Should she turn back now, before it was too late?

She climbed into her car, waited for a break in traffic then pulled back onto the highway heading for Madden.

The Twin Pines Motel was the recommended reunion accommodation. It was also the center of activities, including registration. When Joan turned into the parking lot she was taken aback by the changes. In the days when her mother had worked there it had been a respectable but modest establishment. Now it was a full-sized resort. The small cabins, which had formed the original motel, had been completely renovated and re-faced in gleaming logs. The new hotel addition stretched up six stories. Clearly the tallest structure on the Madden skyline, it housed a dining room, conference centre and a cavernous grand ballroom, the location of the evening's Welcome Soirée. The clock on Joan's dashboard read 6:56 PM If she hurried she'd still make it to the registration desk, but wouldn't have time to change out of her muddy clothes. When she reached to grab the invitation from the dash, it wasn't there. Damn it. She felt around the shadows of the seats but could only find loose cheese snacks and a tepid apple core. It must have fallen out when she stopped to change the tire.

A lump rose in her throat as she pushed the lobby door inward and entered a crowd dressed in their casual best. Madden High had served the entire region and there had been over seven-hundred students when she had been here. The huge size of the crowd wasn't the only jarring aspect. Joan had expected people to look older, but not this much. Nobody looked familiar at all. Maybe they were here with some other event, a wedding or powerboat convention? Joan did a quick reality check. Vi and Leo had been her age when they'd lived here thirty years earlier. These had to be her peers. Avoiding eye contact, she braced herself and walked directly to the ornately decorated table below the sign that read MADDEN 30th HIGH SCHOOL REUNION. If she was fast, maybe she wouldn't see anyone she knew until she'd had a chance to change her mud-caked clothing.

A stern woman with salt-and-pepper hair looked up. "Can I help you?"

"Joan Parker." She felt as though she'd just crawled out of a dumpster, but smiled meekly, wondering if her name would ring a bell. Had she known this stiff-looking woman as a laughing teenager? But Salt-and-Pepper showed no sign of recognition and went directly to the box of registration cards marked N–Z. Nothing. She riffled through the A–M box. Still nothing.

"Would it be under any other name?" There was impatience in her tone.

"No. It's always been Parker." Joan mentally kicked herself for announcing it so loudly. It had never occurred to her to be sensitive about keeping her own name. She'd never even considered taking Mort's. In Vancouver no one ever raised an eyebrow. In Madden she was sure it would make a difference. Everyone would think she'd never had a date, let alone been married. "My husband has a different name, but he couldn't come."

The woman was ignoring her and flipping through the cards again. Now Joan was sure everyone would think that she was making it all up. She stopped herself from rattling on that, actually, she and Mort were separated and discussing divorce. "My registration came in a bit late," was all she said.

The woman pulled a binder out from under a pile of papers, opened it and ran her finger down a column. She met Joan's eyes. "You're not on the invitation list."

"But I received one in the mail."

"Do you have it?"

Joan panicked. "No, I don't. I must have . . . " Stumbling over her words, she realized that she was living her own nightmare. The murmured conversation in the room was becoming overwhelming. Now it looked as though she was crashing the party where she had no right to be. Another woman joined the first. They were both staring at her. "Peg called me." She couldn't remember Peg's married name but her old one came easily. "Wong."

The second woman smiled warily. "You mean Peg Chalmers. She came down with the flu. She's going to try to make it tomorrow."

But Joan was no longer listening. As her eyes grazed the registration list one name leapt out at her. Gabriel Theissen. She caught her breath. Gabe was here in Madden. In this situation he wouldn't care what anyone thought and would seize the moment to let them know it.

The woman examined Joan. "You are a graduate of Madden High?"

She could turn around and head home or do what she came for and face her fears. She knew what Gabe would do. She knew what she'd do if she were on her own turf, in her lab, where she supervised a dozen senior-level scientists. Forgetting her bedraggled hair and mud-spattered coat, she pulled herself up to her full five-foot-eight.

"If I hadn't been invited I wouldn't have driven for eight hours to get here. My name tag, please."

The woman shrugged, uncapped a black felt pen and wrote on one of the blank badges.

Joan took it from her and read "June". "It's Joan," she said.

Without a word the woman took the name tag, crossed out June, wrote Joan, then handed it back to her with a schedule of events.

Joan examined the blotched piece of pink cardstock. It was a mess, just like her. Without a word she left the registration table and went to the hotel reception desk. She managed to check-in and escape the lobby without running into anyone she knew.

Since she had reserved late, she'd been assigned one of the old motel cabins on the far side of the parking lot. As the wheels of her suitcase jostled across the gravel, she breathed in the air scented by the pine forest that gave the resort its name. Then a flood of familiar smells hit her all at once and a tangle of feelings welled inside her. Here she was, back in Madden after thirty years. When she looked up at the same old moon rising above the hills across the river, it seemed as though time had stopped.

If Gabe was here, maybe Hazel had made it too. One of them would have brought some pot. It had been years since she'd smoked dope but tonight she was ready. They'd sit out back by the dumpster, smoke a joint, and laugh it all away, just like in the old days. She imagined Hazel with tattoos, pierced eyebrows or a lip ring and promised herself that no matter how outrageous her friend had become, she wouldn't blink, wouldn't pass judgment. The three of them had always been the odd ones out. Tonight it would be their strength.

When she reached her room she opened her suitcase to decide on an outfit for the evening. Everyone in the lobby had been attired on the dressy side of casual. She put aside the pink satin pants with matching vest that had cost her a week's salary and reached, instead, for a more conservative tweed skirt and sweater, an outfit she usually saved for managerial meetings. Tonight she didn't want to raise any eyebrows or be accused of not acting her age. Her concession to fashion would be the custom-made silk panties and bra, her gift to herself for completing the Hint of Midnight project. The set was pale green with black trim, in tribute to the product packaging. "Incredibly sexy and nobody will even know." She sighed.

Joan was digging in her suitcase for her jewellery bag when, tucked away in a side pocket, she found the bottle of lemon gin, Mort's gift. With a wry smile she unscrewed the cap and tilted the bottle into her mouth. Avoiding her tongue and holding her breath, she managed to down a hearty swig. Now she felt seventeen again.

CHAPTER THREE

WHEN JOAN STEPPED INTO THE BALLROOM her nose twitched at the combination of perfumes blended with the smell of hotel gravy. She was late and only a few diners were in the buffet line, scavenging for second helpings among the remains of wilted greens and chicken bones. People laughed together in small clutches but nobody and nothing seemed familiar. To her dismay, none of the women had shown up in the microfibre pantsuits she'd seen in the registration line-up. The swirl of materials and fashionable lines before her now would fit any upscale New York cocktail party. In her sensible skirt and sweater, she felt like someone's great-aunt. Before she could retreat to do a quick change, a big-haired blonde bounded toward her like a friendly poodle.

"Joannie Parker! I can't believe it!" She instantly recognized Candy Dirkson. Only relief that somebody recognized her surpassed her amazement that the former bully seemed happy to see her. She returned Candy's boisterous hug, stretching her arms around the ample woman. So even cheerleaders grew up. But her relief was cut short. A few feet away stood another woman, smugly smiling. The last person Joan had wanted to see was one of the first to appear out of the shadows, and after all these years, Marlena still couldn't hide her contempt. Unlike Candy, she still had the taut body of an athlete, which she was proudly displaying in a fitted cocktail shift.

"Well, look who's here."

The greeting sounded like a challenge, but rather than grab the bait, Joan decided to take the high road. "Marlena, you look fantastic." She knew by looking at her old nemesis that the fastest way to her heart would be through her ego. Nobody looked that good without arduous effort.

Marlena was stunned for a moment, but Candy filled in the dead air: "Doesn't she? She works out constantly. She and Ray both."

"Ray?" Although the name sounded familiar, Joan couldn't make the connection.

"You remember Ray," chimed Candy. Joan was still drawing a blank. "Drummer for Rank?"

It suddenly fell into place. Ray Stanfield had been a sweet guy who had played with the "hot" local band. In the seventies Rank had made a name for itself from Kamloops to Vancouver. He'd been a year ahead of them but his girlfriend, Sarah Markle, was in their grade. News of their lavish wedding had reached Joan through Vi. The high school sweethearts barely waited until graduation. Within eighteen months they'd had the first of several children.

"What happened to Sarah?" It was out of Joan's mouth before she could catch it. No wonder she preferred the social solitude of the lab, where nobody could witness her ineptness. A pall fell over the conversation.

"What about you, Joan? Are you married?" Marlena asked.

God, Joan wished that Mort were there. "Oh, you bet!" No need to mention the breakup. "Over ten years. But Mort couldn't make it. An emergency at work." She saw Marlena glance down at her naked ring finger. Damn! She'd meant to put it back on before she left the city to disguise her transient marital situation.

"Kids?" asked Marlena.

"No. Career first. You know how it is." She was sweating under Marlena's interrogation. Marriage and kids were still a primary measurement of a woman's worth down the gravel roads of rural British Columbia. Did she have "inadequate" burned on her forehead?

"What do you do?" Candy asked warmly. "I bet it's something interesting. You were always sooo smart."

After all the years Joan had spent loathing her, she decided she liked Marlena's old sidekick. "I'm a chemist. I develop flavours and scents for the food industry." She smiled.

Marlena snorted like a small, muscular bull. "Is there such a thing? I've never heard of it."

Joan had seldom been confronted with this kind of abrupt cruelty as an adult. Despite how plain stupid it was, she'd forgotten how deep it cut. Had she always been this vulnerable? And why did Marlena, as an adult woman, still have to do this?

Candy started to ramble about her job at the Co-op, her softball trophies, her four grown kids, and her baby grandson. It was all a fog to Joan as she stared, wounded, at Marlena.

At that moment firm hands landed on Joan's shoulders. A male voice, familiar after so many years, growled into her ear. "And who's the fairest in the land?"

Joan spun around and stood speechless as she absorbed the vision of Gabe. She'd been rescued. But, God, how he had changed. As a teenager he'd been a string bean with the soft body of a "thinker." Still lanky, he now towered over her with the posture and physique of an outdoorsman. The only hint of his horrible teenage acne were the faint scars that added to his rugged appearance.

"Gabe!" She felt tears spring to her eyes and threw herself into his protective embrace, then pulled back to look at him again. "So are you out there planning a revolution? Plotting to overtake the government?"

Gabe grinned awkwardly.

Marlena snickered. "Get up to speed, Parker."

"Actually, Joan, I'm the sergeant over at the RCMP detachment in Elgar."

"You're what?" How on earth could Gabe Theissen have become a cop?

Marlena was enjoying her shock. "The rest of us have moved on, kiddo," she said.

Gabe gently grasped Joan's arm and steered her away. "You don't have a drink. How can we toast reconnecting?" His slightly crowded front teeth showed when he smiled. Good old Gabe, still watching her back. Over her shoulder she saw Marlena's eyes narrow.

As they made their way to the bar, he politely acknowledged greetings from half the people they passed but didn't engage in conversation. Their unspoken conspiracy to ditch this place pleased her. When he asked what she wanted to drink she hesitated, then blurted, "Gin. With tonic, I guess. Thanks."

They made their way out of a side exit near the stage where the band was setting up and found a log bench under the pines. For a moment they just stared at each other.

Joan broke the silence. "A cop?"

He responded lightly. "Change from inside the establishment. All part of the plan."

"Has it worked?" She smiled but she was serious. She'd forgotten how protective she felt toward this boy, this man.

He nodded thoughtfully. "I like to think so. Kept a few kids from jail. Made sure a few real baddies are gone for a long time. Hopefully was right about which was which."

Sitting with her shoulder touching his, she could smell the fresh soap scent emanating from his skin. Then she glanced down and saw the gold band on his left hand. "Gabe, you're married." She meant to sound pleased but it came off as stunned.

He nodded slightly, twisted the ring around his finger, then said a soft, "Yeah." He paused. "You were smart to miss the opening speeches. Remember old man Sawatsky, our grade nine social studies teacher?"

"Sure I do. Quizzes every Friday afternoon. Didn't that qualify as torture?"

"He's one of the few faculty left that can still stand. He went on reminiscing for about fifteen minutes before someone interrupted to tell him we're the class of seventy-nine, not sixty-seven."

Joan laughed but she knew he was avoiding talking about his family. After all these years, she could still read him. "Is she here? Your wife?"

"Naw, she's not into these things. Neither am I, usually. She went down to the University in Kamloops this weekend. Our son starts his undergraduate program in the fall."

"A son," she said warmly.

Gabe nodded shyly. "He's our only kid."

So many years, so much life had passed. It seemed surreal that they were back here in Madden together. Through the drooping branches of the huge pine she could see the "Welcome to Madden" sign on the opposite bank of the river. Party central when they were young, it now seemed an eerie reminder of how many years had passed. For the next hour time stood still as they began to fill in the canvas of their lives for each other.

Gabe's passion for social change had led him to the Department of Political Science, and an elective in criminology steered him toward a Master's degree at the University of Calgary. That's where he met his wife, Betty. She was a social worker. They lived together for years before he took a job with the Calgary Police Force. The work was related to his thesis on the psychology of social fraud. When Betty became pregnant, they got married and both agreed that the country would be a better place to raise kids.

Gabe stopped talking and stared into space. Joan followed his gaze and realized that he was looking up at the Welcome sign. "That was just about the last thing we agreed upon."

"I'm sorry," she whispered.

"Betty never wanted to get married. I insisted, with the baby coming. Sometimes I think I should have left well enough alone."

His career, on the other hand, had gone surprisingly well. His anarchist ways helped him rise rapidly to sergeant. It appeared as though the RCMP actually appreciated someone who questioned the way things were done and wasn't afraid of taking risks. When he was offered a promotion to inspector, he refused. He didn't want to get stuck behind a desk. Now he lived in Elgar, twenty minutes down the road, worked, took his son camping. He'd transferred some of his old passion to collecting rare books.

Both their drinks were empty and the music drifting from inside was causing Joan to sway involuntarily. She felt a surge of warmth through her body. The most unexpected phenomenon had occurred. She felt as though she belonged somewhere for the first time in a long time. Here, with Gabe, in Madden. There was only one thing missing. "Let's go in and see if we can find Hazel."

"She said she'd try to make it," Gabe said.

"You've kept in touch?"

"She and Lila come to town at least once a year, sometimes more. Whenever she can get away from the church." He read her shock. "Hazel is a minister with the San Francisco Free Metropolitan Church."

Joan had heard of the FMC. Known for its liberal attitudes and work with the urban poor, it was huge. That position would make Hazel one of the most influential religious leaders in North America. It all made perfect sense. Hazel had always been intelligent, kind, and fearless. She was perfectly capable of taking on the American right wing. "What are we waiting for?" She and Gabe shared a grin.

When they entered from the side door, they stepped directly onto the dance floor, that was vibrating with a mass of writhing bodies. Joan had a rush of claustrophobia. She was jostled by a grey-haired woman in a mauve boa and tripped against Gabe. He caught her and left his arm around her shoulder, holding her close. She scanned the crowd, worried that the small minds of Madden would interpret his gesture as something more than platonic protection. But everyone, thankfully, was focused on the stage and the loud rock and roll that blared through the speakers. The sound was familiar, an echo from the past, but she couldn't quite place it. It wasn't Queen or the Bee Gees. She turned and gaped at the sight of the Mick Jagger of Madden High, Roger Rimmer. Still in tight pants and with blond curly hair framing his face, craggy lines accenting his high cheekbones, he was as good-looking as ever. Loathing rose in the back of Joan's throat.

CHAPTER FOUR

THE LABOUR DAY WEEKEND OF 1978 had been imprinted on Joan's mind forever. The WELCOME sign, large wooden letters set against the hills on the far side of the river, had long been the location for momentous events in the lives of local teens. Engagements, breakups, conceptions, and even a birth in the mid-eighties, all took place in the gravel parking lot and woods behind the sign. After Jerry Weiss leapt to his death from the letter 'O' in the mid-eighties, there'd been talk of tearing it down, but the community rallied and, instead, gave it a fresh coat of paint.

The kegger up at the Welcome sign had been planned to celebrate the beginning of the final year in high school for Joan's class. For many it would be the last year in Madden. The population of young people had been declining for two decades and anyone with a whiff of ambition or ability would be gone in a snap, as soon as they could, by whatever means. Like most bush parties in most small towns, the weekend bash had the potential to be the event of the season. Candy's older brother agreed to pick up the keg and deliver it in his Ranchero to the party site. A couple of football players offered to protect the beer before the party, since the keg had to be tapped hours in advance to keep it from foaming. Everyone realized, though, that the two burly youths, despite their best intentions, would probably drink most of it before the party started, so Gabe had offered the services of himself, Hazel, and Joan. The keg would be safe with them since they by far preferred a couple of joints to a case of beer. The prospect of spending a sunny fall afternoon up at the Welcome sign, overlooking the river, with a tray of cinnamon buns and Hazel's guitar, was their idea of Shangri-La.

The one glitch for Joan was that she had already agreed to go halves on a forty-ounce bottle of lemon gin with Daphne Pyle. Joan wasn't much of a drinker, but when Daphne approached her, she'd decided that this would be her breakout weekend. Daphne's parents were Christian fundamentalists and they policed their only daughter to the point of tyranny. But Daphne was open, warm, and adventurous. Shifts, thought seventeen-year-old Joan. She'd hang out with Gabe and Hazel for the afternoon, then get Daphne to meet up with her at the Welcome sign. Later, she couldn't recall when she had started drinking the lemon gin or where Daphne had gone or whether or not she'd had anything to eat besides the cinnamon buns. There were two things, however, that she did recall. After she had puked up the sweet buns and gin, she had continued retching. She had never been so sick in her life, before or since. The second thing she remembered was that Roger Rimmer had tried to rape her and had nearly succeeded. She had never shared this secret with a soul.

Even in the strobing light of the ballroom, Joan could tell that the rest of the band members hadn't aged as well as Roger. Candy happily informed her that this was a twice-in-a-lifetime reunion for Rank. Roger occasionally came to town to visit his parents, but this was the first time they'd seen Rudy Weiss, the keyboard player, since the tenth reunion. Rudy, who had driven in from Prince George where he worked as an accountant, had developed a double chin, and a huge belly that hung over his waistband. Of course Marlena's husband Ray lived in Madden, as did bass guitarist Steve Howard.

Ray, probably under the supervision of Marlena, clearly worked out regularly. He was muscular for a man of fifty, but it hadn't saved his hair, which was now a fringe decorating his neck more than his head. Steve Howard, thick around the middle, had shaved his head to hide the fact that he was balding. His dad, Chuck, had worked for Joan's dad then started his own company after Leo died. He'd accepted equipment in lieu of several weeks' pay. She still felt terrible about this, but was glad Steve had carried on the tradition and was still roofing the houses of Madden and surrounding communities.

As the band ended its song, the room vibrated with applause and a wave of women moved toward the stage. Joan smiled. It was a known fact that when people heard music from their adolescence, it triggered a surge of hormones similar to those created by lust. It didn't matter how old they were. Surprisingly, Marlena, the one person usually at the head of any crowd, had held back. She was smiling seductively toward the stage, but she wasn't sharing the moment with her husband Ray, who was preoccupied with his cymbal. She was looking directly at Roger Rimmer, and the lead singer was leering back at her.

Joan turned toward Gabe and shouted over the crowd noise, "I can't believe that the women still fall all over him."

"What?"

She was about to repeat herself, then turned to indicate Roger. Now, though, he was only ten feet away and moving directly toward them. She shook her head. "Never mind."

The two men slapped each other on the back. "Hey, man. How's it going?" asked Roger. "Where's that beer you owe me?"

Joan was taken aback as the easy rapport continued. Obviously Roger and Gabe were friends. Even though she had never told Gabe about the near rape, she remembered their shared, mutual distrust of Roger. Well, if Gabe liked him, maybe Roger had changed. She'd do her best to start fresh.

He held out his hand. "Hi. I'm Roger Rimmer."

"I know who you are." She smiled, slow to take his hand, expecting that he'd remember and be embarrassed.

"It's Joan, Roger. Joan Parker," said Gabe.

Roger grinned, then pulled her into a hug. "Joan! How are you?"

Did he really not recognize her? His image was emblazoned on her memory card. That bush party three decades ago had permanently coloured her worldview. For years she'd been afraid to walk past treed areas alone at night. She'd avoided men with fair, cupid curls and had turned off Mick Jagger because of their remote resemblance. Now here he was in the flesh. They did the sixty-second "This Is My Life." Roger had moved to California, playing with different bands through the late seventies and early eighties. After that he had done some vague work in the renovation business. It was clear that he hadn't hit the stellar heights for which he'd aimed. As his recap floundered, Gabe shuffled uncomfortably and finally interrupted.

"Okay, I declare a moratorium on discussions of the past. Here's to the now!" He raised his glass.

The three toasted awkwardly, then Joan excused herself to go to the ladies' room. As she departed Roger laughed warmly and warned her not to write anything on the stall that she'd regret later.

Joan felt a strange discomfort as she made her way through the ballroom. Had she distorted the entire episode up at the Welcome sign? Had the fear that had weighed her down her entire life been her own creation? They'd been a couple of kids at a bush party who had had too much to drink. She stopped for a moment in the midst of the crowd, shook her head. Maybe she should have returned to Madden years before to gain an adult perspective.

Her thoughts were interrupted when she noticed several people turned toward the ballroom entrance where a figure was backlit in the doorway. The dramatic, poised woman, with shiny black hair piled on top of her head, let the doors slowly close behind her. There was something familiar about her, not necessarily from years ago but from a recent encounter. Ah, the woman who had passed her on the highway earlier. She couldn't place her, so shrugged it off and made her way to the washroom.

Looking at herself in the mirror, she did the same self-examination that she was sure all the others were doing. How did her wrinkles compare? Was the slight thickness around her lower abdomen worse than the average in the room? Did her short bob-cut make her look matronly? Did the burgundy rinse seem as though she was clutching too tightly to youth? If Mort had made this journey with her he would have reassured her, but since he wasn't here, it was up to her. She thought of her expensive mint-green underwear that nobody would see and smirked at her reflection. If nothing else, she was ready to be hit by a truck and really, what did it matter? She'd be driving home in thirty-six hours. Joan dabbed her mouth with the lipstick she'd bought in France on a promotional junket earlier in the year. It tasted slightly of butterscotch. Not the overwhelming flavour of American glosses popular with adolescents, but a whimper of sweetness, demure, sensual, and barely noticeable.

The washrooms were down a tangled web of corridors, a result of the many additions made to the original motel. Heading back to the ballroom, she couldn't remember exactly how she'd come. After venturing down a long, dark hallway, she ended up at the kitchen. Trying to retrace her steps, she found herself under the dim light of the alarmed emergency exit. Turning abruptly, she almost collided with Roger.

"Thought you might need a guide, Joannie." His breath announced rye and his eyes were glossy.

"Direction isn't my strongest sense but I think I know where I am now." As she tried to walk past him he slid his arm around her shoulder.

"I just wanted to tell you how gorgeous you look."

Her shoulders tensed. "Thank you." She tried to pull away.

His grip became tighter. "What's the rush?"

She removed his arm from her shoulder but he stretched his arms out to block the narrow hallway, then purred, "Joan."

As she tried to slip under his arm he pushed her to the wall. She instinctively turned her face away from his hot breath but he caught her jaw in his hand and forced her to look at him.

"How come we never screwed?"

She struggled to keep her voice calm and firm. "Let go, Roger."

He kissed her neck and the smell of onions mixed with rye made her gag.

"Why, Joan? Why should I let go? The others all want me, you know. What's wrong with you?" He slid his hand onto her thigh and moved it up under her dress. She pulled away. He lunged toward her and she kicked hard with her pointy-toed shoes.

"I'm not the others," she replied sharply. She pushed open the fire door. The loud clanging alarm shook him. It was a harsh exclamation of his failure. She knew he wouldn't follow her. As the emergency door closed on its pneumatic hinge, she looked over her shoulder and caught a glimpse of Marlena at the end of the hall, her mouth agape at what she had witnessed.

Joan hurried across the brightly lit parking lot, avoiding the shadows cast by the large pines. Through the plate glass window, she saw Gabe emerge from the din of the party and look around the lobby. She stopped to compose herself. Just like thirty years ago, she wouldn't mention Roger's drunken, fumbled advance. She'd handled it and didn't want it to sour the joy of seeing Gabe again.

"I was starting to wonder if I'd been dumped," Gabe called out as she approached. She just smiled. Over his shoulder, the beautiful, raven-haired woman who had stopped the party with her entrance was ending a conversation with an older man. As the woman quickly strode through the automatic doors and into the night, the man turned. Mr. Fowler. Stooped shoulders, unkempt, thinning grey hair, an elderly man.

Thirty years ago Ed Fowler had been hip. His hair had brushed his collar and he'd worn corduroy pants instead of the suit-and-tie uniform of the other male teachers in Madden. Slightly younger than her parents, he'd always made Joan feel special. All the kids viewed him as cool, for an adult. After her dad had died, Mr. Fowler had made a point of singling her out with praise for her work. He'd listened kindly to her excuses for being late and missing assignments after she'd started working long hours at the gas bar.

"Mr. Fowler!" He looked up with cloudy blue-grey eyes. "I'm Joan Parker, Mr. Fowler. I've come back."

"Why, how cool is this? If you wait long enough, the nicest memories come chase you down."

Gabe nodded and held out his hand. "Ed."

Fowler took Gabe's hand in both of his and grinned broadly. "And look at you two. Still hanging out after all these years." Gabe and Joan shared an awkward glance. "And Daphne Pyle making it back too. I knew you girls would fare okay. Why, it didn't take a genius to know who'd survive."

Joan was gobsmacked. So the dark-haired beauty was Daphne Pyle. She should have seen it. While Marlena's taut body and trendy style came from obvious effort, Daphne's seemed innocent, right down to the pink blush in her cheek. She was still the prettiest girl in the class.

"My mother sends her regards, Mr. Fowler."

"Vi Parker. What a girl. She's fared all right, Vi has?"

"She's fine."

"You tell her hello from me. From Ed Fowler."

"I will."

"You make sure you do." Then their former teacher shuffled off through the doors and into the darkness.

Riotous applause and drunken cheers rose from the ballroom as, with a rumbling drum solo, Rank rolled into another song. Joan and Gabe shrugged at each other then decided to call it a night.

When they reached the parking lot he offered to walk her to her cabin but she insisted he get on the road. The rain was threatening to return and the highway to Elgar would be treacherous with drunk drivers racing to the next pub before last call. Gabe put his hands on her shoulders. His breath on her cheek smelled of gin mixed with mint gum. Not her brand, but an old-time competitor's product. She wasn't sure what to expect, but he simply kissed her cheek and strode toward his SUV. As he drove away she wondered if she could convert him to Hint of Midnight.

A sudden breeze caught her off guard and sent a chill down her back. So much had changed, so much hadn't. Gabe was a cop and friendly with Roger. Marlena still had a hate on for her. The gin on an empty stomach had hit her hard and the visceral memory of Roger's onion-and-rye breath made her want to vomit. She turned on her heels and headed across the parking lot toward her cabin, sidestepping puddles and digging the key out of her purse as she went. It had been a long time since she'd stayed in a hotel that used a metal key. As she fumbled with the lock, she heard a crunch of gravel and looked up toward the motel units near the woods. Nothing but shadows. Her hands were shaking as she jiggled the door handle. "C'mon," she whispered and was relieved when the lock finally responded with a click.

The air inside the cabin seemed mustier than it had earlier. After double locking the door, she pulled her dress off her shoulders and stepped out of it. Leaving it in a pile on the floor, she flopped onto the bed in her underwear. She was exhausted. The room was spinning. Placing the pillow over her head didn't help. She stumbled to the bathroom, knelt in front of the toilet and lifted the seat. Instantly the gin came up. After heaving until there was nothing left, she laid her face against the cool black-and-white linoleum and closed her eyes.

A heavy knocking vibrated beneath her cheek. It took a moment before she could assemble all the pieces. Someone was pounding on the cabin door. She got to her hands and knees. "Who's there?"

Slowly pulling herself to her feet, she steadied herself against the wash basin, glanced in the mirror, then wished she hadn't. Her left leg had pins and needles, thanks to wrapping herself pretzel-like around the toilet on the cold linoleum. The clock on the microwave said 1:37 A.M. She toddled delicately to the door then opened it a crack. Through the narrow slat she saw Roger Rimmer. He pushed his face toward her. Scotch, aged single malt, peaty and smooth, if her nose was on the mark.

"Joan, let me in," he said drunkenly.

The sight of him was sobering. "Go away," she croaked.

Despite his condition, he managed to shove his hand between the door and the jam just as she slammed the door. "Ah fuck, ah fuck, ah fuck!" he hissed.

Repulsed, she opened the door enough to release his hand, then slammed it shut and locked it.

"C'mon, Joan." He slurred with the composure of a practiced drunk. "I came to apologize."

She didn't believe him and didn't want to engage in an argument.

"Please, Joan, just listen a minute. I'm sorry about tonight. I really am."

She spoke through the hollow-core door. "You're drunk, Roger. Go away." There was silence for a moment then mumbling. Joan put her ear to the door and realized that he was still talking but his voice had slid lower. He was sitting on the pavement, leaning against her door, continuing his monologue.

"The liquor kills the pain, Joan. I'm seein' ghosts here."

"Ghosts?" she asked. "You're hallucinating." What was she doing? Now he knew he had an audience.

"Not like that. My own ghost. You think I don't know how stupid I look? Leaping around on stage like an old billy goat, with that smart-ass eighteen-year-old rock star laughing from the footlights?" He paused and Joan thought he had gone. Then he started again.

"I don't know what hurts more, my back or my fucking ego. Coming back to Madden like this, just shows what a loser I am." He was just getting started. Joan sat on the floor beside the door and listened as he described how, after high school, he'd scraped by playing rock 'n' roll in clubs up and down the California coast. When heat from US immigration got to be too much, he married one of the girls who hung with the band.

"You had groupies?" This surprised her even more than the fact that he'd been married.

"Funny, hey? Oh, we thought we were hot. We travelled in an old VW van with my picture painted on the side. I saw a photo of it later, the van. I looked like a fucking girl in a shampoo commercial." He was silent a moment, finding the thread of his thoughts. "The bitch of it was that we weren't all that great. The kids that followed us, they were as lost as we were." He continued quietly. "Crystal should have known that the marriage was a big sham. I just did it for my green card. We were living in a motel in Yakima. We were both so strung out. When we did sleep, it was coma-land, the sleep of the dead. One morning, I just slipped out the door. I made sure I left her enough smack for a morning hit and cash for the Greyhound back to Oklahoma. If I'd woken her, she would've made a scene. You know what I mean?"

"You're a coward," she said through gritted teeth.

"Oh, c'mon. It would've been hard on everybody." His voice became a mumbling whisper as he momentarily drifted. "Little Crystal. Last I heard, she was hooking in Seattle and surviving downtown. She'd be in her forties now." He paused. "If she's still alive. But, hey, s'not my problem. I have a hard enough time holding my shit together."

At that, Joan heard him get up and stumble away. He hadn't come to apologize. He'd just wanted an audience. She gazed at her hand to confirm that she was trembling, and wondered if it was more anger or fear. Roger had had so much going for him. He was an adored only child; his dad was the kind but befuddled town doctor, and his mom had always stayed at home, always fussed over him. And he'd been undeniably handsome. How could somebody who had been handed so much make such a mess of it?

Finally, Joan crawled into the hard motel bed and pulled the covers over her head, but sleep didn't come as easily this time.

A scream woke her. As though to confirm that it wasn't a dream, another scream punctuated the silence. And another. They sounded close, from the trees outside or from one of the nearby cabins. She didn't know how long she had slept but it was still dark. Her head was clearer than it had been. She wiped the raccoon circles from under her eyes and threw her coat over her shoulders. By the time she stepped outside there were lights on in a couple of cabins, with others flicking on as though a sequential switch had been flipped. The screaming was coming from a figure outside of the farthest cabin. Joan recognized Marlena as the slight woman collapsed into a fetal crouch. Slipping mud-caked runners onto her bare feet, she rushed to Marlena's side as others appeared in the parking lot. Blood was streaked across her high-heel sandals: so much blood. Joan put her arm around Marlena's shoulders, but the panicked woman pulled away.

"You," she hissed. "You did this. You killed Roger."

Joan slowly rose to her feet as Marlena continued with a string of loud, hysterical accusations.

DEATH CHANGES THE RULES

Chapter Five

Gabe settled into his favourite chair with a mug of tea and a signed, first edition of Robertson Davies' *The Cunning Man*. He knew he wouldn't be able to sleep right away. All the way home he had thought about Joan and even now couldn't keep the grin off his face. She was the one who didn't live here anymore, yet he felt as though *he*'d come home. He couldn't remember the last time he'd had such an easy conversation with anyone. At work there was always a hint of formality. The other cops liked him fine, but there was always a distance, possibly because of his time in the city. He had a solid relationship with his son, but never completely revealed himself. And Betty — well she'd be happy if she never had to speak to him again. Tomorrow he would let Joan know how happy he was to have a real friend back in his life. He was about to put his book away when the phone rang.

"Gabe, it's Des." The corporal sounded shaken. "There's been a homicide."

Joan looked at her watch. It was two-fifteen in the morning. As soon as the RCMP car pulled into the motel parking lot, Marlena ran up and screamed at the husky young officer as he climbed out. "I saw them making out in the hallway," she screamed. She pointed at Joan. "Her! Her and Roger!"

If Joan had swilled four G and Ts, Marlena had soaked in a bathtub of rye. Would anyone believe her accusations?

Through the rain she saw Marlena's husband, Ray. He'd joined the growing circle of onlookers, but didn't do anything to stop his wife's ranting, nor did he offer her any sort of comfort.

Gabe's SUV pulled up, splashing through the pitted gravel. He climbed out, nodded in Joan's direction but didn't stop, didn't smile, and went directly to have a word with the young cop.

Marlena immediately draped herself over him like a sodden rag. "It was awful, Gabe. I walked in, there was blood all over the place. All over the bed."

"I gotta take a look around, Marlena. We'll take your statement in a bit." He gently peeled her from his arm, handed her back to Corporal Des Cardinal, then headed to the cabins. The door to number 23 was hanging open. As with all the motel units, there were signs of forced entry from years of drunken parties. Bikers, rig workers, and high school kids, they'd all left their mark: old damage, painted over, but not completely erased. The clientele of the rejuvenated Pine Tree Resort was more upscale: convention delegates coming for the upgraded facility, families enjoying the close proximity to the lake, faculty visiting Lakeview College that had been established in Madden the previous year. Inside each one-room cabin were a bed and dresser, a kitchenette area with a microwave and small fridge, a table and a sofa. Entrances faced the parking lot, but each unit also had a sliding patio door leading to a picnic area by the woods.

Gabe braced himself before crossing the threshold. The smell of new murder blasted him as he entered the room. He was accustomed to the iron scent of blood. Although homicides were not all that common in Lakeview County, death came regularly by way of accidents and suicides. This, however, was different. He had never investigated the murder of someone he'd known since childhood. That their relationship had been such an emotional one made it even stranger. Roger lay slack-jawed, with his head hanging over the end of the bed. A butcher knife protruded from his chest. Forensics would identify the exact number of wounds, but Gabe instantly knew that someone had savagely stabbed Roger multiple times. All he had on was a worn pair of boxers decorated with cartoon reindeer. Pale and skeletal, the rocker looked impossibly old. His famous curls appeared more white than blond in this light, at least the locks not soaked crimson did, and his outstretched arms were etched with the road map of drug abuse that had spanned his adult life. The amount of blood sprayed on the wall above the headboard and over the bedside lamp was startling, even to a seasoned cop. Somebody had been angry with Roger, angry enough to kill him over and over again. Or afraid, wanting to make certain that he wouldn't get up again. It didn't look as though he had struggled. Whoever it was had surprised the rock star. But he'd been awake when the knife went in the first time.

Marlena was slightly more sober a half hour later when Gabe questioned her in the lobby of the resort. Her statement would have to be weighed against her inebriation and her tendency to exaggerate.

"It was open when I got there," she said.

"Open, as in 'wide open'?"

"No. Open as in it sort of opened when I knocked, like it wasn't closed tight."

"And what did you do next?"

"I called, quiet, you know, like: 'Roooger'. Like that."

"And?"

"I went in." She shuddered. "And saw him there on the bed."

"Did you hear anything?"

Marlena shook her head.

"Or see anybody?"

Her eyes snapped toward him. "Of course I did. Don't try to get her off the hook, Gabe. I may not have seen her in his room, but I know bloody well that Joan did it. I saw Roger come out of her room. And I saw them making out in the hall by the bathrooms when the band took a break."

Gabe talked to Joan next. She stood looking out of the large lobby windows. But there was little to see in the darkness. More likely, she'd been watching his mirrored reflection as he questioned Marlena. He handed her a coffee.

"She says you and Roger were . . . " She was watching him as he groped for the most delicate words. "Being intimate in the hallway by the johns."

"What exactly did she say?"

"That you had your hands all over each another. Listen Joan, I'll end up questioning dozens of people. Roger had a lot of friends and even more enemies. Could you just tell me what happened?"

"When I went to the washroom, Roger followed me. He came on to me in the hallway and he wouldn't back off. I left through the emergency door. That's what set the alarm off last night."

Gabe remembered that she'd done the same thing when they had gone to a Led Zeppelin concert in Vancouver. They had tried to be cool but couldn't stand the crowds and smoke. Escaping through the exit door, the blaring alarm had exposed them. They'd been seventeen years old. This time the escape had been more serious.

"Why didn't you tell me?"

"Because you're his friend and it was nothing. He'd been drinking and I'd handled it. At least I thought I had. Just after 1:00 AM. he knocked on my door."

"Why?" he asked.

"He was drunk, he didn't need a reason although he said it was to apologize."

"That possibly makes you the last one to see him alive." They were both silent.

She looked at the Styrofoam cup in her hand. "I better not finish this. I doubt that the reunion dinner will happen now. I'll need a nap before I head for home."

"Peg Chalmers is head of the organizing committee. She won't let a little homicide mess up her plans." His effort to make it less awkward landed badly. "Besides . . . " He felt the line between them shift. "It would be better if you didn't leave town just yet. We can't officially ask you to stay."

"You mean I'm a suspect?"

"Hell, Joannie, we're all candidates. Someone killed Roger." He took the cup from her hand. "You better get some rest. Do you want me to walk you to your cabin?"

When they reached her door, Gabe simply put a hand on her shoulder, gave her a sad, lopsided smile, then walked away. She bolted the door and added the chain latch for extra measure. She checked the patio door to make sure it was locked then looked in the bathroom and under the bed. She changed into her yoga pants and a sweatshirt in case she had to make another instant appearance. As she was crawling under the covers she noticed the message light on her phone blinking. Had it been on when she got in last night? She followed the recorded instructions for retrieving voicemail.

"Hey, babe." It was Mort. "Checking in on my favourite gin tanker. I tried your cell. Hope you're not too bored out there in the boonies."

"Bored," thought Joan. As she closed her eyes the early morning sun was already cutting a razor of light across the ceiling.

CHAPTER SIX

THE COFFEE MAKER GURGLED AND HISSED while the hot water dripped through a generic pre-packaged coffee filter. Joan was accustomed to a rich dark Italian roast brewing, but the scent of any coffee was better than none and essential to the beginning of her day. She sat on the edge of the bed and searched the impossibly thin Madden phone book for Peg Chalmer's number. After four rings, a young woman answered.

"Peg?"

"I'll get her," was the response. The phone clattered onto a hard surface.

After a long wait the receiver at the other end was picked up. "Hello?" Peg sounded quiet and tired. She explained that she'd been hit hard with the flu and a blinding headache. Normally wild horses couldn't have kept her from the reunion. She'd been heading the planning committee for three years. Peg was beside herself over Roger's death. Never in a million years had she expected anything so horrible to happen. She'd braced herself for a fist fight or two but never death, never murder. "And it's totally my fault."

"Your fault?" asked Joan.

"The entertainment committee didn't think we should spring for a motel room, that he should stay with his parents," said Peg. "We're running on a skeleton budget. I agreed with the committee at first, but Roger wouldn't let up about it. Let him feel like a star, poor guy. That's what I thought. If I hadn't caved at the last minute, I bet he'd still be alive." She'd already said that to the police. Corporal Cardinal had called first thing this morning to ask her to pull together a list of reunion participants, but she didn't have an actual list of who had shown up. The women at the registration table weren't certain that everyone had signed in last evening. They knew for sure that some people had arrived late.

"I was almost one of them," said Joan. Remembering the young woman who had answered the phone, she remarked on how fortunate Peg was to have her daughter helping her.

"That wasn't Tabitha." Only Peg would have named her daughter after a 1960s television character. "It was Daphne. She's staying with me. We've been yakking away. Thirty years is a lot of catching up."

"Don't overdo it."

Peg gave a weak laugh. "I'm fit as a fiddle. It's just a little bit of flu."

At the other end of town, a less friendly conversation was taking place. In the hills high above Madden, Marlena Stanfield was punishing her bow-flex for everything that had happened the night before. With each sit-up she seemed more agitated.

Gabe stared out through the wall of windows of her exercise room. A fog had rolled in and hidden the valley below. He could just make out the outline of the Welcome sign on the far bank of the invisible river. Ray stood waiting in his work clothes. His fleece, bearing the Stanfield Developments logo, was zipped to the neck to protect against the morning frost, rare at the end of May. His face reddened with frustration when Gabe spoke.

"If you don't mind, Ray, I need to speak to Marlena on her own."

"You want to know what she was doing at Roger's cabin at two in the bloody morning? Well, so do I."

Marlena let them stew another moment, probably deciding between a good offence or defence. Gabe knew that if this marriage fell apart neither could abide the loss in economic stature. Like so many couples, they'd grown dependent on the comforts of life and would rather suffer the daily unhappiness they knew than the unknown of a more modest existence.

Her reply came out like cold syrup, thick and sweet. "Darling, he was a guest in town. I was checking on everyone." She continued pulling on the weights.

"The whole world knows you have a thing for Roger," said Ray.

"Had," she stated flatly.

"What?"

"Had, Ray. Roger is dead, remember?" She sat up and wiped her armpits with a towel.

"Oh you mean there is a place you draw the line? Hell, Marlena, the whole time he was here rehearsing you dressed like a teenager." Gabe had never seen the usually soft-spoken man so angry. "Your boobs were pushed up so far, they looked like they'd pop right out of your shirt."

Gabe had often wondered if it had been the thrill of the hunt that had attracted Marlena to Ray. When Ray was married to Sarah, he basked in her glow. His high school sweetheart had been beautiful and selfless. Sarah was loved by everyone, and beside her Ray shone like a knight. Marlena had relentlessly preyed upon him.

Their own two daughters, now twelve and fourteen, were miniature versions of their mom. The youngest, Mandy, was already on a diet. At a softball tournament a couple of weeks ago Gabe had heard Tanya cite Marlena, insisting that eating disorders were bullshit and the best lunch was a SlimFast bar. Both girls treated their dad as though he was a bank machine.

Ray finally grabbed his hardhat and briefcase, and stomped up the stairs.

Gabe waited until he was sure Ray was out of earshot. "Who else did you check in on, Marlena?" He hoped to get straight answers now that she was sober.

"I checked on everyone last night. Well, damn near. Mary and George Armitage, Gerald, the Galatis. Next I was going to see Joan Parker. But it looks as though she got to Roger first."

Marlena swung her legs around to sit on the bench.

Her words came in a measured tone. "I never screwed, Roger. I would've." She took another drink. "But I didn't. "

"How's the apartment hunting?" Gabe held his kitchen phone with one hand and rubbed his neck with the other. He needed sleep. He'd only managed to catch twenty minutes of shut-eye since the murder.

Betty laughed in reply. "Teddy hates everything. He says he'll get distracted in residence and finds something wrong with all the basement suites. Apparently the last one smelt funny." For someone who was known as a tough ass among social workers, Betty was all tapioca when it came to their only child. "He thinks we should wait until August, but I'd hate to get stuck in the last minute rush. We have a few more places to check out. I doubt we'll make it home before Monday night."

Gabe had been the one maneuvering to keep them all close, trying to save the marriage, the unit. Now he was glad to hear that his wife and son wouldn't be home until the end of the long weekend. Betty was resentful when he had to work overtime, and Roger's death guaranteed that life wouldn't be simple for the next few days, perhaps longer. But as quickly as he thought of work, the image of Joan came to mind. He realized that he was jealously hoarding the little time they'd have together.

"How's the reunion going? Did you and Roger make up?" Betty was asking out of courtesy, not any real concern. In retrospect the incident with Roger had been so stupid. Two middle-aged men letting their tempers flare. Gabe decided not to alarm her. He'd tell her about Roger's death when she was back in Elgar. He should have patched things up with Roger, apologized for threatening to arrest him last week. Now he'd never have the chance.

"Just be careful on the highway," he warned. "It's supposed to rain all weekend." He hung up and headed for the shower. He'd left instructions that everyone who had been at the reunion, guests and staff, should be asked to congregate at the high school gym at ten. He'd be surprised if his officers were able to get everyone there. There was no record of where his former classmates were staying. There was the hotel and Riverside RV Park; they'd also have to match attendees to relatives in the phone book. They couldn't order witnesses to stay in town. Pretty soon people would start spreading like buckshot. When that happened, the chance of solving Roger's homicide would become exponentially more difficult. They had their work cut out for them.

There were patches of blue peeping through the clouds as Joan walked from the motel to the new high school. "New" was a relative qualifier since it had opened almost twenty years ago. The sprawling complex served the vast surrounding region of logging towns and the nearby nickel mine. Madden was also the regional seat of provincial government. The school served a cross-section of blue- and white-collar families. Her old school was diminutive in comparison. Those grounds had been turned into a pretty park, and the sign in front of the old red brick building identified it as the Madden Cultural Centre and Day Care. It was much smaller than Joan remembered.

A small group of smokers congregated outside the new school. Thirty years ago they would have been laughing and posing. Now they huddled in social banishment. She heard a shout from behind her.

"Joan!"

Even after decades, she recognized the warm contralto voice. She turned and grinned at Hazel, who was moving toward her with open arms. Except for forty extra pounds, her old friend hadn't changed much. Her dark hair, flecked with grey, was in the same Beatle bob that it had been thirty years before, and her heavy-rimmed glasses had been replaced with a frameless pair. She wore a straight silk shift that hung to her ankles and Joan was certain the pattern of bright tangerine and teal swirls was an original hand-painted design. They fell into each other's arms and Joan felt herself pushing back tears again. It was either pre-menstrual or pre-menopausal, this constant urge to cry, compounded by the stressful night. There was comfort in the incensed silk shoulder. She held Hazel at arm's length.

"It's quite a shock, isn't it?"

Hazel nodded. Her eyes were swollen red, as though she'd been crying for hours. She took the tissue that Joan offered and wiped the tears from under her glasses. "He'd been unhappy most of his life, Joannie. Maybe now he's found peace at last."

This seemed a strange reaction to Roger's murder. Hazel was a minister, and even when they were kids she'd been the rational one, but it was a placid position in the face of such violence.

The crowd was filing into the school. Hazel took Joan's arm and they entered together.

The gymnasium stink rushed at Joan. A hundred windbreakers, rain jackets and sweatshirts, a hundred pairs of running shoes, rain boots and loafers crammed into close, airless quarters permeated the room, along with variations of soap, shampoos, and colognes. The worst, though, was the smell of sweat pouring from bodies that had consumed far too much liquor the night before.

Gabe stood at a podium set on the floor instead of up on the stage. Just like Gabe, she thought, to want to be on the same level as everyone. She let escape a small smile.

"He's changed some, but not in the important ways," Hazel observed.

Gabe thanked everyone for coming, introduced his team, then proceeded with official business. The RCMP knew little more than they had in the wee hours of the morning. It was important to the investigation that they talk to everyone and get the necessary contact information before anyone left town. Joan wasn't sure she'd get away that easily, given Marlena's insane accusation that she had murdered Roger.

The woman Mr. Fowler had identified as Daphne raised her hand. Of all the women in the room she seemed the most perfectly made-up today. Her hair was precisely sprayed in place. "I can't stick around," she called out. "I have to get to Calgary by six o'clock." Her voice was abrupt and impatient this morning. This was a far cry from the timid girl Joan had known in high school. Gabe told her that an officer would take her information right away, and they'd see what they could do about getting her on her way as soon as possible.

Gabe then singled out Peg. She looked pale and unsteady. He reminded her that they needed a complete list of reunion guests. Then he thanked everyone again and left the podium.

Before anyone could get away, Ed Fowler hurried to the microphone and announced that he had organized an evening of board games at the old school, now the cultural centre. The caterers had agreed to set-up in the hallway there for an Italian-themed buffet. His cheery smile belied the tragedy that was keeping them all in Madden. One would have thought that this recent turn of events had created a wonderful opportunity. Joan had no idea whether or not Mr. Fowler had a wife and kids or any social circle, but he was obviously enjoying the company from his past.

Ed Fowler had been kind to her mother, her brothers, and her. He had made them feel as though they belonged in Madden when the common attitude was that the Parker family had made their own bed because her father had spent beyond his means. She recalled Fowler quoting Robert Kennedy, insisting that they all had the potential, through small actions, to change the world. He applauded moral courage, and outside the classroom, he practised those teachings by supporting her family despite community disapproval. People in the gym were grumbling at his suggestion of Scrabble and rummy. Although she usually avoided large social gatherings, she would make a point of showing up at her old teacher's tournament. It was time to repay his kindness.

She still hadn't touched base with Peg in person, so she hovered near while the reunion chairperson met with Gabe. The only thing that looked healthy about her was her generous head of silky black hair. When she started to waver, Gabe helped her to a seat. It certainly looked worse than a twenty-four hour bug.

A flurry of activity caught Joan's attention. People were gathering around a small table as though it was an end-of-the-year clearance sale. Over their shoulders she could see that they were flipping through the 1979 Madden yearbook. She felt a heavy weight in her chest. Her family had left town before she could pick up her copy. Although she'd paid for it, she'd never even seen it. She wondered again if her photo had been included or if all record of her time at Madden High had vanished. She felt as though she was intruding on a private ceremony and turned toward a display of student art, staring at the charcoal sketches of motorbikes and flowers until the crowd around the yearbook began to thin.

Once everyone had drifted away, Joan went to the table. The book, bound in the navy-and-gold school colours, was open to photographs of a school production of *The Princess and the Pea*. She recognized Rudy Weiss sitting on the edge of the stage holding a ukulele. The next few pages featured athletic teams. A fuzzy shot of Hazel lifting the regional volleyball trophy above her head, the photo poorly framed and out of focus, was credited to "Marly", some aspiring photographer who, hopefully, had developed more skill over the years. Joan tentatively flipped to the headshots of the graduating class. There she was, in the middle of the bottom row. She stared into the eyes of her younger self. This girl's entire life was about to change seconds after the picture was snapped. Had already changed, but she hadn't known it. She scanned the page and saw both Candy and Peg. It was odd how they had switched personalities. Candy was the bouncing and familiar middle-aged woman. Peg was now tired and unsettled looking. Joan turned to the next page. The smell of the old high school overwhelmed her as it wafted up from the pages. With a certainty that she couldn't explain, she felt that the solution to Roger's murder was in the pages of this book but, as she scanned the rows of faces, nobody whispered any clue.

Joan hadn't been in a high school washroom in years but the aroma hadn't changed: heavy bleach and hairspray. She found Peg dabbing at her eyes with a long tail of toilet paper. After polite comments about Joan's purple hair, Peg broke down in tears again.

"This flu makes me madder than a drunken, tired hornet. I've spent three years planning this reunion. Three years. I thought it would be a party — *my party*." She stopped then blurted out, "I haven't had a man since one of my patients took me out five years ago. What if that was my last sex? I thought this weekend would change all that. One more romance, even a weekend fling, that's all I want! Hell, I even fantasized about ol' Roger. Until he was so rude to me about paying for his motel room." She blew her nose. "I feel so stupid. Please don't tell anyone."

When Joan emerged from the bathroom, Gabe took her arm and steered her away from the crowd. "I know it was hard for you to come back to Madden. It shouldn't have happened this way." He spoke breathlessly, as though he had to rush the words out or they'd get stuck behind formality, dissolved by the light of day. "But I'm glad you're here. I woke up thinking about you."

She was floored by his candor. Joan was accustomed to erecting steely walls of propriety when it came to professional situations. It flustered her that he was so open, especially at the centre of a murder investigation. She wanted to know if "thinking of you" meant he was plotting her arrest or imagining her dancing naked. As he asked her about Roger, she suppressed the questions that she had for him.

No, she hadn't had contact with Roger since leaving Madden thirty years before. No, she hadn't kept up with anyone. Several times Gabe had to repeat his questions because Joan's mind was wandering. What kind of relationship had developed between him and Roger? And there was one question she was most interested in having answered. Finally she blurted it out: "Do you believe what Marlena told you last night, Gabe, about Roger and me?"

He looked awkward. "I can't answer that. It's my job to listen." He was embarrassed, which worried Joan. If Gabe doubted her, what chance did she have of convincing anyone else?

"You know it isn't true." She watched his tortured expression and could tell it was hard for him. "Roger the Dodger?" she laughed nervously. "Me and Roger? Can you even begin to imagine it?"

This dragged a crooked smile out of him. He told her he had to meet with his officers to go over all the interview material.

"When can I go home, Gabe?"

"Soon. Soon." He closed his notebook, briefly put his hand over hers where it rested on her knee. "Can we get together later?"

Before she could answer, Hazel joined them. "Hey, Hazel," Joan instinctively asked, "do you want to get together with us for coffee later?"

"Hell, I'll need a beer by the end of today."

Hazel had held onto her best qualities; her sense of humour, her lack of criticism and judgment, her thirst for a good time. The three of them agreed to meet at a place called Jacques Bistro. Gabe went to his next interview. Hazel said she had visiting to do in town. Her parents had died many years before and Joan wondered who it was that she still visited in Madden. She looked around for Peg, but she had disappeared. With several hours to kill, Joan decided to go back to the motel for a warm sweater, then she'd grab lunch and go for a long walk to let the spring air fill her nostrils.

Chapter Seven

An earlier urban planner at Madden City Hall had the foresight to protect the riverbank as recreational property. The core of the plan was a web of trails connected by rustic bridges and stairs. To make room, the city had bought up Vern's Wreckers, two old farm sites, and had arranged a public path through the old Madden Mobile Home Park. The trail started behind the motel and ran through the forest of pines and poplars all the way to the railway tracks, where it joined the far end of Main Street.

Joan picked up a map of the parkway from the front desk of the Twin Pines and decided to walk into town. She passed a sign warning cyclists that the path was steep and rocky. Soon after that the trail dipped abruptly down the riverbank. Luckily the pathway had been spared the pine beetle infestation that had devastated so many forests in the West. The thick trees met overhead and Joan was soon walking through a tunnel of green. On one side the river rushed by, and on the other large rocks and dark clay created a natural, crumbling wall. Except for the distant highway sounds, she might be a million miles from anywhere.

She'd been walking for several minutes when she realized that she wasn't alone on the path. Quick footsteps pattered ahead. As she rounded a curve she saw a figure: a woman, rather tall, hoodie drawn up over her head, was slipping and sliding in flimsy footwear. Joan couldn't make out the face. The woman sped up and Joan lost sight of her. But when she rounded the next corner she could see the woman trying to climb down the path toward the river. With a sudden cry, she slid down the lower bank and landed with a thud. As Joan raced toward her, she recalled last night when she'd tried to assist someone in peril. Marlena had turned on her. With care, she approached the spot where the woman had disappeared and saw arms and legs tangled among branches and deadwood. The woman looked up. It was Daphne. Her sunglasses were askew on her nose and her backcombed hair stood up from her head like a rooster's plume. She smiled meekly. "Hi there, Cupcake."

As Joan pulled Daphne up the bank, it became clear that the other woman had no idea who she was.

"I'm Joan." The reminder elicited a blank stare from Daphne. "Parker. Joan Parker."

"Of course. Joan, Joannie. How the heck are you?"

She suspected from this over-enthusiastic but hollow response that Daphne still didn't recognize her. It was a blow. Was she so unforgettable that even someone who had been a friend, one of a very few, couldn't remember her? Not only had they had several classes together, but they'd also shared the lemon gin fiasco.

As she helped Daphne to her feet and brushed the dead leaves from her jacket, she had a closer look at her former classmate. The heavy makeup had made her look older under the harsh light of the gymnasium, but in the soft light of day and with her sunglasses perched comically, Daphne looked far younger than her years. "What kind of life," she wondered, "had left so few lines and scars?"

They walked together along the path. Joan did most of the talking. Although Daphne was vague about many things, she did remember that Joan had left in November before they graduated. Daphne too had left early, in May. This was news to Joan and she felt a sudden bond. It was the first time either had been back to Madden. She asked Daphne what changes were most surprising to her.

"The school seems bigger, especially the gym. But it's been so many years." She spoke haltingly.

Joan was puzzled. "But that school wasn't built until a dozen years after we left." She looked at Daphne with concern. She had heard of people with early onset dementia. Was that what was happening to Daphne? Was it safe for her to be out on the paths by herself? "Daph, are you okay?"

The other woman shot her a nervous glance. But there was something else in her eyes. Anger? "It hasn't been a walk in the garden, Joan. After I left Madden, I got sick. Encephalitis," Daphne offered curtly.

Joan knew of this condition, the devastating swelling of the brain. The effects were frightening. A lot of patients died. One woman she knew, a lab technician at Constellation, had been a victim of West Nile virus that resulted in encephalitis. It had taken months for her to regain her speech, and now she was confined to a wheelchair.

Daphne continued. "They never found out why or how I got it, just one of those things. It destroyed my long-term memory. Besides that, I'm fine. Better than anyone expected."

"I'm so sorry, Daphne."

Daphne brushed it off. "I'm one of the lucky ones." Then she chuckled, almost to herself. "I prefer not to live in the past

– because I can't. It makes for some awkward social situations. I almost didn't come to the reunion."

So the prettiest girl in high school had also had reservations about returning to Madden. Joan didn't usually take the initiative to make physical contact, but she felt drawn to thread her arm through Daphne's arm. Silently, she reprimanded herself for her own whining about making the trip. What a self-pitying loser. Her life had only improved since she left town. Her hurdles led to accomplishments. Daphne was far braver than she. She would forgive her for looking so great.

"You're staying with Peg. How did you guys reconnect after all these years?"

"She called me out of the blue," said Daphne. "I have to say, I was surprised to be invited since I wasn't on the graduating list."

"Same here," added Joan. She marvelled at the similarities in their journeys to Madden.

"She even invited me to stay with her. By the time I got here, though, she was puking all over the place. Poor Peg. Knocked the stuffing out of her going out this morning. I had to put her back to bed before I came out."

The two women decided to have lunch together. As they walked through the woods, then into the modest downtown core, Daphne shared her story. She had married less than a year after leaving Madden. Then she got sick. After her recovery, she had a little girl. She hardly mentioned her husband, an insurance salesman, but spoke dreamily of her child and their fairytale relationship. Patti had excelled in school and gone onto college. Patti could have done anything, but had settled on hair and esthetics. She now owned her own beauty salon. Daphne worked with her, scheduling appointments and ordering supplies, keeping the place spick-and-span.

In their youth Main Street had been the only commercial street in Madden. The gravel road had been muddy in spring and choked with dust in the summer. On either side of the street there had been modest shops: a hardware, sewing-machine shop, drug store, all practical, nothing more glamorous than an occasional new awning. All that had changed. Main Street was now one of several streets alive with business. Flower baskets hung from stylish lampposts. Garbage cans were hidden in wood-picket containers that matched benches on the corners. A computer shop sat next to a trendy café, the old Royal Bank building housed an upscale clothing store, and at the far end of the street, Jack's Chinese and Western Restaurant had been transformed into Jacques Bistro. Joan was in awe of the change. Enough of the structures remained to keep it familiar, but now it had a manufactured small-town prettiness that it hadn't in the past.

By this time they were both relaxed and laughing. Neither had mentioned the murder. They decided to try Jacques Bistro for lunch, even though Joan knew she'd be there later with Gabe and Hazel. No scent of the deep fryer. No thirty-five cent coffee. Caffeine now came in Americanos at two-fifty a pop. Both women ordered the spinach salad with strawberries, and the greens and berries were plump and fresh. This was a far cry from the iceberg-and-radish salad drowned in French dressing of thirty years ago.

Joan couldn't be sure, but the Jacques who served them now, with diamond-studded eyebrow ring, could very well be the annoying toddler who used to hide under the tables and tie their shoelaces together when she and her friends were sipping cokes.

For a while Jack's had been their battlefield. Gabe, Hazel, and Joan would hang out, stack coffee creamers and plan their getaway from Madden. Marlena and her gang, including Candy and Peg, would come in with the jocks. Sometimes Daphne would be with them. Inevitably Marlena would throw insults at Joan's table. Usually Joan and her friends would clear out, determined not to admit that the nastiness bothered them. On one occasion, though, Jack Sr. had become so infuriated that he'd marched right up to Marlena's table and, in his heavily accented English, had given her the boot. He'd then poured Joan and her friends a free refill. Daphne hadn't left with Marlena and the others, but had come to Joan's table to apologize, then had sat down with them. She'd been one of those people who was decent to everyone.

"What are you smiling about," asked Daphne.

Joan shook her head. "Just remembering."

"Lucky you," joked Daphne.

"You were a nice kid, Daphne. You may not remember, but you were."

Daphne smiled and the pink blush rose in her cheeks.

"We hung out together at a bush party once at the beginning of grade twelve. I had a run-in with Roger Rimmer that night." It was the first time either had mentioned Roger.

Daphne lowered her head. "He wasn't very nice, was he?"

"You remember that?" asked Joan.

Daphne shook her head. "No, but people don't want to talk about him, not the way you'd think they would after someone . . . " she paused, " . . . passes away."

They were both silent for a moment, then Daphne looked up with a bold smile. "The lemon gin!" she exclaimed.

"You remember?" Joan asked.

Daphne nodded and added, "It's one of the few things I do remember."

Joan wasn't surprised. She was still overcoming her re-acquaintance with the scent of that odious liquor. Despite working with scent for years, Joan still marvelled at the noble, underrated nose. Its true beauty was as a channel to the powerful olfactory channel. It leads us to our mates, warns us of our enemies, and is the memory sense. One whiff hurls us back decades to mints from grandma's pocket, smoke from a deadly fire, or fumes from a pungent bottle of lemon gin.

Daphne popped the last strawberry into her mouth and pushed her salad plate away. "I'm embarrassed to say I don't remember anything at all about Roger. What was he like?"

Joan chose her words carefully. "He wasn't afraid to follow his dreams, whether it was music or girls. He loved them both." Joan paused. "His parents must be devastated."

"They're still alive?" asked Daphne.

Joan nodded. "Hazel said they're still in the same house."

Daphne stared into the distance. "I never even talked to him, to Roger." Tears welled. She dabbed at her eyes with a crumpled tissue, missing a tear that created a rivulet through her caked makeup. "I wish I'd at least talked to him."

The two women sat in awkward silence. It struck Joan as odd that, until now, they'd been able to carry on as though it was just another day. But they'd landed in the middle of a murder investigation. As Daphne put the tissue back in her purse, Joan noticed the ripped lining and broken zipper. Everything about Daphne had given Joan the impression that she was well off, but maybe that wasn't the case. This trip to Madden may have been difficult for Daphne for other reasons. Not everyone can take time off and rent a car to drive to another province. Was that why Peg had insisted that Daphne stay with her? "My treat," Joan hurriedly said, placing two twenties on the table.

They said their goodbyes on Main Street. Daphne was headed up the hill to check on Peg and to see if there was any message from the police about whether or not she could leave. "I was scared to come," Daphne said, "but I thought, somehow, it might help me remember. Instead it all seems brand-spanking new." She took Joan's hand and looked her in the eye. "But in a good way. Now I hardly want to leave."

Joan felt guilty as she passed by the cultural centre, or the Couch, as it was now known. She knew that Mr. Fowler was inside preparing for his big games night. She would have stopped to help, but her head was spinning from lack of sleep. She convinced herself that he'd have corralled enough people to give him a hand and vowed that she'd catch up with him later in the evening. She needed to close her eyes before meeting with Gabe and Hazel.

As she approached the Twin Pines, she had a sudden memory of her mother coming home in her chambermaid uniform, lighting a cigarette and rubbing her tired feet through the reinforced toes of her nylons. Vi didn't like to bad-mouth anyone. She avoided the neighbour ladies who counted their currency in gossip. On one particular evening, Joan recalled her mother laughing about "the shenanigans of Maddigan."

"People think they're invisible once they're on motel property, even in the light of day. Management should install revolving doors in those cabins so those people having affairs wouldn't need to stop to unlock doors." Never once, though, did she divulge any names.

Inside her cabin, Joan stripped to her bra and panties then curled up under the orange-and-brown bedspread for a short nap. Her last thought before drifting off was that the Twin Pines Resort, despite its facelift, was still steeped in scandal.

Chapter Eight

A SHARP KNOCK AT THE DOOR roused her. She glanced at the clock and groaned. She only had twenty minutes before she was supposed to meet Gabe and Hazel. Damn! Why hadn't she set the alarm? She slipped into her clothes and buttoned her blouse. Carefully, she cracked open the door and saw a tall, stern-looking policeman. Behind him stood Des Cardinal, who nodded a silent "hello."

"Mrs. Parker?" asked the officer.

Joan was about to correct him with "Ms" but stopped herself. It wasn't the time to appear argumentative or raise feminist alarms. She just nodded.

"I'm Staff Sergeant Smartt from the Major Crime Unit in Kamloops. You know Corporal Cardinal. I need to ask you a few more questions about the Rimmer incident."

She stepped out of the way. It made her uncomfortable having the two strange men in her messy motel room. She wished that she had at least picked her panties up from the floor. She considered kicking them under the bed. Would this Smartt assume she was hiding some sort of evidence? She smiled involuntarily then realized that both men were watching her. Now, she thought, they either think I'm guilty as hell or a loon.

Smartt immediately made it clear that he leaned toward the former. "We understand that you were not originally on the invitation list for the reunion."

She looked from Smartt to Cardinal.

"Margaret Chalmers gave us the invitation list. Your name had been added to the bottom in pencil, yours and one other. All the other names were typed."

"But Peg — Margaret — is the one who phoned me. She invited me."

Smartt ignored her. "We compared the list to school records. It appears you weren't in the graduating class of nineteen seventy-nine."

She could feel herself getting red in the face. "Is this about Marlena Stanfield?"

Des Cardinal spoke up. "Sorry, Ms. Parker, but we have to follow up on anything we've got. Which isn't much." He was silenced by a glare from Smartt.

"I think she's said enough." Gabe stepped into the room and put a hand firmly on Joan's shoulder. "You all right?"

She nodded, forcing back tears of relief.

"I'm leading this case now, Thiessen," Smartt said. "It's clearly a homicide. My division. You're out of bounds."

"Out of bounds?"

"You heard me," retorted Smartt.

"Okay, then, as of now I'm removing myself from the case entirely. So I'm here as Ms. Parker's friend. It's up to her, not you, whether I stay." He paused. "Unless you're charging her."

It sounded as though Gabe was asking for trouble, then Joan realized that he was calling Smartt's bluff. She wondered about their relationship. There wasn't a spark of warmth, no professional courtesy between these two men.

Gabe went on to suggest that the investigators question Peg again and ask her why Joan's name was added in pencil.

The officers were barely out the door when Gabe firmly closed it behind them. Joan and he stood face to face, neither saying a word.

He gripped her arms. "You're shaking."

She nodded. It was all so weird. "I'm the suspect in a murder investigation."

"And I'm here to help. Marlena mentioned the bit about the guest list."

"Marlena?"

"I thought I'd better get over here. I know you didn't do anything wrong. I know you too well."

Where was this leading? Too much was happening too quickly. She was in a fog. "We don't know each other, Gabe. It's been nearly thirty years since we've even spoken."

"Last night, for the first time, I realized that I've been friendless a long while. Friends in the way people ought to be, laying the bones bare, telling the truth, sharing secrets. Maybe it's because we were kids together. Kids talk about things that adults don't dare. Maybe it's because we shared those wild years. But last night, last night thirty years washed away." He brushed the hair from her face.

The sensible, analytical part of Joan's brain calculated the risk, then the hormones kicked in. Their lips came together and their mouths began exploring, tentatively. As she breathed in the scent that was all Gabe, she heard the police car drive away, crunching on the gravel outside her cabin. This was too fast, too risky, too insane. It was so like the old Gabe to tread this close to the edge. She pulled away.

"We can't. This is going to get us both into trouble."

He ignored her protest, folded his arms around her, and drew her into him. When he leaned in to kiss her again, she welcomed the force of his body. Then the phone rang, shattering the moment like an air raid siren, and she had to steady herself.

She lifted the receiver and heard Mort on the other end. "Hey, babe. How's the holiday?" His cheery voice hit her like a chilly wind. Instinctively, she turned her back to Gabe, then stammered that she'd call back.

By the time she hung up, Gabe was at the door. The interruption had killed the moment. Embarrassment hung between them. She wasn't practiced at having an afternoon rendezvous in a motel room. Nor, it appeared, was Gabe. They haltingly agreed to meet at Jacque's Bistro. Gabe promised to apologize to Hazel for the delay.

Through the crack in the curtains, Joan watched him cross the gravel parking lot. His loping gait was still familiar after all these years. It continued to puzzle her, though, how Gabe and Roger had ended up as friends. What could they possibly have had in common? She resolved to ask him.

Before leaving for her drink with Hazel and Gabe, she had a call to return.

"Hey, you, where have you been hiding?" Mort's tone was light, but beneath the question was concern.

She felt a numbing guilt. Despite the wall that had grown between them, they were friends and she appreciated Mort's gentle bruin warmth. He was always there to protect her. They'd never completely severed their tie even after the separation.

The final dagger in their marriage had come six months earlier. Joan had phoned home from Tokyo, at dinnertime in Vancouver, and heard a woman's voice in the background. Mort casually volunteered that he was entertaining some friends, barbequing in the rain. He happily rattled off the names of his guests and she realized she knew none of them. Worse, she didn't care. Their lives had grown completely separate. Yes, they occasionally exercised their libidos together, but it was a friends-with-benefits deal; a stress relief, warm and perfunctory, like a good pedicure.

She told Mort about Roger's death and the police questioning her.

"Damn, I should never have let you go on your own, Joannie."

He updated her on the store fire. Arson wasn't suspected. Carelessness appeared to be the culprit. He'd been asked to attend the employee interviews to provide support.

As he spoke, she imagined what it would have been like if Mort had come with her to Madden. He would have charmed everyone in a way that Joan never could. Roger probably wouldn't have hit on her, and Marlena wouldn't have had reason to be jealous. She wouldn't have connected with Gabe. They wouldn't have spent the evening together reliving their youth. She wouldn't be breathless from being alone with him in her motel room just now. In that moment, she vowed that she'd never sleep with Mort again. It wasn't a thread keeping them tied together. It was a chain that kept both of them from moving on.

"Don't worry about me, Mort."

"Of course I'll worry about you. Now, call when you get on the road. I'll go stock the fridge at the condo, cook you some grub . . . "

"You don't need to do that," she interrupted abruptly.

"I don't mind at all. It's not a problem," he replied.

"It's starting to be. It's my fridge." She told him she'd call when she got back to Vancouver.

After hanging up, she looked out at the familiar dark pines, She cracked open the window and breathed deeply until she could taste the forest air, and wondered, for the first time, where home was.

Staff Sergeant Smartt's jaw muscle was working overtime. While the homicide cop from Kamloops seemed to be offering an olive branch, his unconscious clenching told the truth. Smartt had no option but to ask Gabe to rejoin the Rimmer case. The Elgar RCMP detachment that served Madden was understaffed. Gabe ran a tight ship and the only way they'd make any headway in a timely manner was if he rallied his officers.

Gabe knew that his relationships with his old classmates weighed in his favour. While his connection to the reunion could be construed as a conflict, it was also a bridge. He hadn't been Mr. Popularity in high school, but now he was trusted. He hated playing games, but he wasn't shy about using a trick or two if it helped move an investigation forward.

The central area of the Elgar station was hushed. Everyone was waiting for him to respond to Smartt's offer. He waited. The air crackled with tension. Des's spoon clanked against his mug as he slowly stirred his coffee. Janine, the high-strung receptionist, didn't pretend to look away. Gabe's silent gambit wasn't for the entertainment of those watching but for the autonomy that he needed so he could make decisions quickly and command the respect necessary to run this investigation. Second ticked away. The LED display on the clock announced another minute.

The Kamloops homicide officer sputtered out a blast of contained breath. "Whatever resources you need . . . "

Gabe smiled and held out his hand to seal the deal.

Every time the door to Jacque's Bistro opened, Joan looked up. She wished she had brought a book to hide behind. Normally it didn't bother her to sit alone in a restaurant. She'd spent hours in airport hotel dining rooms with her laptop, the blend of foreign languages and music creating a comforting hum, in pleasant contrast to a Spartan, silent hotel room late at night. Being alone in that context, one in an army of jet-lagged people, defined her as part of that cultural milieu, an essential piece in the mosaic. The rules were different in Madden. Here "alone" was just "alone". Out of place. Unwanted. Thirty years were suddenly sucked away in a vacuum. Once again Joan was the girl who didn't quite fit. She picked up the menu one more time. If Gabe and Hazel took much longer, she'd have the house specials memorized.

As she went down the now familiar list, she caught herself comparing it to the old menu of Jack's Café. Instead of chicken chow mien, there was chicken with braised pea pods and lemon grass. She could imagine its delicately scented perfume. Roast lamb with curried cranberry compote had replaced Jack's artery-clogging cheeseburger, and vanilla ice cream had given way to fresh raspberry gelato. She was taking solace in the fact that the menu had changed as much as she had, when Gabe walked though the door.

As he slid into the booth across from her, she had an overwhelming sense of déjà vu. It was like living in two worlds at once.

"Smartt saw the light. I'm back on the case." It was obvious that he was enthusiastic about the change.

Joan, though, was disappointed. They'd spend less time together. The line would be drawn between them – he the law enforcement man, she the murder suspect. She gave herself an inner slap for selfishness. Of course Gabe should be running the show. That would achieve the best outcome. It made sense. She straightened her back against the booth and forced her biggest smile. "That's great, Gabe."

He saw through her lame imitation of happiness. Reaching over, he squeezed her fingertips, an ambiguous physical gesture that could mean just about anything.

"What's the matter?" he asked.

Words were slow to come. They shouldn't be alone together. The optics were bad for both of them, but for the first time in her life, she couldn't control herself. As a teenager, her hormones had run high, had ruled her life, but she couldn't remember ever wanting him in this way. Neither of them had resembled a teen idol. Physical desire hadn't been part of the equation — at least not for her. Now Gabe was married, a father. She sensed danger in the air and put up a shield.

"How did you and Roger end up as friends?"

He leaned back with a weary sigh. He explained that Roger boomeranged between California and Madden, returning frequently to visit his parents. "It became difficult to avoid him. The pool hall, the bar." He grinned. "My work takes me to all the best places."

"Go on."

"One time, when Hazel was in town, she asked me to watch out for him."

"Hazel? But she loathed Roger."

The incident that had brought them to a boil over Roger and had tied the three outcasts even closer as friends had been an offence directed at Hazel. She had been the star center on the girls' high school basketball team. After the Madden Rockets had won the Regional Division tournament, their team picture had been posted outside the school office. Steve Howard, who had just joined Rank as bass player, had drawn a penis protruding from Hazel's shorts. Sweet Hazel, who'd never hurt anyone, spent a weekend in tears.

Joan had called Gabe and together the three of them had plotted. On Monday, Hazel led the charge. In her firm, controlled manner, she marched into the school office and demanded that the principal deal with the incident. It was as much a political statement about tolerance toward gays and lesbians as anything else. The school administration balked at her demand so the three of them had banded together in protest, refusing to leave the front office until justice was served.

Eventually Mr. Fowler and one of the bachelor trustees came forward in support of Hazel. The principal had no choice but to confront Steve. The teenager caved, revealing that Roger had forced him to do it, had threatened to find another bass player if he didn't. Steve wasn't a bad kid and had been wracked by guilt. Roger never denied any of it. He made a mocking apology that just reinforced that he had minions to do his bidding. That was all the administration expected, and it was never spoken of again.

"Roger became a project for Hazel. In the past few months he had been coming to town more often and seemed to be straightening out. He was excited about playing with Rank again. Couldn't get enough rehearsing in. They'd jam up at Ray and Marlena's."

"Were you close?" asked Joan.

"I'd stop to chat when I saw him on the street. We played a few games of pool. Truthfully, that's as close as I wanted it. Then it got complicated. Earlier this month I was called over to Mountain View. You remember the seniors' home?"

She nodded.

"Roger was caught with his hand in the cookie jar. At the front desk there's a box to pay for raffle tickets. It's an honour system. You put five bucks in the box and write your name on a ticket stub. There's a monthly prize, dinner for two at the local pizza joint, handmade quilt, that kind of thing. I guess Roger couldn't resist all those fivers staring up at him."

"He was caught red-handed?"

"He tried to bullshit his way out of it, said he was putting money 'in' the jar." Gabe sighed. "Maybe I should have brought him in. None of this would've happened."

"Why didn't you?"

"There was a lot of pressure to let it slide. Roger may not have had a lot of friends, but his father is still a pillar here. There was a time when Madden wouldn't have had a doctor if Tom Rimmer hadn't stuck around. He and Laura could've been soaking up the winter sun in Mexico rather than shovelling snow. There's a sense around here that he's owed."

"So Dr. Rimmer applied pressure?" asked Joan.

"Oh no, never. The doc didn't expect Roger to get special treatment. Didn't want it either, if you ask me. That's just how it is here."

"What was Roger doing at the seniors home?"

Gabe shrugged. "He wouldn't say."

As they sat in weighted silence, the waitress came to their table. Young, hip, and svelte, she could have been serving in any downtown Vancouver restaurant. This pleased Joan. She was developing an odd sense of pride in her old hometown.

"Hey there, Gabe. Someone named Hazel left a message for you. She can't make it for dinner. She said something's come up."

As the young woman took their orders, Joan realized that she was pleased that Hazel wouldn't be joining them. Every moment alone with Gabe felt delicious, like stolen time.

They ate their dinners in easy companionship. Gabe fed her a sample bite of his dinner and smiled as she confidently identified the tastes. His beef tenderloin was seasoned with a delicate mix of ground peppercorn, black, green, and red, but the sauce had been prepared with an artificial beef base added to the fine masala, which to her seemed a culinary crime. He parted his lips to taste her mango salsa, and she felt a sensual thrill run up her back and into her breasts as she slid her fork into his mouth. She could hardly get the words out to describe how the salt of sun-dried tomatoes and the bite of the fresh cilantro combined in perfect harmony with the ripe fruit.

By the time dessert arrived, they were laughing happily at their teenaged antics and sharing anecdotes about what had happened in the intervening years. Although both told stories of funny and horrific dating disasters, neither spoke of their spouses. Before coffee arrived, Joan saw that Gabe was glancing at his watch every few minutes. Their time was coming to a close.

Gabe sat up straighter and his voice became more formal as the conversation turned to work. He talked about the many interviews he still needed to do and the paperwork that would keep him up until late. When he tried to wrestle the bill from her, insisting that she was on his turf, she argued that Madden belonged to both of them.

She'd spent so many years feeling as though she were faking it, as though luck had been the essential element in her success, whether at university in the chemistry faculty "pretending" to be a scientist or at work posing as a team leader. During the past thirty years her memory had filled with grey clouds when her thoughts turned to Madden. But now she knew that this town, with Gabe and Hazel, was the last place that she'd really felt she belonged.

She was disappointed when he stood up to leave. A corner of her mouth turned up in a half-smile that pleaded "don't go."

He bent down. Instead of repeating the brotherly kiss on her cheek, this time he touched his lips to hers and held them there for the briefest moment.

"See ya'," he whispered in her ear before standing.

As he walked out she was sorry that she'd driven downtown. If she'd begged a lift it would have given her an excuse to be alone with Gabe in his truck, driving down Main street at his side, parking at the Twin Pines . . .

God, she laughed to herself. I really am an emotionally stunted juvenile.

The young waitress cleared Gabe's coffee cup with a clatter and Joan noticed her abrupt critical glance. The bottom dropped out of her stomach. So this is how it happens. She'd trespassed into illicit territory. This could mess things up big time, for Gabe's reputation, for the investigation. She didn't understand what was behind his public show of affection, but next time she'd control herself.

CHAPTER NINE

GABE PARKED HIS SUBURBAN BETWEEN TWO RCMP cruisers in the Twin Pines parking lot. The crime scene squad was busy at work. It was hard to believe that only twenty-four hours earlier Roger had been prancing across the stage under a pulsating light show. Although it was almost eight o'clock on Saturday evening, it was still broad daylight. At this time of year, a month before summer solstice, it wouldn't get dark until almost eleven. The long, hot summer evenings were something Gabe had missed during the years that he'd lived farther south, and the barely dark night skies would always bind him to this place.

Pulling on a pair of translucent latex gloves, he walked toward Roger's cabin and considered how Roger's choices had been responsible for determining this fate. The singer had known that the reunion committee was trying to save money, but he'd insisted they put him up at the Twin Pines so he wouldn't be forced to stay with his parents. Undoubtedly, he'd hoped to score — women, grass, coke, something — and his parents had laid down the law years before. Although Mrs. Rimmer doted on him, the doctor was hard as nails. Making up for past leniency, Gabe figured. At any rate, if Roger had been in bed up on the hill on Friday night, he'd probably still be alive.

Gabe stepped over the threshold and surveyed the room. A team member, wearing white coveralls, knelt on the floor, scraping up one of many blood samples. On the other side of the bed, Corporal Pam McFarlane was slowly tracking a light over the carpet, checking for blood splatter. She was a scrawny little thing who looked as though she should still be in high school, but she was the most thorough and dedicated cop he had, destined to climb the ladder quickly if RCMP politics didn't fail her. Gabe went to the bedside table where two glasses sat undisturbed. The first, a typical motel waterglass, held a bridge of four front teeth. Obviously Roger wasn't expecting company when his killer arrived. It ruled out a date gone bad.

"McFarlane," he said, "could you please make sure these get checked out before the funeral. Can't let his last appearance be without his famous smile."

She nodded solemnly as she took the glass. "When will that be, Gabe?"

He sighed. They both knew the answer depended upon their investigation. "Let's hope it's soon, Corporal."

She nodded and went back to her task.

Gabe lifted the second glass with his gloved hand. It was a highball tumbler from the lounge. As he waved it under his nose, he recognized aged single-malt scotch. Roger would have been drinking the best since the tab was on the Grad Committee. On the dresser, several items were secured in labelled plastic bags laid out in tidy rows. One item in particular caught his eye. He raised the bag to examine the contents. Inside was an eight-by-ten colour print that had been ripped down the middle then taped back together. Holding it to the overhead light, he recognized the faces. It was a group photograph taken on the afternoon of their high school grad, thirty years before.

The graduation ceremony had been held in early May. After certificates had been handed out, a formal prom had allowed parents either to revel in the glow of their bright lights or to sigh with relief that barely literate offspring had the paper to prove they'd made it through twelve years, or more, of public school. The evening after-party belonged to the kids and was a tribute to debauchery. Designated drivers and dry grads wouldn't be introduced in Madden for another ten years. Seat belts hadn't been mandatory and were usually ignored. Parents waited at home in fear. They listened for the sound of sirens, and were thrilled when drunken sons and vomiting daughters staggered through the door. This photograph, though, was taken at the beginning of it all. Fresh-faced girls, long-haired boys, all in their best outfits, posing for the camera, daring the world to come at them.

Gabe shook his head at the tall beanpole in the back row, pimples glowing orange in the faded colour of the old print. He felt sorry for the awkward youth he'd been. Joan, of course, was absent. There, in a tall, stiff shirt collar, head slightly cocked, was Roger, the best looking of the bunch. With curls hanging in golden ringlets to his chin, he had a feminine quality that had always appealed to the girls. Had he tried to destroy the photograph or had it ripped by accident?

Joan left her car on Main Street and walked the few blocks to the Couch for Mr. Fowler's games night. It was a beautiful evening. The rain shower earlier had washed the sand and salt from the streets. Ancient, twisted lilac trees crowded the stone steps leading to the front door of the old brick building. The bold scent of the white and mauve blossoms announced that the valley was on the brink of summer.

As soon as Joan entered the hallway, she saw that the interior of the building had been entirely renovated. It barely resembled the school where she had lived out long days for almost three years. Vibrant murals covering the halls from floor to ceiling had replaced institutional pink and green paint. Entire walls had been knocked out, resulting in an open lounge in the middle of the building. One door was propped open and she was drawn to the sound of the party. Her first impression was that she was entering a teepee. Three classrooms had been combined to create a large, informal space that was much larger than it appeared from the outside. Hanging lights with colorful paper shades gave the impression of a lower ceiling and made the room warm and intimate.

Mr. Fowler appeared to be in his element. He roamed the room with his glasses pulled down on his nose, chattering away to his guests, providing instructions and advice. There were four card tables set up around the room and a game of chess was in session on a coffee table over by a worn couch. Rank guitarist Rudy Weiss and his wife Monica were playing Monopoly with two other couples at one table. Undoubtedly it wasn't what they had imagined themselves doing on this Saturday night, but they probably welcomed the chance to get out of their hotel room. Their drive home to Prince George would be long and monotonous. Although the police couldn't officially hold anyone, most alumni were staying out of courtesy, or curiosity. There were a couple of others she vaguely recognized, people who as kids had been bussed in from farms and smaller towns to attend high school.

When Mr. Fowler caught sight of Joan, he came over, hooked his arm into hers, and led her to a table occupied by Daphne, Candy, and the stern-looking woman with salt-and-pepper hair who had intimidated Joan at the registration desk the night before.

The woman was introduced as Tracey. She had moved into town at the beginning of grade twelve so their paths had hardly, if ever, crossed. Ed Fowler happily crowded in with the four women.

The only game they all knew was blackjack. Joan wasn't much of a card player, and was relieved: blackjack was something she could bail out of easily. She planned on staying no more than fifteen or twenty minutes. It had been a long and stressful day and she was determined to get a good night's sleep.

Once the cards were dealt, Candy pointed out some of their former classmates in the room. Sarah Markle, whom Ray had dumped for Marlena, was seated with her handsome husband who looked several years older than his wife. Sarah was round, stylish, and comfortable looking. Candy whispered that they were both in the Foreign Service and spent a lot of time in Paris.

A man who looked too old to have been in their class made a beeline for Joan.

"Did ya' miss me?" The man pointed a finger like a gun. When he smiled, a row of too-bright teeth glistened.

Joan smiled awkwardly.

"Oh, c'mon Joan. It's me!" He opened his arms as though giving her a better look at his forty-eight inch chest squeezed into a sweater two sizes too small would trigger her memory. All it did was send a wave of Hugo Boss cologne directly up her nose.

"I'm sorry," she stammered, holding back a sneeze and hoping she'd be rescued by someone at the table. She looked at Candy, but the blond card shark was concentrating on her hand.

"A boo, boppa-boo, boppa-boo?"

"I beg your pardon?" His scat reference meant nothing to her.

He repeated "A boo, boppa-boo, boppa-boo, boppa boo," this time slapping his legs to keep time. When her helpless expression didn't change, he finally introduced himself. "C'mon, Joan. It's Gerald. Gerald Gillespie."

"Gerry?" This man couldn't be the quiet boy who sat behind her all through grades 7 and 8. They exchanged a few words then he went back to his seat, despondent that she hadn't recognized him. For a fleeting moment Joan envied Daphne. At least she had an excuse.

Three hours later Joan watched Candy draw another stack of chips toward herself. Every time she won, she pumped her fist up and down hissing "yes" with tremendous satisfaction. Although they were only playing for quarters, Joan figured Candy would soon be able to put that grandson of hers through college. It was time, the women decided, to call it a night. Daphne had already tried to escape twice, pointing out that she'd left Peg all alone up at her house, but Ed Fowler had been eager for them to stay. Everyone else had cleared out half-an-hour earlier.

"I derive immense pleasure from having you girls here." He took Daphne's hand on one side of him then reached for Joan's on the other. "It's hard to keep tabs on you all from a distance. Though with the internet it's much easier than it once was." He looked at them soulfully. "I know it hasn't always been easy for you girls."

Daphne looked as awkward as Joan felt. She pulled her hand from his. "I should really get back to Peg's. What kind of house guest am I if I come tromping in at midnight? Especially when she's not feeling so hot."

Mr. Fowler jumped right in. "Let me give you a lift."

Daphne smiled awkwardly. Joan tried to rescue her by offering to be her chauffeur, but Mr. Fowler was adamant.

"But I go right by there," he insisted.

Joan watched as a weary Daphne followed Ed Fowler to his car.

Raindrops the size of jelly beans splattered Joan's windshield and slid down the side windows in dense rivulets, distorting the outside world. When she parked her car at the Twin Pines a young police constable was strolling the grounds, huddled into his dark slicker. So, she wasn't the only one worried about a killer lurking behind the trees. Glancing in the direction of the swollen river, she noticed that the lights were still on inside Roger's cabin. She didn't envy whoever was left to guard that place on such a bone-chilling night. After securing the door lock, the deadbolt, and the chain, she quickly changed into her nightgown, wrapped herself in her pashmina shawl, and slipped under the covers. She regretted not packing her regular camping pajamas, a pair of adult-sized sleepers with feet and a trap door. The exhaustion she had felt while driving deserted her. She lay stiff as an ice cube waiting for the sheets to warm, conscious of the humming refrigerator, distant traffic, and the rushing river. She listened for the comforting crunch of boots on gravel as the young policeman patrolled and was almost asleep when she realized that his steps hadn't returned to her end of the complex for some time. Had it been seconds? Minutes? An hour? While she lay with her ears tuned to every sound, she heard footsteps again, but this time quieter, as though someone didn't want to be heard. And heavier. This wasn't some lightweight boy in uniform. Joan tried to will the footsteps away, but instead they moved closer and closer. A soft, slow rapping at the door had her choked with fear. She pulled the covers to her ears, afraid that the slightest creaking of the

GLYNIS WHITING

bed would expose her presence. Why *her* door again? Last night it had been Roger and that hadn't ended well, at least for him. A whisper broke the silence.

"Joan." A single syllable, drowned out by rain and the rushing river. It wasn't until the second "Joan" that she bounded out of bed, unfastened the three locks, and threw the door open to Gabe. He glanced carefully back into the yard before slipping into the room. He pulled the door closed behind him.

Furious, Joan slapped his chest. "You scared the b'Jesus out of me."

Besides a glint of light through the crack in the curtains, the room was dark and warm. She could make out the curve of Gabe's nose and the broad outline of his shoulders, but she couldn't read his expression.

"Do you want me to go?" he asked.

She was silent. Every neuron of logic screamed "Get out." In a town that had eyes and ears everywhere, just yards from the spot where Roger was murdered, was the last place they should meet. His presence, though, made her skin tingle.

He gazed down the length of her body, then looked back into her eyes, reached out and pulled her toward him.

She heard his moan as he folded his arms around her, pressing his body into hers. His coat smelled of wet wool tinged with old coffee. He was soaking wet and she was shivering. When she pulled away, he tugged the damp nightgown over her head. At that moment she was thankful that she hadn't been wearing the sleepers with feet that made her look like a gigantic beige rabbit.

Although network television and *Cosmo* would have the world believe that woman over forty are all prowling for younger men, most of those women know that with the older lover comes sensitivity, technique, and a sense of humour.

Besides, they share cultural references. They know that Paul McCartney was with a band before Wings.

Gabe held her beneath the covers and she felt the chill leave her toes. He warmed his hands before cupping her breasts, and as her eyes adjusted to the silvery light, he kissed each nipple. He moved down her body with his kisses, looking up every so often to check her reaction. She could only think, "I could eat him alive, every morsel of him, and not leave a trace." It had been a long time since she had been with anyone besides Mort. How different Gabe's body felt. She didn't want to let go of his buttocks. The way the muscles tightened with his movement. As she explored his body further, she burst out with a playful laugh.

"What?" asked Gabe.

"I expected you to lean to the left. Ah."

His gentle hands had found her sweetest spot. He rolled on top of her and their bodies moved in slow unison. Arousal ran through her like an electric current. Her hips moved involuntarily, cuing him to quicken his pace. She forced him onto his back and rolled on top of him, forgetting the modesty of her half-century-old body as she arched her back to invite him in further. If sex had ever been this good with Mort, it had been long, long ago in another galaxy.

An hour or so later a snore woke her abruptly and she realized she'd made the loud snort. When her eyes adjusted to the dark, she saw Gabe on his elbow, smiling down at her.

"We've waited approximately thirty years, eight months, and nineteen days for this," he said.

"We have?"

"C'mon, you remember. Our deal?"

"I need a few more clues, Gabe. What deal?" Then it came rushing back. As teenagers, they'd joked about helping each other lose their virginity if they hadn't had sex by the time they got to grade twelve As far as she was concerned, it had been a perfunctory matter, something to check off the list as a step toward adulthood.

Gabe now nodded down at her. "You do remember, don't you? We were going to do it that weekend. I knew you weren't serious, so I wasn't totally surprised when you chickened out and went into hiding." He traced her lips with his finger and she lay there thinking about the awful end to that evening. She had to tell Gabe about Roger's attempt to rape her, but now was not the time. Gabe said, "It was serious to me, Joan."

Chapter Ten

Joan woke with a smile on her lips on Sunday morning until she realized that Gabe, very sensibly, had slipped out before the sun was up. She reached over, touched the bed where he'd lain, and breathed deeply to hold the memory of him. A single dark hair lay on the stiff cotton of the hotel pillowcase. She carefully pinched it between her fingers, then ran it across her lips as the reality of the day bombarded her. She debated with herself about visiting the Rimmers. It was more complicated now that she had to weigh the Gabe factor. If anyone found out they'd spent the night together, the investigation would be headed toward disaster. If it was only Marlena accusing her of murdering Roger, she wouldn't worry about it, but Staff Sergeant Smartt seemed to think she had potential as a killer. In the end she decided that she would only reinforce suspicions if she didn't show up. Although Roger hadn't been a friend of hers, Dr. Rimmer had been the Parker family physician all through Joan's childhood. It would be natural for her to pay a call of respect. If she went early she might miss the inevitable crowd.

On the way to the Rimmers', Joan stopped at a dead-end road high on the hill facing the river. She had a stunning view of the Welcome sign, and it seemed to be one of the few places in the county with full cell-phone coverage. She turned the phone over in her hand, watching the illuminated green bars denoting perfect reception. The logical thing to do would be to leave town right after she visited the Rimmers. She should call the Elgar RCMP detachment to see if they wanted her to stay in Madden any longer. It wouldn't be wise to ask for Gabe. If word got out about them it would fuel the rumour mill and set tongues wagging up and down the aisles of the Co-op Store. That, however, wasn't what was needling her. The stakes, in this situation, were much higher than town gossip. Could Gabe get fired because of her? The RCMP brass could sure put the screws to him for sleeping with a suspect. Although he was equally to blame for their indiscretion, she felt responsible. She hadn't discouraged him. What was even more disturbing was the cold fact that she might be thrown in jail. Was that possible? It wouldn't be the first time that an innocent person was accused of doing something they didn't do. Would it look even worse that she had been angrily rejecting Roger on Friday, and not embracing him passionately, as Marlena had described? And if it was discovered that Roger had tried to rape her thirty years before, would that go against her? She should have told Gabe right after the murder. Coupled with the confusion over whether or not she'd been on the invitation list, it made her look plain bad, as though she'd been withholding information. Thankfully, Peggy could clear up that misunderstanding.

As Joan stared at the phone, silently daring Gabe to call her first, she allowed herself to remember the details of her night with him, the tender touching, the fevered intimacy, the aftermath of lying in the arms of someone who knows you so well. Slowly, she admitted the truth to herself. She didn't really want permission to leave. She wanted to stay in Madden for a while longer, but not under suspicion of murder. She couldn't just wait for someone else to make her life right. Research was her specialty. Nothing could keep her from digging around for information on her own, doing her own private investigation. She'd do what she could to get both Gabe and herself out of this mess.

It wasn't much different than what she did in her lab. There she used the process of induction, combining information in the form of scents and tastes to make best-selling products. Now she would turn to deduction, deconstructing the murder, isolating the ingredients that made someone want Roger Rimmer dead.

DETECTIVE PARKER

CHAPTER ELEVEN

PEG CLIMBED BACK INTO BED AFTER opening the blinds to let in more of the gorgeous sunlight. The quiet of an early Sunday morning reminded her of floating on a cloud. Although she still felt a bit dizzy, today was the closest she'd come to feeling herself since Thursday. Yesterday her legs gave out and her whole left side was black and blue from the fall. Now she knew that she should have had the flu shot. All the other homecare nurses were so against it. She figured they knew best. Too late now.

Yesterday was mostly a blur. She had tried her best to answer all of the questions that the police had asked, but she wished Gabe had been the one to question her. That Sergeant Smartt person made her nervous. He was so abrupt and darned unfriendly. She wasn't sure that she'd been clear about a few things. When she talked to Des Cardinal later today she'd make sure they had it right.

By yesterday afternoon she had been feeling nauseous and lightheaded again. At first she worried it was her heart, but it hadn't felt the same as before. Two Christmases ago she'd known that the heartburn wasn't simply from over-indulging in eggnog. As a nurse she knew the symptoms. She hadn't told a soul when her doctor diagnosed her with heart disease. That was an old person's sickness. She wanted one more fling, one more romance, before she told the truth to anyone. No, this had to be a flu bug. She couldn't eat yesterday when Marlena had dropped by with sandwiches and those herbal supplements she was always pushing. It was kind of her, except that any conversation with Marlena was all about Marlena and it made her head spin. Besides, that Extract of Oregano just made her want to barf. It was so much easier being with Daphne. Thank goodness she'd stayed in the afternoon to help out. Peg could tell that she was used to being around sick people. She knew how to sit quietly. She plumped her pillow, told her all about the reunion "meet and greet", what everyone was wearing. It sounded as though it was going just as she'd planned, except for Roger getting himself killed. Hearing Daphne tell it was almost like being there. Daphne was sweet, and she had a natural beauty with all that black hair and old-fashioned curves, but she didn't need to wear so much makeup. Peg was glad she'd told her that if she wasn't careful, she'd have that same artificial look as Marlena.

Maybe, though, she shouldn't have told Daphne so much about Madden's personal affairs, about Linda Howard's miscarriages early in their marriage, the details of Candy's divorce, the tension in Marlena and Ray's relationship. Although anyone with eyes could see that the young Howard children looked nothing like Steve, that Candy should've dumped her brute of a husband years before, and that Marlena had had the hots for Roger since they'd been kids. But it was just her personal opinions. Daphne would be gone from Madden in the blink of an eye. Peg decided to put it out of her mind and just enjoy the view: the two pagoda-shaped bird feeders outside of her window, and the lovely breakfast tray Daphne had left by her bed. A bit more rest then she'd get up.

When a searing headache attacked the back of her skull, she reached for the painkillers. She couldn't remember how many she'd already swallowed this morning. Two more couldn't hurt. This was the worst bug she'd ever had.

Old Doc Rimmer was respected in the community the way that you respect an old guard dog. A dog that, simply by existing, has kept thieves at bay for a lifetime, but has never gone out and done anything splashy, like catch a bank robber. In addition to setting bones and writing prescriptions, Dr. Rimmer served the community in many respectable, unexciting ways, such as sitting on the school board. His most notable achievement was serving as chairman when they voted in construction of the new school. He steered the board quietly. "Hard work without hullabaloo" was his motto. When the board wanted to design a plaque in his honour, he refused with a shake of his head.

When it came to raising his only child, though, Dr. Rimmer had been a drowning man. In his day, during the war, there hadn't been all these street drugs. Well, not in the schoolyards of small towns like Madden. When he and Laura realized that the beautiful green palm under the grow light in Roger's bedroom was marijuana and that he was supplying the junior high school, Laura started reading books about drugs while he buried himself in work. It turned out to be the beginning of Roger's long road that ended with hard drugs and the destructive behaviour that went with addiction. The doctor couldn't admit it out loud, could barely admit it to himself, but he was relieved that his son was dead. It had been an exhausting, terrifying twenty-five years. His wife and he could now sleep through the night without worrying. He wished it could have come some other way, that it hadn't had to be so violent, but at least it was over.

Candy was breathing heavily by the time she reached the top of Peg's front stairs. She shifted the box of Co-op pastries to her other arm and knocked with her free hand. There was no answer so she tried the door. It opened easily. The house was silent, except for the hum of the refrigerator and the Chinese wind chime above the door. When she called out, there was no response. There wasn't even a sign of Peg's old cat, Me-Me, who was usually quick to greet guests in anticipation of treats.

Candy made her way down the hallway to Peg's bedroom, making as little noise as possible in case Peg was asleep. She entered, then stumbled backwards in shock, dropping the bakery box. It broke open, scattering pastries across the broadloom. Me-Me was beside the bed greedily eating the remains of Peg's breakfast that had spilled onto the floor.

When Joan arrived at the Rimmers', there were already several cars parked at the curb and in the driveway. One, she noticed, had rental plates. As she walked up the path toward the tidy split-level home, a couple of older women were leaving. There was one thing in Madden that hadn't changed. In the event of tragedy, you were never alone, at least for the first while. The casserole brigade bolted into action and tea flowed like the Nile. She remembered how it had been when her dad had died. Swallowing the lump in her throat, she rang the bell and Hazel answered the door.

"C'mon in. Glad you made it."

Eau d'egg salad assaulted Joan when she stepped into the house. Hazel took Joan's coat and eased the introduction. "Laura, look who's here. It's Joan Parker."

Mrs. Rimmer, wearing the sagging look of suppressed anguish, fawned over her. "It's good to see Roger's friends here."

Joan felt like a fraud, but this wasn't the time to correct the mourning mother. She sat down next to Mrs. Rimmer with a plate of shortbread and a cup of Earl Grey.

"Except for the members of his band," Mrs. Rimmer said, "I never knew who his friends were. I never met any of his girlfriends, not even his wife."

"Crystal, wasn't it?" asked Joan.

Laura Rimmer nodded. "He didn't tell us that he'd been married until it was over." She dabbed at a spot on her skirt with a napkin. "I felt badly about it, but it was probably for the best."

"How long were they married?"

"I'm not sure." She looked embarrassed. "It's been over for years. There were no children."

Throughout Joan's visit, Dr. Rimmer was robotic in his responses, smiling when spoken to, obediently holding his cup out for a top up when the pot came around, but mostly his tired eyes rested on the television, where herds of elephants silently crossed the savannahs of Africa.

Hazel easily navigated her way around the Rimmer house, directing guests to one of three bathrooms and pulling extra cotton napkins from a drawer in the buffet. Joan chalked it up to her friend's experience as a minister. This kind of pastoral visit must be second nature. But when Mrs. Rimmer caught Hazel's arm and requested that she bring her pills to her, Hazel went directly upstairs without asking where to find the medication.

When a chair became vacant beside Roger's father, Joan perched on the edge and leaned over to get his attention.

"Can I get you anything, Dr. Rimmer?"

His automatic response was to shake his head, but then he pursed his lips and really looked at her. "Joan?" he asked.

She nodded, shocked that he recognized her so easily.

"It's good to see you. How is your mother?"

Joan brought him up-to-date, but was surprised that not much was necessary. Not only had Vi been sending Christmas cards, but Dr. and Mrs. Rimmer had had lunch with her in Vancouver.

"Must have been a dozen years ago," he calculated. "But, when you get to our age, that's like yesterday." He filled Joan in on their day-to-day lives. Both Mrs. Rimmer and he kept active in the community.

"But you're retired?"

"Trying to be," he answered. "Stepped down as president of the Rotary last year, but still busy as past-president, and we both volunteer at Mountain View. There are two other doctors in town now, but some of the older patients still call for a second opinion now and then. "

By the time Joan left him he'd filled in the fine strokes, but they'd never once mentioned his only child.

Later, Joan walked with Hazel to their cars. Here they were, two middle-aged women. So many years had passed. This block-shaped, grey-headed women in African dress was a complete mystery to her. She asked her about her partner, Lila. Joan knew from Gabe that the two women had been together for nearly twenty years, had contemplated marriage. It was a committed relationship.

Hazel hesitated before answering. "We drove up to Madden together, but Lila's cloistered in our hotel room. She's grading papers for the Russian lit class she teaches at UC Berkley."

Joan suggested that the three of them get together for dinner.

Hazel shook her head. "Lila's grumpy with me at the moment." She looked at Joan, assessing whether or not to say more. "The reason I didn't get to the opening night reunion bash was because we pulled over to the side of the road to decide if we should end it."

"End it? You mean the trip?" asked Joan.

"The relationship. The whole bag. She thought I had a thing for Roger. Can you believe that?"

"Did you?" asked Joan. She was beginning to feel like a cop.

Hazel paused before answering. "I went from hating Roger to feeling sorry for him. I guess I did love him, the little boy in him. But not the way you mean or Lila feared. It's my work to be there for people and it's work that I'm cut out for. Keeping their confidences is another part of the job. I'm good at that too." She put an abundant arm around Joan's shoulder and gave her a friendly squeeze. "I'll see if I can get Lila to quit whining and have dinner. You'll love her. I've always thought that she's a lot like you."

Joan smiled. "What does that mean?"

"Why, intelligent, honest, a bit of a prig . . . " Hazel held her at arm's length, "And still hot after all these years."

As Hazel climbed into her rental car, Joan called out: "How long are you staying?"

"Don't know. The most I can hang around is till mid-week. How about you?"

"I have no idea," Joan responded, but she had an overwhelming sense the decision was no longer in her hands.

Peg lived in one of the older neighbourhoods, where boulevards separated the sidewalks from the roads, wide porches overlooked the street, and people still walked to the corner store. It gave Joan comfort to see that some parts of Madden hadn't changed. Peg would be able to clear up the misunderstanding about the invitation list, and then she'd be able to return to Vancouver. As she turned the corner onto Peg's street, an ambulance passed her headed in the opposite direction. Joan's stomach lurched when she saw a police car parked in front of a hot pink bungalow. Candy Dirkson sat on the curb, tears flowing, her generous body heaving with uncontrolled sobbing.

Joan parked and went to her. "The ambulance. Is it Peg?"

Candy nodded. "I haven't been to visit Peg all weekend, after all her hard work to make this reunion happen. She would have had so much fun with us last night. I'm a horrible friend!" she wailed. "And she was probably feeling terrible about what happened to Roger." Between sobs she tried to describe what had happened when she arrived an hour earlier.

"Me-Me was eating Peg's breakfast."

"Who's Me-Me?"

"Peg's cat. Peggy was all twisted around."

"And she was hurt?" asked Joan.

Candy shook her head. "No, Joan. She was dead."

Ray couldn't believe his luck as he watched Daphne at the end of the bed slowly unhooking the clasp of her bra. When her generous breasts were unleashed, her nipples pointed toward him as though begging for him. He couldn't help but compare them to Marlena's tiny breasts that matched the rest of his wife's boyish, athletic body. Goddamn, Daphne looked great for her age.

They had driven to a motel on the other side of Elgar. He wasn't quite as well known there, and the unkempt young man at the front desk didn't look familiar. The guy didn't seem to give a shit anyway. Unlike a lot of men he knew, Ray wasn't experienced at adultery. Marlena liked sex and besides, basically she scared the shit out of him. She yelled at him if he even told a dirty joke to another woman. When Daphne had come on to him at the gas station that morning, he couldn't resist. How lucky is that, a good-looking broad asking if you want it at nine o'clock in the morning? She even bought him a coffee and muffin. Marlena would never know and Daphne would be gone from town by tomorrow. While driving, she had unzipped his fly and pulled his schlong out of his pants. He'd just about spilled his coffee on her head. Now, straddling him on the motel bed, she was making him crazy by flicking her tongue in and out of his ear.

"You stay in shape to play with the band, Ray?" she whispered. "I heard Marlena stays in shape to play with the band, too."

Ray corrected her. "Oh, Marlena doesn't play with the band. She just . . . "

Daphne interrupted, "Maybe not the whole band, but at least one member. One besides yours."

Before he could respond, she slid her head under the covers. Oh, God! Oh God, this was payback time. Whether or not Marlena had ever screwed Roger, she'd wanted to. Ray knew it. Everyone knew it. Even Daphne knew it, and she'd been in town less than a week. That hurt.

When Joan returned to the resort she went into the hotel lobby to let the staff know that she wouldn't be rushing off. The front desk clerk was glad that not all of the customers were being chased away by the murder. Joan nodded robotically. It wasn't her place to start spreading the word about Peg's death. She'd left a message for Gabe and was afraid to say anything until they talked. Her stomach grumbled and she was light-headed. Although she didn't feel hungry, she had to eat something if she was going to keep her mind clear. She was heading toward the dining room for lunch when the clerk called, "Oh, Miss!"

She turned.

"I forgot to tell you. I put calls through to your room while you were out. One of them sounded urgent."

Her cell had been on silent when she visited the Rimmers. She turned it on. Still no reception. She wandered the lobby until two green bars appeared on her phone. Wedged between the front desk and a potted fern, she checked her voicemail. The first message was from Mort.

"Hey, babe, just checking in. You sounded stressed earlier. Let's talk about it."

The second call was from work. It had to be important for Ted to call on a Sunday. His message was brusque. Tony was having difficulty figuring out her market analysis and could she please call.

The last message was from Gabe. He'd be busy for the next couple of days and didn't know when he'd get to see her. He didn't mention Peg but she assumed that was one of the cases now consuming him. He asked her not to leave town without letting him know. "It's a personal request, Joan, not an official one."

She punched in the number to Constellation Inc. reception, then the three digits to reach Tony's direct line.

"Hey there, it's Joan. What's up?" Tony admitted he was lost. As she listened it became clear that, as she suspected, she needed to be there to finalize the project paperwork or there would be delays in launching Hint of Midnight in the Southeast Asian market. Ted wanted Joan to come back as soon as possible. She glanced at her watch then across the lobby. Time-zone calculations clicked through her mind. If she left now she'd be back in Vancouver by dinnertime. She and Tony could work through the night then email the documentation to their Mumbai lawyer before he left his office. She could feel her heart start to race. This was her usual cue to run back, not because of how badly they needed her but from her underlying fear that they'd find out that they didn't.

"Joan, are you still there?"

Before answering, she took a deep breath. "Sorry, Tony. You're going to have to deal with this one on your own for now." She gave him a list of instructions and said she'd call in a couple of days to see how they were doing without her. Just before she hung up, she added, "And get Rosy to help."

"Rosy? The receptionist?"

"She's enthusiastic and smart. She deserves a chance."

On the way to the hotel restaurant, Joan slid a copy of the *Madden Monitor* from the stack on the reception desk into her purse then frowned into her wallet when she went to pay. A lonely twenty remained. She mentally revisited her purchases since leaving home yesterday, added in her poker loss, and calculated that she was missing about forty dollars. It was too much to have accidentally overpaid. It must have fallen out of her wallet, or maybe she'd bought something and forgotten. She'd physically retrace her steps this morning and at the same time, start to gather information on who killed Roger Rimmer.

"Why the hell did they haul her out of the house before we got there? Is everyone in this town trying to make rat shit out of this case?" Staff Sergeant Smartt's fury hung in the air like an avalanche ready to rumble down a mountain. He cursed the local ambulance service then screamed at Gabe.

Gabe knew that if Smartt didn't keep his mouth shut, or at least his voice down, nobody would get this job done. Why did the yellers so often rise to the top positions?

"It appears to have been a stroke, natural causes." Gabe said calmly.

"She was a goddamn witness in a goddamn murder investigation that's not even two days old. That makes it a suspicious death. Period. I want an autopsy and I want to know where her classmates were this morning," demanded Smartt.

Again, they had an audience in the office, and this time Gabe wished they hadn't. He knew that Smartt was right. Nobody should have touched Peg's body. He hadn't been called until after she'd been moved. It had been dealt with as a normal death, despite her involvement with the reunion and Roger Rimmer. No matter, Smartt lacked the sensitivity to work in such a small community. There was barely a person in town that didn't know either Roger or his parents, and everyone knew Peggy. This situation touched everyone.

Smartt wasn't finished. "And what about that woman from Vancouver, Parker? Do you have any more on her?"

"Nothing of interest," replied Gabe.

He had been uncomfortable running a check on Joan. Part of him had been afraid that he'd find information that he didn't want to know. Not criminal activity, but personal stuff that she had a right to keep private, like the fact that her car was still registered in her husband's name. What made him feel particularly awkward was that another part of him wanted to know. He wondered just how separated Joan and Mort were. But who was he to question her personal circumstances? Betty would be home by tomorrow evening, and all he could think about was how he could arrange to see more of Joan before then. It all seemed impossible with the murder investigation and now Peg's death.

"The dead woman, this Chalmers, she said Parker contacted her and asked to be included in this reunion," said Smartt.

"Where did you get that?"

"I interviewed her myself, yesterday at her home."

It irritated Gabe that Smartt was duplicating their efforts. "When she was at the school yesterday she was confused. She was sick, obviously worse off than we all knew, and she'd had a lot on her plate for the past few months with this reunion."

Smartt grumbled as he skimmed through his notes. "Says here Cardinal called her late yesterday. He was going to her place today to go over her statement one more time, get it all straightened out."

"*My* notes say Peg contacted Joan Parker by telephone and insisted that she come to Madden."

"You're certain?" Smartt asked.

Gabe nodded but didn't mention that it was Joan who had explained to him the sequence of events that got her to the reunion.

"How close are the two of you?"

Gabe thought he knew where the Superintendent was going with this and that he'd be ordered to avoid her. "We were friends in high school, but we haven't spoken in almost thirty years."

"Good. I want you to make a point of talking to her. Keep tabs on her as long as she's in town," ordered Smartt.

"Done," said Gabe then he turned away so that Superintendent Smartt wouldn't see him smile.

Joan walked into the arts centre to find several teenagers in the hallway running lines from *Little Shop of Horrors*. A good-looking boy with shaggy hair and a tight T-shirt broke into song to the appreciative swooning of the all the girls and at least one of the boys. He reminded Joan of Roger. How little the world changed. She found the door to the games room open and went inside.

One window blind was up so there was plenty of light to guide her to the table where they'd played blackjack the night before. If she'd dropped her cash while playing cards, it might still be there. She passed the couch and stopped. A chill ran down her spine. Mr. Fowler's motionless body was stretched out on the floor. She calculated what to do first, call the police or check to see if he was still alive, then she stepped toward him and bent to feel his pulse.

Suddenly his eyes shot open and she screamed.

"Oh, Joan, I'm so sorry. I didn't mean to scare you." Mr. Fowler clambered to his feet as quickly as his aging joints would allow. "My back's bad. I like the floor for a nap." As she gasped to catch her breath, he continued. "It's nicer here than at my place." He smoothed his hair and buttoned his sweater. "There's nobody there since my wife passed on."

"I'm sorry I woke you," Her heart was still pounding. "I've misplaced forty dollars."

"Oh, dear."

"I thought it might have fallen on the floor when I was paying Candy out last night."

He grinned impishly. "She's quite the shark. Wouldn't have expected it." He shook his head. "I tidied up this morning but I didn't find any cash. There were other things people forgot. In the old days it was faded jean jackets and textbooks. Now it's reading glasses and cardigans."

They both smiled then spent a few minutes together looking under tables and the old, sagging couch. Finally they gave up. The money wasn't here. Joan said goodbye and turned to leave, but Mr. Fowler stopped her.

"Joan, I have something I need to tell you." His tone was serious. He directed her toward the couch. "It's about me, my life. But it's also about you."

She perched on the edge of the sagging sofa and Mr. Fowler closed the door. She wondered what could be so important. He stood before her, as though at the front of a classroom, cleared his throat and began to tell her a story.

In 1973 Ed Fowler was a twenty-eight-year-old Madden schoolteacher with radical ideas. Half-a-dozen years earlier he'd left Portland at the height of the Viet Nam War. "That war was unconscionable. But it wasn't just the war, it was the number of people in my country who supported it and refused to listen with grace. It's a sinking, lonely feeling when you realize you don't belong in the country of your birth."

"I can't imagine," said Joan.

"It was a horrible era for the United States of America, no question, but leaving it was the best thing that ever happened to me. It set me free." He paused for a moment to wipe his glasses. "I left with a duffle bag and a degree from Oregon State and I crossed the border into Canada."

"You dodged the draft?" asked Joan.

"Technically, although I don't think they were that interested in someone my age, at least not at that point in the war. Eventually I wound up in Madden. Property was cheap and I knew they got a good deal of sun. I met Suzette, my future wife, through friends. She had the skills to live an alternative lifestyle; she gardened and sewed and made the most whimsical quilts on a frame that dominated our living room."

"Hippies. You were hippies," said Joan.

"I suppose we were, although we never would have described ourselves as such. Labels were verboten back then, a sign of the establishment." He chuckled at the memory, but she detected melancholy in his voice. "A dozen of us like-minded souls plotted out a communal farm where we would become self-sufficient. Our cropland was cultivated in a large circle with pie-shaped plots. I can't quite remember why we did that," he said shaking his head, "but we grew everything imaginable: potatoes next to beets next to carrots next to soybeans, and so on. In the centre of it all was a large ramshackle house that we built mostly from found materials. At any given time there were seven or eight adults and a half-dozen or more children living there, including our twin girls, Sky and Summer. The revenue from the farm was paltry, not enough to pay for gas or sugar or to buy shoes, so I took a job teaching math and science at the school in Madden. One of the first parents I met was Vi Parker." He looked up at Joan with watery blue eyes. "I was smitten. Immediately and irreversibly smitten."

Joan was stunned. "My mom?"

Fowler nodded again. "Vi was a few years older than I was, but to me she was eternal youth. I found reasons to talk to her whenever she came to the school, and that was often since you and your brothers were there."

"I don't remember her being so involved with the school," said Joan.

He stopped for a moment and stared out the window as though it framed a view of Joan's mother as a young woman. "Oh, she wasn't one of those parents who sat on committees to demand newer equipment or more library books. She was more likely to appear in a flowing skirt with crepe paper and balloons to decorate the gym for a spring dance, or with a towel, bathing suit, and a bucket of chicken to lead a group of kids to the swimming pool. She'd be right in there, splashing and playing while the other mothers lounged on the sidelines." As Mr. Fowler spoke, the years fell away and Joan was transported back to those hot June days at the pool, a memory so visceral that she could smell the chlorine and coconut oil and see her mother in her bright-skirted bathing suit and turquoise bathing cap, snapping the caps off Coke bottles, and encouraging their burping contests. She couldn't remember Mr. Fowler at the poolside, but then she'd been so absorbed with her own life.

"Do you remember that, Joan?"

She nodded slowly. "I do." She remembered her mother, and an image of the young schoolteacher began to emerge from a corner of her memory. They had all admired him, but never suspected that he had passion beyond his social causes.

"I made excuses to be around your mother whenever I could." He described her sparkling energy and the sound of her melodious laugh. "I grew as a human being from watching her. She lived her values, Joan. I never heard her pass judgment on another person. She went out of her way to be kind to everyone."

"She still does," added Joan.

He nodded with a sad smile. "Within a very short time, I fell deeply in love with her and she knew it. I began creating elaborate, transparent opportunities to be near her. One time I wrangled an invitation to a party where I knew she'd be. My grand plan was to insinuate myself into her social circle." He chuckled. "How odd I must have looked, the left-wing teacher among the blue-collar workers of Madden. I'm sure they all thought I was a communist."

"Weren't you?" asked Joan.

He shrugged, then, as though it was an afterthought: "I guess maybe I was." He looked at Joan. "Once I even danced with her." His eyes shone. "I still remember the feel of my hand on her waist." He stared down at his hand, now crisscrossed with blue veins. "Your mother broke my heart gently. She reminded me that I had a beautiful wife, and she rhapsodized on Suzy's best qualities, even though she hardly knew her. She talked about your father, about how he was her one true love. After he died, I thought I'd have a chance. I offered to marry her, to take care of all of you. Once again, she reminded me about my dear Suzy. She was right." His next words caught Joan off guard. "Your mother is one of the bravest people I've ever known."

All of her life Joan had tallied her mother's weaknesses. The person Fowler described was definitely Vi, but from a different angle, illuminated by a shift in light, through a prism that gave her image a thousand sparkling colours. Her mother might have had an easier life and not lived the past thirty years in poverty as a single woman. Joan felt a weight lift. Her mother had chosen her life.

Marlena Stanfield scrutinized her reflection in the mirror, silently cursing herself for eating garlic toast with her salad at lunch. It wasn't just the carbs that angered her. For the first time in years she had come close to having sex with someone whom she found intensely desirable and Roger had to go and get himself killed. She kicked herself for not acting faster, for all the missed opportunities, for her miserable life. She felt stuck.

She turned sideways to better examine her shapely biceps. She was more powerful than a lot of men she knew. Did her physical strength scare them off? Whatever sexual opportunity was going to happen in her life, she'd have to make the first move. And she'd have to act fast while there was all this party action in town. It amused her that the man who tickled her erotic imaginings the most this weekend, besides Roger, had been living down the highway in Elgar all this time. Betty Theissen was out of town for a few days. If Marlena played her cards right, she might end up with a hole in one, so to speak. Maybe a little handcuff action. She smiled to herself then posed in front of the mirror for one last look to see if she could still pull off a convincing wet-lipped pout, then she carried an armload of fresh linens to the guest room.

"You're welcome to stay as long as you like." She relished the look of awe as Daphne set her small suitcase on the king-size guest bed. Marlena swept open the curtains for the full effect of the view of Madden below. "You won't be disturbed down here at all. The other bedrooms are all two floors up. You can make all the noise you want. Ray leaves early and I sleep like the dead." She was momentarily embarrassed by her insensitivity after what Daphne had been through this morning. "I just about fell over when I got your message. It must have been horrible, walking into that house with a dead body lying there and all those police." She gingerly placed an arm around Daphne's shoulder. The physical connection felt stiff, but she knew it was probably the appropriate thing to do.

"It was the last thing I expected," Daphne whispered. "Truly, the very last thing I expected."

Chapter Twelve

THE FIRST PERSON GABE INTERVIEWED ON Sunday afternoon was Candy Dirkson. She lived in the house in which she had grown up, a two-story place that was old but well maintained. Old-fashioned flowerbeds along the front walk were starting to blossom with vibrant purple irises and snowy white lily-of-the-valley. Candy had ranched with her abusive, alcoholic husband for over twenty years, then finally divorced him after her own parents passed away. She told Gabe that she'd realized that life was too short. Recently she had started to exercise and watch her diet. As two divorced, middle-aged women, she and Peg had bonded more tightly than they ever had as teenagers. Peg had taught her how to power walk and supported her struggle to change her eating habits.

"I knew she was dead, but she looked so uncomfortable." Candy sobbed anew then blew her nose into a wad of damp tissue.

Gabe waited her out, avoiding the temptation to put words in her mouth. Candy was a mess.

"I had to make her comfortable, so I stretched her legs out."

"So you moved the body." He corrected himself. "You moved Peggy before anyone else came?"

Candy nodded. "I can't believe Peg died before me. I've been waiting for a heart attack to strike me down for ages with all this excess weight. She was so skinny. A stroke." She shook her head as though she still couldn't grasp that her friend was gone.

"You're sure she was dead?"

"Yeah." Although her lower lip trembled, she managed not to cry and her voice was more controlled. "She wasn't cold yet, but she wasn't warm either. There was no question that the life had gone out of her." She described the cat-eaten breakfast on the floor and the spilled glass of water.

Gabe knew she'd be familiar with death from her decades ranching. "And did you touch anything else?"

"Of course! I had to clean it up. Peg paid a fortune for that new carpet." The thought was enough to send her into heaving sobs again.

He cringed at her answer and handed her another tissue. "I have to take you back to Friday night, Candy. You okay?" She nodded and he continued. "Can you tell me again what you did after the band quit playing?"

"Marlena wanted me to hang around for a drink so we went into the lounge. It was past last call but Nick gave us a shot of rye anyway." Her eyes went wide. "He won't get in trouble will he?"

Gabe shook his head. Serving after hours was the least of his worries.

Candy blew her nose. "I hadn't had rye in years and I couldn't finish mine so Marlena did. Then I went to pick up Maryanne, my daughter. She was babysitting for Steve and Linda Howard. Steve usually gives her a ride but he was still hanging out at the hotel with the other guys in the band. I brought Maryanne home. We made popcorn without butter, and watched TV for a while, some stupid zombie film. We both fell asleep on the couch."

Candy confirmed that it was about twenty after one in the morning when she had collected her daughter. She remembered calculating how much Linda had to pay Maryanne for babysitting.

That meant Candy would have left Marlena at the Twin Pines at about 1:15 AM, forty-five minutes before Marlena found Roger dead. What, wondered Gabe, had Marlena done in the intervening time? "Candy, I need to ask you about your relationship with Roger. Were you . . . ?"

A laugh bubbled up and she blew her nose. "Gabe, are you asking if I slept with him?"

Gabe smiled wryly. "Yeah."

"Of course I did. But that was thirty years ago. All of us did, all the girls. He told us to keep it quiet so it wouldn't affect his image. He insisted that rock 'n' rollers had more sex appeal if they were single. Who knows if that was the real reason. And, Gabe, you gotta know," she smiled coyly, "now I like my men with a bit more meat on them."

After Joan left, Ed Fowler wondered if he should have told her the entire story but comforted himself by remembering Vi's advice. She believed that people owned their secrets and this, he thought, applied to the dead as well as the living. She had promised that she would leave sleeping dogs lie and he would do the same. Now he questioned whether or not inaction had been the honorable choice. Sometimes one had to make things right, no matter what the cost. As he tidied the lounge he carried on a wild, silent debate between himself and the Vi that he knew thirty years ago. Once again, she won.

After vacuuming the entire lounge of the Couch, he started to take down the decorations then stopped himself. As far as he knew the police were no closer to catching Roger's killer.

Madden may be keeping its visitors for a while so he may as well be ready. He taped the crepe paper back onto the wall.

Marlena mixed martinis for herself and Daphne and then, once her girls were out of earshot, provided her assessment of what had happened on Friday night. "Obviously old Joannie Parker wanted in Roger's pants. He rejected her and whamo, knife in the chest."

"But they would have arrested her, wouldn't they, if she'd done it?" asked Daphne.

Marlena took another drink and shook her head. Poor little Daph. Even though she lives in the city, she's still a rube. She explained the situation. "It's Sergeant Gabe. He's doing her, in return for letting her get away with it. That's how it works. And I have to say," she leaned forward and spoke in a hushed voice in case her daughters were within earshot, "I'd do Gabe Theissen at the drop of a hat."

She took Daphne's glass and went toward the open kitchen. Just then the doorbell rang and she called for Daphne to get it.

Daphne opened the door to Gabe Theissen.

Marlena purred, "Well, come on in, Gabe. We were just talking about you. Let me mix you a drink."

Gabe shook his head, then looked from one woman to the other. "I'm here on business."

"Again?" asked Marlena.

He took a step inside. "I have to ask where you were this morning, and I'm reviewing statements about Friday night. I need to know if you've recalled anything more."

Marlena sat on the couch and patted the seat beside her. "Come sit, Gabe," she ordered.

Gabe chose a straight-back side chair and silently evaluated the situation. He needed candid answers quickly and it wouldn't happen with these two women together. Just then Ray walked into the house, carrying a gym bag.

Marlena toasted him with her martini glass. "Hey, Ray, we've got company."

When Ray saw Daphne and Gabe, the colour drained from his face.

Gabe made a mental note. As a cop he was used to getting an uncomfortable reaction from people, but this was different. Gabe could have sworn that Ray's shocked response was to Daphne and not him.

Marlena didn't appear to have noticed. She went to her husband and looped her arm through his. "Gabe's here to find out where we all were this morning."

"This morning? Why?" he stammered with an uneasy smile.

Daphne answered. "Peg died this morning. There was an ambulance there when I got back to her house." She choked back tears.

"Not . . . she wasn't murdered?" asked Ray.

"There was no immediate evidence of a struggle. Looks like a stroke and she was being treated for a serious heart condition," Gabe said. "We're not labelling it as suspicious, but we do have to investigate, given . . . "

Marlena finished his sentence. "Given someone offed Roger. Someone we know." They all knew that she was referring to Joan. There was an embarrassed silence. Marlena became defensive. "What?"

Daphne turned to Gabe. "Peggy never told me she had a heart condition. But she did take a lot of pills."

"Hell, at our age we all do," said Marlena. She started down her long list of supplements, then broke off. "So, Gabe. Let's get on with this interrogation. What do you need to know?"

"I have to interview each of you on your own. Is there someplace I can do that?"

"Oh, that's ridiculous, Gabe. We're all friends."

He did a soft-shoe around his request, joking that it was to protect their friendships. When Marlena finally accepted that they couldn't all be questioned together, she suggested that Daphne be interviewed in the living room, Ray in his downstairs office, and Gabe could talk to her in the kitchen.

Gabe started with Ray downstairs.

Ray said that this morning he'd gone for a drive to look at some of his properties then had gone to the gym. Nobody had seen him on his drive, but he'd talked to a lot of people at the gym.

"You do that often, Ray, do your rounds on a Sunday morning?" Gabe watched him shift his body to a more protected position. This could be defensiveness, as though he was shielding a secret, but he chalked it up to Ray always being slightly awkward in his own skin. He hadn't been that way before he married Marlena.

"I like to see the properties when there are no crews, inspect them without eyes watching my back."

Gabe nodded, thinking that it was probably one of the only times Ray wasn't in line for criticism. He then asked Ray to recap what he did on Friday night. Ray told the same story that he had the day before. He'd had a drink with the band but was one of the first to leave. He'd had enough after hanging with the guys all week, and he had business to attend to the following morning. The girls had been asleep and, no, they hadn't woken up when he'd come home. He drank a couple more beers and watched some TSN.

Gabe waited to make sure he was finished, then broke the brief silence with another question. "How'd you end up back at the Twin Pines, Ray?"

"Steve called me. He'd gone up to Rudy's room for a nightcap and to practise the chorus of 'Crossroads'." He looked up at Gabe. "A Cream song."

Gabe nodded. "I remember. It was a Rank classic. I'm curious, why didn't you go with them? You already had it down pat?"

Ray shook his head. "Rog thought the two of them should do the chorus without me."

"But you used to do it with them."

"Rog did that a lot, shut me out on vocals. But, hey, I was dog-tired. Happy to go home."

"So Steve phoned your cell?"

"On the house line," corrected Ray. "When all the screaming started, he went out and saw Marlena. That's when he called me."

"Why do you suppose Marlena was there?"

"C'mon, Gabe. We've already done this. You know she said she was checking on the out-of-town guests." Ray looked down at his shoes.

"Do you believe her?"

"Would you?"

Gabe looked into the eyes of the man he'd known all of his life. "I need to ask you, Ray. Did you kill Roger Rimmer?"

Ray looked up at Gabe, shook his head and responded with a quiet but firm, "No."

Gabe sat on a stool across the kitchen island from Marlena while she chopped vegetables.

"Is there a reason to believe that Peg died from anything except a stroke?" she asked.

He shook his head. "Not at this point, no. We're doing a full autopsy so we'll know in the next few days if anything smells bad."

Marlena mapped her morning for Gabe. She'd run with both the girls, gone for an iced coffee then come home. She also stuck to her story about Friday, with one slight amendment. "Gabriel, my boy, what if I went to Roger's room looking for something more? Would that make me a suspicious character?" Her cynical, steely gaze was meant to challenge him. That look, he thought, was sharp enough to cut flesh.

"Did you?"

She paused a moment, lifted an eyebrow and spoke slowly. "Like I said, I was just offering a little old-fashioned Madden hospitality."

"What about the time between one-fifteen, when Candy went home, and 2:00 AM, when you found Roger?" He held her gaze and she didn't flinch.

"I waited in my car until I saw Roger go into his cabin. Then, believe it or not, I didn't go in right away. I almost chickened out. I watched the light go out, then I waited awhile longer." Her admission put her outside the cabin when the murder took place. It also placed her there when Roger was lolling drunkenly outside Joan's cabin door.

This was sticky territory. He trod cautiously. "You said that you saw Roger leaving Joan's cabin?" He left it open ended so that she could fill in the blank without him directing her.

She blew out a mouthful of air. "Okay, I didn't actually see him come out of Joan's cabin. He was sitting outside on the ground. Am I going to get into trouble?"

Gabe forced himself to remain calm and kept his expression blank. "It was a stressful night for everyone." He flipped to a previous page in his notebook, then back to his fresh scribblings. "Did you see anyone go in or out of Roger's cabin?" He watched her eyes flicker.

She shook her head and answered carefully. "Of his cabin? Not a soul."

If she were telling the truth, her answer suggested that the murderer had used the patio door on the side facing the river to gain entrance to Roger's cabin. Patio doors were a common point of entry for burglars. They were the doors most likely to be left unlocked and were shielded from view. In the case of the Twin Pines, that side of the buildings was pitch dark.

"One more thing, Marlena."

"Yes?"

"You'll be up the creek if you keep accusing Joan without grounds." He kept his tone neutral.

Marlena made a face that Gabe thought was intended to look like a pout but came across as a sneer. "But Gabriel, won't you be in that creek along with me for playing favourites?"

He knew she was right, but he was determined not to lose this stand off. Smartt didn't have the same experience with Marlena that the rest of them did. If she didn't withdraw her accusation, Joan would remain a target. Everything he wanted to say at that moment would sound defensive, juvenile, or both. He silently turned and walked down the three steps into the living room to question Daphne.

She was obviously uncomfortable with Marlena lingering in the adjoining kitchen, so Gabe suggested that they go sit in the police cruiser. Daphne pulled on her sweater, smiled meekly at Marlena, and followed him out the door.

Daphne had never been in a police cruiser before and marvelled at all the bells and whistles. She smiled at Gabe as he settled into his seat.

"Everyone is so comfortable around you," she said. "You seem like a nice man."

"So you don't remember me?" he asked.

She shook her head timidly.

"We graduated together, in the class of '79." Gabe pulled out his pad and pen. "Joan tells me you were sick, meningitis or something?"

She corrected him. "Encephalitis. It's affected my long-term memory from before I got sick, but my short term is fine. Very good, in fact." Her face suddenly lit up with recognition. "Gabe, Gabe Theissen!"

"You do remember?"

"Yes, no. I mean, I remember your picture. From the yearbook." She seemed genuinely pleased by the connection. "And now you're a cop."

"We went to school together for twelve years. I know it's been a tough few days, for everyone, but I have to ask you a few more questions."

She nodded.

Gabe confirmed the statement Des had taken about Friday. She'd gone home before the music ended that night because she didn't want Peg to be alone. She'd brought her a piece of lemon cake from the buffet wrapped in a napkin, but Peg hadn't wanted anything to eat. Daphne had urged her to see a doctor and offered to go with her in the morning, but Peg had refused,

134

insisting that it was the flu and would pass. Gabe noted that as Daphne told the story she became increasingly distraught.

"On Saturday, yesterday, Peg said she was doing better. Tired, she said, that's all. She was so insistent that I go out to the games night. She didn't want to hurt Mr. Fowler's feelings." Daphne looked up. "She was always so thoughtful." She sniffed and caught a tear on her cuff. "I thought maybe she wanted some privacy. We'd spent so much time together since I got here. It was so kind of her to invite me to stay with her. I couldn't have afforded the trip otherwise. I decided to be a good guest by giving her some space. Once I got to the Couch I had a really good time. I connected with so many people." She became wistful. "It was all a bit odd, though. People knew me, but it was like I was meeting them for the first time. Mr. Fowler drove me home last night. Peg was asleep when I got in."

"Did you talk to Peg this morning?" Gabe asked.

Daphne nodded. "She was awake when I got up and chirping like her old self. She talked about getting up. I made her a boiled egg and toast before I left and told her she should just stay in bed and rest."

"Was she expecting anyone that you know of?"

"No. Oh, except Officer Cardinal."

"Anyone else," asked Gabe. Daphne shook her head. "And the door, did you lock it when you left?"

"Oh, no. Peg never locks her door."

"And you came home just before noon," said Gabe, referring to the police report.

"I could see the police car when I turned the corner. They'd taken Peg's body away. She hadn't seemed that sick. I wouldn't have left her otherwise." Daphne trailed off. Tears were streaming down her cheeks, leaving rivulets in her caked makeup. He handed her a tissue and she dabbed at the muddy tracks of mascara. "I'm so selfish. I should have stayed."

Gabe asked, "Where did you go?"

She looked at him, then blurted it out. "You'll find out anyway. I was with Ray. At a motel." The tears gushed forth. She confessed that she had put so much stock in returning to Madden. Her own marriage had faltered after she got sick. It had just withered away. Her husband just left one day. They had never actually divorced.

"My daughter, Patti, she deserved so much more than I could give her. It all makes me feel like such a loser, my whole life. I dreaded making this trip." She hung her head and avoided looking at him. "But there's another part of me, the part that wants to fill in the blanks. I feel so empty inside."

"How did that happen," said Gabe gently, "with Ray?"

"Friday, when the band was on a break, Ray gave me directions to the bathroom. Afterward he asked if I was having a nice time."

"He was flirting?" Gabe was surprised.

"No. Oh, no. He wasn't trying to pick me up or anything. He was just nice, a nice normal guy. From what I could see, he was by himself." She looked up from beneath thick false eyelashes. "Plumbers, they don't wear rings you know."

Gabe watched her fold her manicured hands on her lap. He hadn't known Daphne well when they were in school. Her parents were strict about her associating with boys. She still had a shy, girlish quality about her.

"This morning I saw Ray at the gas station and I recognized him from Friday. I suppose you'll have to tell Marlena. She'll be devastated. Really, really choked."

Gabe responded that it wouldn't be necessary, at least not at the moment.

"You're sure?"

He nodded.

"You're a very nice man, listening to me like this," she said, as she dried the last of her tears.

"What about Roger, do you remember anything about your relationship with him?"

As far as Daphne was concerned, Friday night was the first time in her life that she'd seen Roger.

Gabe watched her walk to the house. He could swear that she'd been almost disappointed that Marlena wouldn't hear about her fling with Ray. His job, however, was not to enforce the moral code of Madden.

Chapter Thirteen

Hazel and Lila occupied a suite on the top floor of the Twin Pines Hotel. The six-story tower, added to the original motel in recent years, made it a skyscraper in local terms. When Joan called up to the room, Hazel asked if she would mind coming up. They could have coffee in the room.

Joan gasped when Lila answered the door. Standing almost six-feet tall, with a mane of wavy auburn hair over her shoulders, she wore slim fitting blue jeans and a cashmere sweater that hugged her fit but ample torso.

"I have waited so long to meet Hazel's best friend from childhood," Lila gushed in a lush southern accent, then hugged her.

Joan did a double take at the heady fragrance of angelica and fern fixed with the violet tones of orris root. She couldn't place the perfume; it might have been a custom blend, but she would've expected a delicate magnolia or some other floral scent. In all her musings, she hadn't imagined Hazel's partner to be so striking or so young.

Hazel was working on her sermon for the following Sunday. She explained that her church was part of an inter-denominational rally for peace and it was quite a big deal. She stacked papers and books on the small table by the window. "How could our lives have become so busy that we haven't reconnected until now?"

Joan wondered if it had to do with Lila. Did she keep Hazel on a short leash? Did Lila's jealousy extend beyond Roger? Just as likely, though, that Hazel's prominent work kept her frenzied.

"I can't believe Marlena accused you of stabbing Roger to death," exclaimed Lila. Hazel and Joan grimaced at one another. It didn't surprise either of them.

"What worries me," said Joan, "is that Staff Sergeant Smartt is on my tail. He seems to think that Marlena is credible. Peggy was the one person who could have cleared me."

"How's that?" asked Hazel.

"The cops have the impression that I crashed the reunion. I didn't even want to come, and I don't want this mess to bite me in the butt when I get back to Vancouver. I have to clear my name."

Hazel handed her a coffee. "So, what can we do, Joannie?"

"I need to know more about Roger." She looked into her friend's grey eyes. "Haze, how did you reconnect with him? It's the last thing I would have expected."

"When I first joined the First Metropolitan Church I was an associate minister. My duties included going out onto the streets to help those in need. Boy, I was young." She shook her head at the memory. "And naive."

"From Madden to San Francisco. Must've been huge culture shock," said Joan.

Hazel nodded. "One day, nearly twenty years ago, I was at a San Francisco hospital doing rounds, listening to lonely lost souls and finding out what I could do to help. Usually it meant hooking them up with social service agencies that deal with housing, mental-health care or addiction treatment. I was on the psych ward. Some patients were in such bad shape that they had to be strapped to their beds to keep them from ripping out their IV tubes or trashing the room. That's when I saw him."

"Roger?" she asked.

Hazel nodded. "It was the hair that caught my attention. The bond curls. They'd lost their luster but those ringlets still made him stand out, especially in a crowd of drug addicts. There he was, sitting on a hospital bed, hooked up to an IV, chatting up a cute little Asian nurse. He didn't look so bad then. All I could think about was that stupid basketball photograph. Oh, Joannie, I knew that I should've been able to look beyond that, to have mercy, but..." Hazel shrugged.

"What happened?" asked Joan.

"I couldn't bring myself to approach him." She bent her head and stared at her lap. "I turned around and walked out of the room before he saw me." She paused. "Anyway, months passed and I forgot about it."

Lila sniffed impatiently and moved away.

"We have a soup kitchen at the church. One afternoon, after we'd finished serving lunch, I went out to deliver a meal to an AIDS patient a few blocks from the church. On the way there I heard all this screaming. There was a crowd gathering on the street around a man lying on the sidewalk. There was a syringe hanging from his arm. It was Roger. He was a skeleton."

"He became her hobby," said Lila. "Like some people collect pretty pieces of glass. They might cut you but they're mesmerizing." There was a savage tone in her voice.

Hazel ignored her. "I resuscitated him, called 911. Then I got him into a rehab program."

"It wouldn't be the last time," Lila said.

"I always believed that if I'd talked to him that day in the hospital I could have kept him safe."

"You gave him a chance," insisted Joan.

"Roger made me understand my mission in life," said Hazel. "He taught me the most important lesson I'd ever learn. Forgiveness. We came here to visit his parents. They became a surrogate family for me. I quit hating this town." She gazed out the window overlooking the rooftops of Madden. "Sometimes we get the most from where we least expect it."

At that moment there was a knock at the door.

Lila opened it.

"Gabe!" said Hazel.

"Well, it looks as though this has become reunion central." Lila's voice was thick with sarcasm.

His wool-and-coffee smell sent Joan back to the previous evening. She gave him a weak smile.

"Ms. Parker," he said.

She felt herself blush and hoped that neither woman noticed. Lila had distanced herself from the door and Gabe. She had greeted Joan so warmly. Maybe she just didn't take well to men.

"I'll be in the restaurant reading the newspaper," said Lila, grabbing her wallet.

Hazel didn't try to stop her. Now, finally, they were together again, just the three of them. Though Gabe had come on business, he dropped his formal demeanor immediately. Flopping down on one of the double beds, he stretched out completely.

Hazel laughed. "Hey, Theissen, the shoes!"

It reminded Joan of the hours they had spent in one another's bedrooms as teenagers. Those had been the only places they could be guaranteed privacy in houses full of siblings and parents. They'd crank up their record players or radios full blast so that their conversations wouldn't be overheard. Discussions about hot crushes, parties, and where to get the next bag of grass were their world. Joan couldn't get enough of looking at her two friends.

Gabe rolled onto his side and looked directly at her. "I'm supposed to keep an eye on you."

"Who says?" she asked, mockingly defensive.

"My boss on this case." He sat up and became serious. "Marlena's not backing off from her story. She's conceded that she didn't actually see Roger come out of your room but is convinced that the two of you were making out in the hallway on Friday night."

"What about hard evidence — fingerprints, blood splatter, all of that stuff? Is my DNA in Roger's room?"

He sighed and explained that all that television detective stuff burned his ass. Everyone expected answers by the next commercial. That kind of analysis could take weeks, some of it months. "Smartt still thinks that you invited yourself to the reunion."

"So what if I had?" argued Joan.

"Did you?" asked Hazel.

"No!" Gabe and Joan replied in unison.

He continued. "The fact that you deny it is what bugs him. Now that Peg's dead there doesn't seem to be any way to prove that she approached you."

"Candy was working closely with Peg planning the reunion," said Hazel. "Has anybody asked her?"

"I met with her but I didn't ask her about the list. I will. I need a statement from you too, Hazel," said Gabe.

"Should I leave?" asked Joan.

Gabe hesitated, then shook his head. Joan knew she shouldn't be there during official questioning but was glad to learn from watching a pro.

"We stopped before reaching Madden on Friday and spent the night at a motel," said Hazel.

"Did either of you leave the room?"

"No. Lila will back me up, if she's in the mood."

He scribbled on his pad. "What time did you arrive in Madden?"

"Sometime mid-morning, I'd say . . . "

Before she could finish, Gabe stood abruptly and went to the dresser. He lifted a sheet of paper and examined it closely.

"What is it?" Joan asked.

"A photocopy of a grad photograph." Gabe held it up. There was a jagged line where the original had been torn and taped back together. "Where'd this come from, Hazel?"

"Roger had the original pinned to his wall," said Hazel. "I asked for a copy."

"Do you know why he ripped it?" asked Gabe.

"He didn't. Said it was like that when he got it."

"From who?"

Hazel shrugged. "I asked but he wouldn't say. My guess is that some girl was pretty mad at him. I doubt it was his wife."

Gabe and Joan again spoke in unison. "Why?"

"Will you two quit doing that? It's cute, but it's beginning to bug me."

Joan and Gabe stole a glance at each other.

"Crystal couldn't have gotten her hands on a grad photo. As far as I know she never came up to Canada."

"Did you ever meet her?" asked Joan.

"Yeah, they were together for a heartbeat, but it's been over a long time. Was really over before it began. Crystal was a junkie for years, scrawny little thing. Her arms and legs looked like a map for Via Rail. She did straighten out. She was in San Francisco a couple of months ago and looking better than I'd ever seen her. Even if she'd had the photo, she never struck me as the jealous type. When I saw her she didn't even want Roger to know she was alive, let alone in town."

"When did you get this copy?" Gabe waved it at Hazel.

"Roger gave it to me in San Francisco. He said he'd carried it around for years. That photo was the only thing he'd kept from Madden.

"Mind if I hold onto this?"

"Sure. I don't know if he still had the original," said Hazel.

"He did." Gabe placed the copy between the pages of his notebook.

When Joan rode down the elevator with Gabe, he put his arm across her shoulder. She looked up at him and he gave her a squeeze. "Just following orders, keeping an eye on you," he reported.

As they stepped from the elevator into the main lobby, it was to the unexpected bustle of activity. Joan had forgotten that the reunion weekend was scheduled to conclude with an afternoon wine-and-cheese farewell. Even with a double tragedy over the past couple of days, the activities continued although with a more subdued tone. Here in Madden their generation still practised the tradition of filling people with liquor before sending them onto the highway.

"I have to get word out about Peggy," said Gabe. "Ask very nicely for folks to stick around for a while longer."

Joan spotted the familiar blonde shag-styled head bobbing through the crowd. "There's Candy," she said. "Could you ask her about the invitation list? Peg was her best friend. She won't be in the mood to hang around here for long."

As Gabe crossed the room he was swarmed. Everyone wanted to know about the investigation.

Joan decided to duck over to her cabin to freshen up and make a phone call.

"Mom, it's me," she said when she got Vi on the line.

She told her mother that she'd seen Ed Fowler. Vi played her cards close to her chest, obviously not wanting to betray Fowler's trust about his crush on her, even after all these years.

It was only when Joan said that he'd told her everything that her mother let out a sigh and exclaimed, "Oh dear. It was so sad. I wouldn't have said anything to him but he asked me directly and I couldn't lie."

Joan thought her mother was confused. "Asked you what, Mom?"

"Suzy Fowler and Dan Prychenko."

"What?"

"Oh, now I've done it, haven't I? You know how I hate gossip."

"Mrs. Fowler and Marlena's dad had an affair?"

"I shouldn't have said anything."

"That was thirty years ago, Mom. They're both dead. It hardly matters anymore."

"There's no expiration date on gossip," said Vi. "I'm sure it's as painful to Ed now as it was the day he found out. A person couldn't work at Twin Pines and ignore the dirty laundry in Madden. You have to understand, Joannie, I tried to turn a blind eye. They weren't bad people, not Suzy, not Dan, not the others. Maybe they did bad things, but they always had their reasons." As Vi spoke, the pieces started falling into place.

"Was that when Mr. Fowler asked you to marry him?" asked Joan.

There was silence on the other end of the line, then a long, purposeful sigh. "He was reacting to Suzy and Dan. You know that two wrongs . . . "

Joan interrupted. "Don't make a right. Yes, Mom, I know."

Vi had brought her kids up on clichéd platitudes. The Lord helps those who help themselves. If wishes were horses, beggars would ride. Count the pennies and the dollars will take care of themselves. People who live in glass houses . . . Joan's moral code had been shaped by proverbs and nursery rhymes. All her life she'd defined her mother by her failings. This visit to Madden, to a past that they shared, was shifting her perspective in so many ways.

"Don't say anything, dear."

"Of course not. Mom, something else has happened."

"And what's that?"

"Do you remember Roger Rimmer?"

"Dr. Rimmer's little boy. Yes. Sweet little guy, all that blond hair, full of beans."

"He's dead. Somebody killed him."

"On purpose?" asked Vi.

"Yes. He was murdered."

"Oh dear. Oh no. Nobody deserves that, do they honey?"

Joan knew that, in Roger's case, more than one person may have thought otherwise. She decided not to mention Peggy's death. Despite the animosity between Joan and Peggy thirty years ago, Mrs. Wong had kept their family in casseroles for a month after Leo had passed away. She didn't want to deliver more bad news over the phone.

Candy Dirkson nibbled on a cracker when what she really wanted was to inhale the entire tray of imported cheeses. She was normally able to turn the worst situation into a laugh, but the reality of finding Peg was sinking in hard. It was the worst thing that had ever happened to her: worse than the end of her marriage, worse than the gut ache she had every time she thought about the downhill slide that her life had taken. Peg had been the light in her life.

Despite what she had told Gabe about her lack of interest in Roger, she had hoped that his return to Madden would turn things around. Roger had kept telling her that large women were hot and he openly flirted with her. She'd trusted him. When he'd asked to borrow a few dollars, she hadn't hesitated. Then it was another hundred, then a thousand. Everyone wondered why he kept coming back. She had a pretty good idea why, and it was reflected in her bank balance. She should have expected what would happen next. Once their former classmates started rolling into town, he hadn't given her another glance. She hated her life of dead-end jobs and one-night stands. She had thought Roger was a ragged second coming. He turned out to be recycled trash.

Peg, too, had started to ignore her. She got so busy with this reunion. With Daphne in town, Peg hadn't bothered dropping into the Co-op for coffee, hadn't even picked up the phone to say, "hi there."

Candy glanced around the room. Coming to the wine-and-cheese reception was supposed to cheer her up. Maryanne had gone to a softball tournament and she hadn't wanted to be alone, but now she regretted that she'd come.

When she saw Gabe approaching, she forced a smile. "Hey, cowboy." There was little enthusiasm in her voice.

"Hi Candy. Are you doing okay?"

"Sure, Gabe. Sure I am."

"There's a loose end that's turning into a snag. I think maybe you can help. Peg invited two people whose names weren't on the invitation list. I know it's probably nothing."

"Joan and Daphne? Oh no, Gabe. It was a problem."

Gabe raised an eyebrow. "In what way?" he asked.

"The committee agreed that only people who had actually graduated with the class of '79 should be invited. Otherwise, where do you draw the line? There were another dozen people who would have been on the list: drop-outs, people who failed and had to return for another year. Peg was firm about it, absolutely hardline."

"So what happened?"

Candy shook her head slowly. "Dunno. When we got together to stuff envelopes, there were invitations for Joan and Daphne. Peg wouldn't budge. She'd handwritten the envelopes. I had the feeling that someone had pressured her to add those two." Then she added, "The invitation committee was very upset."

Gabe asked, "Who was on the invite committee?"

"Besides Peg?" she asked.

Gabe nodded.

"Me, Ray and Marlena, though Ray hardly ever showed up."

Joan drove downtown to buy sinus medication. It was rare for her to get a headache. It would be easy to attribute it to the gin and late nights, but as it moved from behind her eyes to her sinuses, she recognized the familiar light-headedness. She'd been working her nose overtime, and was reacting to some unknown source in the environment. Usually she avoided smells that might shut her down, like bleach, burnt rubber, and sewers, but sometimes she wasn't careful enough. And, normally, she wasn't in such stressful life-and-death circumstances.

On the way back to the motel she saw the moon rising over the Welcome sign. Watching parked cars up on the ridge, silhouetted against the navy blue sky, she shook her head. The world of women had changed a lot in thirty years. Back then it was rare for a female scientist to lead a team of researchers. Offices had dress codes forbidding women to wear pants. And there was worse, much worse. A young woman she'd known had left Madden rather than report a gang rape. She had been drinking and worried that she wouldn't be seen as a victim. In the lingo of those times and this town, she would have been "asking for it."

Joan had never told a soul that Roger had attacked her at the bush party. In those days she might have been blamed. She shuddered as she recalled details that she hadn't thought about for a long time. Her jaw tightened at the visceral memory of Roger's strong musk smell. In minute quantities musk is a sex magnet for a lot of women. Not for her. With her powerful olfactory sense, it reminded her of a dirty litter box. Images rushed at her on the wave of the musk memory. The neurons of the olfactory sense and memory live beside one another in the brain. She was jolted by clear memories of people that night. Peg had worn a pair of pink vinyl hot pants stamped with a lizard design. A fuchsia snake, thought Joan. Steve had been there too. Later that evening he'd asked her if she was okay. Had it been because she was drunk or had he known something? Had he seen Roger attack her? If Roger had no witnesses, nobody would ever need to know about the attempted rape. If someone else had seen or he had bragged to someone and it came out now, it might appear as though Joan were concealing facts for the wrong reason. She didn't know anything about the intricacies of homicide law. Could she be charged with concealing information that was, somehow, vital to the investigation? Her head was still pounding. She chastised herself for her reluctance to share her own story a long time ago, especially with Gabe. She hoped she hadn't now put him in a compromising position. It was time to tell the truth about her first run-in with Roger Rimmer.

Chapter Fourteen

IF THE REUNION WEEKEND HAD SERVED up more than its share of death, it was also turning into an all-inclusive groaning board of food and drink. Marlena had issued an invitation for Sunday-evening cocktails. The reunion guests held captive in Madden by the investigation were to report to her house after the afternoon wine-and-cheese party. To Joan's surprise, Marlena had left a message at the hotel requesting her presence at the soirée. Surely Gabe couldn't have talked her out of the idea that Joan had killed Roger? More likely their hostess wanted to show off her home to everyone, murderers included.

At the afternoon wine-and-cheese, Daphne had confirmed it. "It's right out of *Home and Garden*. Seriously, Joan, she made all the decorating choices herself. Every room is really modern. It's got more chrome than the tail of a '59 T-bird. She spends hours and hours cleaning and won't let me lift a finger. Her girls can't do enough to make me feel welcome." She sighed happily. "They're sweethearts, real sweethearts."

"What about Ray?" asked Joan. She was beginning to wonder if he had a presence in his own house at all.

"Oh, he's doing his bit too. No worries there," Daphne said with a demure smile. Then she glanced around and lowered her voice. "Marlena treated all of us like shit at one time or another, Joan. But don't you think the best revenge is showing up? You've done so well with your life and all under your own steam. If she's changed, that'll make her happy. If she hasn't," her voice was now a low whisper, "that'll burn her to bits." Daphne gave her arm a pat then went to follow the havarti tray.

Still Joan was reticent about going to the Stanfields. She'd never been good with wakes and funerals and was sure that's what this open house would be. She was worried that she'd blurt out something inappropriate and couldn't quite shake the fear that Marlena was setting up an ambush. What convinced her to go was the chance to get closer to the truth. Maybe Marlena knew who had killed Roger, and for some reason was protecting that person, blaming Joan to create a smokescreen. Maybe Marlena had killed him herself.

When Gabe called the Stanfield home early Sunday evening Ray wasn't there.

"I sent him out for a fresh bottle of rye two hours ago," complained Marlena. "He's never around when I need him."

Gabe knew this wasn't entirely true. When they played softball together he'd seen Ray race off more than once when Marlena called him home. The guys joked that the best way to get Ray to make a run would be to have Marlena calling him in from home plate.

"And he's not answering his cell," she continued. "Try the shop. That's where he hides when he wants to avoid me."

Ray had made his mark as a developer in the region and had a gleaming office in the new industrial park on the outskirts of Madden. Gabe knew, however, that his heart had always been more into plumbing than contracting apartment complexes and strip malls. He enjoyed working with his hands.

When Gabe pulled up to the old Stanfield's Plumbing shop, Ray's car was the only one on the deserted downtown side street. Few businesses opened on Sundays in Madden, especially in the evening. It wasn't out of respect for any religion or even so that people could spend more time with their families. Sunday was bonspiel day in the winter and tournament day in the softball season. The common devotion in Madden was to curling and baseball. Even if you didn't play, you showed up to watch.

He tried the front door of the shop, but it was locked tight. Shading his eyes, he peered through the window. The front office was deserted. He made his way around back and tried the door next to the loading bay. It opened easily. Gabe called Ray's name, but there was no response. He walked down the dark hallway toward the sound of a television. Then he saw him. Ray was slouched on a worn sofa in the corner. A beer sat lopsided on his lap as he intently watched the hockey game.

"Hey, Ray," said Gabe. "You know Marlena's ready to knock your balls off if you don't get back to the house."

Ray looked at him, took a swig of his beer then looked back at the television. "She took my balls years ago. What else have I got to lose?" Looking weary and deflated, he turned his attention back to the game. The Canucks were playing the Red Wings. Gabe watched in silence with him for a few moments, glancing at Ray's hand to confirm that, as Daphne had said, he wasn't wearing a wedding ring.

"I've got a conflicting report of where you were this morning."

Ray took another swig of his beer, his eyes on the screen.

Gabe waited him out.

Ray drained his beer. "I don't regret what I did this morning." He put the empty on the floor beside the couch.

Gabe counted three bottles. Ray opened another and held it out to Gabe, who just shook his head. Ray shrugged and took a long pull.

"I've been a fool for a long time now. Ever since Marlena hustled me twenty-five years ago. Did you know that I'm not allowed to contact Sarah and my other kids? I promised Marlena when we first got together." He paused long enough to shake his head. The Canuck goalie let one slide through and the Detroit crowd went wild. "Fool," moaned Ray, "that's what I am. A damned fool." He was looking straight ahead with a dead stare, no longer watching the players skate across the ice.

Gabe nodded then asked, "How did it make you feel when Marlena paid so much attention to Roger?"

"How would it make you feel? Well, I got her good this morning, didn't I?" He took another swig.

"Does she know?" asked Gabe.

Ray looked down at his shoes and shook his head. "I may be stupid but I'm not crazy."

"I need to hear from you where you were this morning, Ray."

"You looking for your jollies? I was in a motel room in Elgar getting humped by a beautiful broad. Happy?" he asked.

"You were on the invitation committee. Do you know how the decision was made to add names to the list?"

"You mean the two girls?"

"Right. Joan and Daphne."

"Peg phoned a few weeks ago and suggested it. And I was madder than a pit bull that she wanted them here. You know why?"

Gabe shook his head.

Ray whispered, barely mouthing the words. "'Cause," he swallowed, "Marlena told me I had to be mad. Personally, I didn't give a shit one way or another."

"Do you think someone might have suggested it to Peg?"

Ray shrugged. "Never thought of it." He considered for a moment. "Don't know why they would."

"And this thing with Daphne?" asked Gabe.

"A few extra pounds on a woman, wow. It makes her feel different. And she didn't put me down once."

"Did she mention Roger?" asked Gabe.

"That's the strange thing. Her hate-on for Marlena is as fresh as yesterday, but she doesn't remember Roger, even though they dated."

"Didn't he date all the girls?" asked Gabe.

"He slept with all the girls. Daphne and Rog, they were actually a serious item. She was the one who broke it off."

"You remember it all pretty clearly," said Gabe.

"When you're in a band together you're like brothers. You love 'em and hate 'em at the same time, but you can't live without them."

"Do you know why Roger and Daphne broke it off?"

Ray shrugged again. "I figured it was her parents. You remember how they were."

Gabe did remember. Mr. and Mrs. Pyle made no secret that they thought Madden High School was Satan's leg trap. He had a vague memory that Daphne was forbidden to participate in field trips or after-school activities. Whenever she hung with the other kids there was the unspoken acknowledgement that her dad might drive up at any moment and drag her away. Daphne didn't fight back. She'd just sneak out the next day, and the next.

"Why do you think Daphne felt so strongly about Marlena?"

"Gabe, you know my wife. She's out to win. If that means other people lose," he looked Gabe directly in the eye, "even better."

The first period of the game ended and Ray started stacking bottles into the case. Gabe helped him lock up and dropped him off at his own party.

Joan hoped that the drugstore remedy would work before she had to go to the Stanfields'. She sprayed her nostrils with saline. This sinus thing, combined with the medication, dulled her sense of smell. She couldn't risk losing it. In the meanwhile it was time to return Mort's multiple calls.

"Hey, babe, I keep trying your cell in case your reception kicks in." Mort was obviously happy to hear her voice.

"The local cell tower is decorative." Joan was bracing herself to make this as painless as possible. "Mort, being away has given me perspective. It makes me realize that we're spending too much time together. We're separated."

"We're still friends. You laugh at my jokes and I give you great back rubs."

Despite his enthusiasm, she could detect the tension in his voice. They both knew what was coming. So much was now clear. Mort had given her a refuge. He'd made her feel safe and comfortable, but he'd never made her skin tingle when he touched her. She'd never felt passion with Mort, or anyone else, like she had with Gabe last night. At forty-eight, she had finally experienced the best sex in her life. It made her take stock.

"Mort, when we get back I think we should not see each other any more."

"C'mon Joan. Don't be harsh. You're over-reacting to the death . . . "

"Deaths," she interrupted.

"What?"

She explained about Peg. "And I'm not over-reacting to anything, Mort. Quit psychoanalyzing me. You're not a shrink."

"No, I'm your husband."

"Give it up, Mort. We haven't lived together in months and I know you're dating other women." She waited for him to deny it, but he didn't. They were holding onto each other for all of the wrong reasons.

She got off the phone and was going to call Vi to find out if there were any other tidbits her mom had left out in their last conversation, but she looked at the clock. She was already late for cocktails at Marlena and Ray's.

As she drove over the tracks and up the hill, she silently reviewed her accumulated knowledge on the case. Scant, at best. Although she had more suspicions, she was no further ahead with actual facts than she had been this morning. Red and blue lights flashed in her rearview mirror. She glanced at her speedometer. No problem there. No playground zone in sight either. Then she realized who it was. She pulled to the curb and waited in her car. Instead of coming to the driver's side, Gabe tapped on the window of the passenger side. Joan unlocked the door and he slid in beside her.

"Is this your idea of discreet?" Her tone was sterner than she'd intended, but she didn't apologize. The weight of the situation was catching up with her.

"I tried your cell," he said.

"Welcome to no-man's land." This time she allowed the hint of a smile. "Sorry, Gabe, but I can't stop thinking about Peg. Was it a coincidence that she died right after Roger?" His silence told her nothing. "She was the only person who could completely clear me."

"Clear you or Daphne," added Gabe.

"Or Daphne," agreed Joan. "What if we're targets of some kind? Has she gone back to Calgary?"

"She wants this cleared up before she leaves town, same as you."

He wasn't telling her everything. She gently prompted him. "And?"

"And there's another reason she's here that has nothing to do with the case." He paused. "And I'm not sharing this with you in my official capacity. I'm not sure it has anything to do with the case, but I trust you and I need that analytical brain of yours." He paused again. "Daphne and Ray . . . have a thing."

"You mean?"

He nodded. "Yeah, they're sleeping together. At least they did. I don't know if it was a one-time thing."

She shook her head in disbelief. Who would have thought that skinny little Ray Stanfield would be the pin-up boy of Madden High? Certainly not her and probably not Ray himself. Sarah, Marlena, and now Daphne? "Must be leftover adolescent hormones," she said.

"Maybe." They looked at each other, the big question hanging silently between them. Is that what it was between the two of them, hormones, a one-time thing? Gabe continued with an awkward, slightly deeper tone, his professional voice. "Spending time with you, re-living those early years, is helping me put the case together."

"That's assuming that the murder is tied to our past," she said. She knew that this was her chance to tell him the truth. She started carefully, reluctantly. "Last Friday wasn't the first time that Roger attacked me."

Gabe's mouth opened, but it was several more moments before he made a sound. "When?"

"The Labour Day Party." She could see him putting the pieces together: her disappearance, her lack of interest in fulfilling their secret pact to lose their virginity together. "He tried to rape me, Gabe."

"What?" His confusion was replaced by anger.

"I went into the woods by myself, to throw up." She smiled sadly. "That damn gin, you know? I heard footsteps behind me. I guess he followed me. He pulled me into the bush. It was so dense and dark." She kept her voice even and calm as she explained how she had barely managed to fend him off. "After that all I can remember is sitting among the trees on the dead leaves, crying. I was too embarrassed, probably too drunk, to move, then I fell asleep or passed out. The sun was coming up and kids were straggling home by the time I had the wherewithal to pull my jeans back on. Then you and Hazel found me."

Gabe's voice was distant. "You had puke all over your shirt."

She nodded. "You took me home. Hazel told my parents that I'd slept at her house. I didn't dare say anything after that. A couple of weeks later my dad died. Life took over. I barely ever thought of it until he tried it again on Friday night."

"Why didn't you tell me?"

She reminded him what the sexual landscape had looked like in 1979. It was rare for girls to complain about being attacked. "You remember Doris?" she asked. She didn't have to say more. The landmark case was imprinted on their brains. Doris Welch had had the guts to try to press rape charges against two hefty teenagers after a night of drinking in a local bar. She'd gained consciousness with a two-hundred pound footballer on top of her. Just when the defence lawyers had started to quake in their boots at the brutality of the crime, the judge came back with a not guilty verdict. He cited the fact that she hadn't been wearing underwear as one of the primary reasons for the rape. In the days before thongs, avoiding panty lines was tantamount to inviting rape. "That kind of court decision is enough to shut anyone up."

Gabe was quiet, then took her hand. "I'm surprised you ever wanted to look at a man again." He looked distracted and worried.

"What's the matter?" she asked.

"The system hasn't changed all that much." He continued carefully. "The fact that Roger attacked you twice, if anyone finds out I know . . . "

"I want to put it on the record, the official record," she insisted.

"I've gotta think about this Joan." He covered his eyes, as though the light was suddenly too much.

"I have to, Gabe. You know I do," she insisted.

He let out an audible breath. "Okay." He nodded slowly. "I'll write up a report. Smartt may want to talk to you again. I'll do my best to keep the hounds from your door."

It frightened Joan that her past might draw attention. She'd always been a private person, more so with age. She nodded firmly, accepting the risk.

"Gabe, if Peg didn't die of a stroke . . . " She paused. "Who would be after both Peg and Roger?"

Gabe shook his head. "Roger, I get. It's unfortunate, but there are several people who might have wanted to see him dead. Peg, that's another story." He shrugged.

"Did she piss somebody off thirty years ago?" Joan ticked off the possibilities: "Or could she have identified Roger's killer? As the reunion chairperson she would have been in touch with everyone who came as well as those who didn't. Or is there some maniac out there randomly killing the Class of '79? "

Suddenly the list of suspects exploded.

Gabe took her hand. "Unless we get confirmation that Peg's death was something besides natural causes, let's not speculate. I'd better drive my own truck to the Stanfields, otherwise the whole town will be talking." He swung open the door, but before climbing out he leaned toward her and kissed her. His tongue tenderly separated her lips. Moments passed until out of the corner of her eye Joan saw a vehicle slow. She gently pushed Gabe away and they both watched Des Cardinal drive past. Gabe winced and climbed out. After the squad car had disappeared around a corner, he dipped his head back inside. "Sorry about that." Then he was gone.

The graduating class had swarmed to the Stanfields. As Joan had expected, it turned out to be more a wake than a reunion. People who hadn't attended the afternoon gathering were hearing about Peg's death for the first time as they came through the door. Despite Marlena's plan to show off to the graduates from out of town, locals invited themselves when they heard that the Stanfields were opening their doors. The day had turned warm and the heat lingered into the evening. People spilled out of the house onto the expansive back deck and throughout the house.

For the moment, Joan and Hazel had the kitchen to themselves. Requisite pies, squares, crustless sandwiches, and other funeral fare were stacked on the table and counters. The scent of lemon meringue and matrimonial bars swept Joan back to her childhood.

"Peg always kept her distance from me," said Hazel, leaning her large body against the island. She popped the last bite of Nanaimo bar in her mouth and licked the chocolate from her fingers. "I used to think it was because I'm a lesbian, that it made her uncomfortable."

"And that changed?" asked Joan.

"Yes it did. I was in town checking up on Roger a few years back. He was staying at his parents. Peg stopped me at the grocery store and was really friendly. She said there were things that had happened when we were in high school that shouldn't have and she was sorry she hadn't been more supportive. I figured she was talking about the modified basketball photo."

"Did she mention Steve?"

"No. She said that Roger should have taken responsibility. I told her not to worry about it, that I'd let go of it years back. Heck, I may not have become politically active if they hadn't tried to give me a penis in tenth grade." Hazel turned her attention to a plate of cookies. "I told Lila I'd bring her something sweet. I'd better get back to the hotel or she'll give me the silent treatment all night."

"Are you two doing okay?"

Hazel shrugged in response. "Her snits don't usually last this long." She held up a paper plate heaped with chocolate pecan cookies and two large lemon squares. "We'll see if this helps."

"I'm really sorry that you got stuck on the road on Friday," said Joan. "It would have been great if the three of us could have caught up together before this became an investigation instead of a reunion."

"Sounds like you and Gabe made out fine without me. Besides, a night at the Elgar Motel is something that Lila and I can cherish in our old age. It was like sleeping in a 1950s time capsule." Hazel grinned and swept out of the room.

Joan had assumed that Hazel and Lila had been stuck somewhere near the Kamloops Airport the night that Roger had been murdered. She wondered why they hadn't travelled the last few miles to the room waiting for them at the Twin Pines. Were they afraid that their fight would become public? Although she hadn't yet schmoozed her way through the twenty or so people in the next room and had only briefly nodded at Marlena and Ray when she arrived, she was ready to duck out the back door. It had been a long day. Her brain was full of details that she needed to process. As she was about to make her escape, Daphne and Marlena, chatting like a couple of chickadees, came into the kitchen bearing empty trays.

"Joannie, are you in here chowing down all on your own?" chided Marlena.

The veiled insult doubled Joan's resolve to leave as soon as possible.

"I bet Joan can eat whatever she wants without a worry. She looks so great!" As Daphne spoke she filled trays with professional speed, laying out attractive arrangements that would make Martha Stewart proud. She popped a plump, fragrant strawberry in her mouth.

"Daph," said Marlena, "haven't you turned into the perfect little diplomat? Didn't get that from your hoot-an'-holler folks, did you?"

Daphne stiffened and faltered. "May they rest in peace."

"Rest in peace? Why, your dad may have mellowed but that's no reason to count him as dead," said Marlena.

Daphne spun around. "What do you mean?"

"I mean he was perky as a chipmunk when I was over at the lodge the other day." Marlena started stacking trays by the sink. "Do you think we'll need more sandwiches? People seem to be going after the squares and sausage rolls more." She started rinsing the trays one at a time.

Joan noticed that Daphne had gone as white as the whipped cream on Marlena's shortcake. "Daph, are you all right?"

Daphne stood silently, staring straight ahead.

"Oh, for God's sake," Marlena gasped impatiently as she grabbed a paper napkin from the kitchen island and held it under Daphne's chin. "Spit."

Daphne remained paralyzed.

"Hurry, just spit it out," said Marlena, hand on her hip.

The memory came rushing back to Joan. They'd all been at Marlena's birthday party, her ninth or tenth. She couldn't remember exactly. The cake was angel food topped with a cloud of whipped cream and stuffed with luscious red strawberries. Although Mrs. Prychenko had scraped the strawberries from Daphne's serving, a trickle of juice had seeped into the cake. Daphne had bitten into it, and almost instantly, her lips had started to swell. Daphne had been more embarrassed than scared, until her throat started closing and she couldn't breath. Ambulance sirens had ended the party. Now Joan recalled that Daphne had had to steer clear of several foods because of severe allergies. More than once she had been rushed to hospital when there was a recurrence of the birthday party scene. Peanuts were one of the worst. Strawberries were another. Joan had always attributed Daphne's parents' strict surveillance of their daughter to their religious fervour. How much of their concern might have been fear? Fear that their youngest child would die before them?

Close to tears, Daphne stared at Marlena.

"Spit? Why?"

Joan stepped in. She could detect the strawberries on Daphne's breath. "Your allergies, honey."

Daphne looked mystified. "I'm not allergic to strawberries. I'm not allergic to anything."

"Yes you are," said Marlena sternly, in a know-it-all tone.

Joan took the napkin from Marlena's hand. "She looks fine now."

There had been strawberries in their salad at Jacques the day before. Daphne had shown no reaction then. But even if she had outgrown childhood allergies, something so severe should be in her records. When Daphne was in recovery from encephalitis someone should have warned her about something as serious as deadly allergies. What kind of man had her ex-husband been to leave her in such a precarious position? How thoughtless they had been. But Daphne hadn't choked or gasped for air. If it wasn't the strawberry that had made her turn pale, then what? It hit Joan like a brick. Daphne was responding to Marlena's comment about Mr. Pyle living in the Lodge. She was certain of it. Daphne hadn't known that her father was alive and here in Madden.

After Marlena left the kitchen, Joan asked gently, "When did you last see him, your dad?"

Daphne was curt. "I don't know. A long time ago. I don't want to talk about it." Beautiful, vivacious Daphne pasted a wide, stiff smile on her face as she went from the kitchen to the crowded living room. Joan followed.

Ray, Steve, and Rudy were standing around the piano trying to harmonize. At the sight of Daphne, Ray jumped on the sofa and drunkenly mimed a rapid drum solo with two satay skewers, oblivious to the chunks of chicken and pork flying across the room. Then he raised his hands.

"Attention everyone." The intro was unnecessary since it was hard to ignore a grown man jumping on the furniture. "Rank rises again. One night only, before Rudy leaves town." He grinned at his fellow band member, who smiled awkwardly.

Rudy's not as pissed as Ray, Joan thought.

Ray continued, his excitement rising. "Tomorrow night at the Madden Couch, featuring a new lead singer." He smiled at his audience. "Me." At that he bowed and fell off the sofa.

Joan could feel someone standing close to her. Gabe.

"It's where all the cool kids hang out," he said.

As Ray pulled himself to a sitting position on the carpet, Marlena looked as though she wanted to kick him. Joan couldn't help but think it was in bad taste to revive Rank so soon after Roger's death.

Gabe interrupted her thought. "Fowler is always happy to have anyone drop in." He looked around. "I'm surprised he didn't show up here tonight."

Ed Fowler typed "Vi Parker, Vancouver" into the search engine, hit "enter" then held his breath as he waited for the results. He spent hours every week Googling former students and faculty of Madden High. It gave him satisfaction to see their successes. He was an Internet lurker, though. Except for posting on Facebook and Craigslist about the reunion, he rarely actually contacted anyone. That, however, was about to change. He slowly exhaled.

Gabe and Joan leaned side by side against her car outside the Stanfield house. The warmth of his hip, where it touched hers, sent an electrical surge through her body. They knew that they couldn't touch further, not under the glow of the plate-glass window. Party sounds emerged from the house. "So Marlena no longer has her sights set on me?" she said.

"She's had time to digest what happened. She knows it's an outrageous idea, you killing anyone."

"I have a hard time believing it's that simple."

"Joan, let it go. I was wrong to get you to dig into this with me. It could be dangerous."

"I'm not stopping now. Smartt still mistrusts me. After you file that report about the attempted rape, he'll trust me even less." She stared into the night, her active brain twisting the clues around like a puzzle. She felt Gabe studying her profile.

He slid his hand down and discreetly slipped it over hers. "I can't let you do it, Joan."

"Yes, you can. You can and you must." She looked up into his concerned eyes and a hot tsunami of lust drowned her reason. She wondered if they'd be able to steal any time alone tonight. An invitation to a night of sensual pleasures was on her lips when the Stanfields' door opened. Ray, keys in hand, stumbled out with Rudy and his wife, Monica. Gabe became a cop, stepped in and offered the Weiss's a ride.

Rudy smiled at Joan. "Aren't you at the Twin Pines as well?"

She glanced at Gabe, who shrugged helplessly.

"Hop in," offered Joan. "Parker Taxi at your service." She mimicked Gabe's shrug, then quickly ducked into the driver's seat to hide her disappointment.

The cold linoleum balanced the heat of exertion as Joan finished her evening exercise routine. She lay back on the floor and looked up through the skylight. Straining to make out the features of the man in the moon, she realized she had been so busy trying to prove her innocence that she had missed something staring straight at her. If it hadn't been Peg's idea to add Daphne and her to the invitation list then someone had gone out of their way to break protocol. What if they had been lured here by someone with a score to settle with them both? What if they were in danger? She needed to warn Daphne. When she leapt up and reached for the phone, she saw that it was almost midnight. Was her imagination getting the better of her? It was too late to call the Stanfield house to warn Daphne on some half-baked intuition. It was also too late to call her mom to ask her about something that had been grinding at her all day. How, exactly, did Vi find out that Marlena's dad and Mr. Fowler's wife were having an affair?

Chapter Fifteen

THE NURSE POINTED OUT HAROLD PYLE sitting in the dining room, then left her standing in the entrance. She hadn't told the nurse her name, hadn't mentioned that the elderly man seated alone at a table, bent over his Monday breakfast, was one of her last remaining blood relatives. He looked nothing like she remembered. He still had a thick head of hair, but it was now white, nothing like the rich black hair in the photograph that sat beside her bed in Calgary. She watched from the doorway, wanting desperately to go to him, but afraid. She couldn't take his rejection again.

Suddenly the nurse was at her side, urging her to go sit with him. "His only visitor lately was that musician, the one who died last week," she said.

"Roger Rimmer?"

The nurse nodded then went to break up a traffic jam of walkers at the door.

"May I sit here?"

Harold Pyle's head tilted up and there was no recognition in his eyes. He nodded once then went back to his porridge. She took the seat next to him, where she could study him from the side. From this position she could see his craggy features without it being obvious that she was memorizing every curve, line, and whisker. His leathery skin had seen too much sun in his youth. The blue eyes sat deep in their sockets, red-rimmed, the whites now a jaundiced yellow. He was so much smaller now. She remembered him as a towering, formidable figure.

After a moment he looked up at her again. "I had a daughter looked a lot like you." He sniffed. "She broke her mother's heart."

He fed himself another bite of oatmeal. She watched him in silence then he looked up again, examining her with rheumy eyes. "My Daphne." His face sagged in sorrow as he spoke. "It took me getting old to realize we should've been nicer to her." His head bobbed in a palsied nod of contemplation. "Our own daughter. Charity begins at home." He paused then asked, "What'd you say your name was?"

Unable to deal with the emotion rising in her throat, she stumbled out of her chair. As she fled from the room she almost toppled an elderly man who was navigating between the tables with two canes.

"Mind if I sit with you, Harry?" asked the man.

When she was at the door, she looked back one last time. Although he'd gone back to eating his cereal, his eyes were on her.

Gabe hung up the phone after leaving a message for Joan then slowly stirred milk into his tea. He hadn't slept well. Although he was enjoying not having to deal with Betty's icy sarcasm at everything he said, the house felt empty. The thought of Teddy leaving made him lonely. Already he missed his son.

He didn't feel any closer to solving Roger's murder. The quiet house gave him too much space to think about the uneasy relationship with his dead classmate. Led by Hazel's example of charity, he had struggled for a long time to put his disapproval of Roger on the back burner. Since Joan had told him about her near rape at the Welcome sign so many years ago, his early dislike of Roger was back. It was hard not to be critical of someone who had been given so many opportunities by so many people and had burned everyone who had ever tried to help him. What hurt more was that Joan had kept the assault a secret. He'd lain awake half the night trying to push back the awful spectre of Roger attacking her. Gabe sipped his tea. She'd been his closest friend. Not surprising that he'd had so few friends, given his cynical wit and black wardrobe, his long trench coat that he wore even in the middle of summer.

He could barely remember the bush party on the Labour Day weekend of 1978. It didn't hold the same violent significance for him as it did for Joan. He'd been disappointed that she hadn't shown up to fulfill the pact of losing their virginity together and assumed that she'd chickened out. Plagued by erupting pimples and a colt-like ungainliness, he hadn't been surprised. A part of him was secretly relieved. Their friendship had been more important to him than anything else. It crushed him now, though, that she hadn't taken him into her confidence. How had she coped, carrying that secret by herself? Then a disturbing thought occurred to him. If Joan hadn't trusted him then, was she withholding information now?

The thought was interrupted by the ringing telephone. It was Chin Lau from the lab in Kamloops. They had results on Peg.

"Hemorrhagic stroke," Chin stated flatly.

"It's what I thought."

"Not so simple," Chin corrected. "The bleeding in the brain, caused by a drug interaction."

"An overdose?" asked Gabe.

"Kind of. A combination of the warfarin she was taking for her heart and cimetidine," said Chin. "Made the effect of the warfarin lethal. She bled to death. Plus, she was bruised up like a boxer. But there's no record of her having a 'scrip for cimetidine. No doc with half a brain would give her a prescription for it, at least not without constant monitoring. There was a lot in her system. Our unit traced Mrs. Chalmers prescriptions. Her GP has no idea where she got the cimetidine."

"What's it used for?" asked Gabe.

"Most commonly, ulcers, heartburn."

Gabe trusted Chin more than any toxicologist he'd ever worked with. He wasn't one to rush to a conclusion.

"Could it have been a mix-up at the pharmacy?" asked Gabe.

"Hey, man, don't diss the pros. This was a lame-o fubar," replied Chin.

Occasionally Gabe had to go through a thesaurus, not for the interpretation of chemical compounds, but to unravel Chin's metro hip lingo. In this case, however, the message was crystal clear.

"And Chin, her doctor, he's local?" Gabe held his pen, ready to write, but he didn't need to.

"That'd be a Dr. Rimmer, Dr. Thomas Rimmer."

Gabe thanked Chin, hung up the phone, then gave himself a minute to absorb the information. The spring groaned as he tilted back in his chair. This would be another blow to Tom Rimmer. The old doc had delivered half the town. Peg had probably been his patient all her life. He made a mental note to stop in on the doctor, maybe distract him with a game of chess and ask him a few questions at the same time. He held the photo from Roger's room up to the fluorescent light. What was the link that delivered death to both Roger and Peg? It didn't look good for Joan: Marlena's claim that Roger visited her room on the night of his death, even if he hadn't gone inside; Roger's attempt to rape her in 1978; Peg, the only person who could have cleared her regarding the invitation. He'd delayed reporting the near rape, but sooner or later he'd have to share the information with Smartt.

He stared again at the fresh faces of the class of '79. Which one of these kids had grown into a murderer? As he studied the photo, he noticed something that had escaped him before. Gabe dialed the Twin Pines Hotel and asked to be connected to Joan Parker's cabin.

Joan turned into the crescent of the Elgar subdivision, checking house numbers against the address scribbled on the back of her grocery receipt. The urgency in Gabe's voice had kept her from asking questions on the phone, but she'd been surprised when he insisted that she come to his place in the middle of the day. The second surprise was his home. The large lot was dominated by an impersonal two-car garage and driveway, and the house was a cookie-cutter suburban design, indistinguishable from the hundred or so surrounding it. Gabe had been a fanatical environmentalist long before curbside recycling had been conceived. As a teenager, he'd picked up litter as they walked, and he had lectured their peers on the dangers of beer cap pull-tabs to wildlife. He'd been fearless in his commitment. Once he'd approached a large pickup truck at a stop sign to lecture the burly driver on the harmful air pollution caused by the blue smoke billowing from his exhaust. Gabe had convinced her that they could truly make a difference. Joan had continued to 'walk the walk' into adulthood. Although she owned a car, she shopped for fuel-efficient models and preferred to cycle or walk when distances permitted. Her neighbours referred to her as the recycling Nazi. Okay, there were lots of people making a bigger difference, but over the years, she had always heard Gabe's voice in the back of her mind, bringing her in line. So where had he become derailed? Now he lived in a house that was an environmental eyesore, with a gluttonous footprint for only three people. Was the house a product of his wife Betty's ideals, or had he changed that much? She toyed with the question, but it didn't dampen her desire. She pushed the doorbell. A long, loud chime echoed through the house. She waited, imagining the eyes of the neighbourhood on her back.

Calling on Gabe had been a daily routine when she was growing up. They'd been best friends since the sandbox and that hadn't changed once they hit puberty. His basement bedroom had been their hangout, When Gabe was twelve he saved for a year to buy his own portable record player from the Eaton's catalogue, chalking up hours babysitting and pushing the mower over every lawn in the neighbourhood. She remembered the day it arrived as though it was last Christmas. They'd walked downtown to pick up the parcel then had run all the way back to his bungalow. With the lid closed, the record player was a small suitcase with a baby-blue faux-leather finish and a white handle. They would sit for hours on the carpeted floor, playing monopoly and listening to forty-fives. As they graduated from singles of the Beatles to long-play albums by Moody Blues and Led Zeppelin, the yellow plastic adapters that fit into the centre of forty-fives became their tiddly-wink collection. Gabe's room was also where she'd hallucinated on acid for the first time and where she'd recovered from her lemon gin poisoning, Gabe and Hazel watching over her, unaware of the violent attack she had survived.

"C'mon, c'mon," she whispered, waffling between the guilty anticipation of being alone with Gabe and the urge to drive off, fleeing while she still could. It was stubborn determination that kept her there. More than anything she wanted to solve this murder. Maybe Gabe's marriage was held together by a mere thread, but he loved his career. He could lose it all if they were caught together. She'd find out what was so private that they had to meet here, then she'd leave. She was discreetly picking a poppy seed from between her teeth when she saw the tall silhouette through the opaque side panel.

"Thanks for coming, Joan." Gabe led her past the living room where she caught a glimpse of family photos along the mantle. Based on the suburban utopian house, she had expected Betty to look as though she came off the rack at Sears. Instead the pictures revealed her to be fit and stylish in a comfortable, friendly way. She was also exceptionally pretty. Their son, tall and lanky, was the doppleganger of Gabe thirty years earlier. He'd inherited Gabe's acne. Instead of rebellious black, though, he wore a preppy striped shirt with pressed jeans. His hair was clipped and clean.

Gabe opened a door at the end of the hall. The space, a den-cum-library, was all Gabe. He'd transformed a corner of this suburban world into a private retreat that would have been suited to a clearing in the woods. The scent of warm cedar panelling and shelves that reached to the high ceilings blended with the musk of old books. It all wrapped around Joan like a down comforter. She collapsed into an inviting leather armchair. Robertson Davies' *The Cunning Man* lay by the phone beside her, bookmarked toward the end.

"I didn't want to meet at my office. I shouldn't be talking to you unofficially at all," he reminded her. His hair was unruly. The stress of concern pulled down the corners of his mouth. For the first time, she saw the years hanging on his face.

"Did you tell Staff Sergeant Smartt about Roger attacking me?" She thought this might be the reason for the secrecy.

"No."

"Gabe, I know it won't look good."

"That's an understatement." He chewed his lower lip, a habit that he'd had since boyhood. "I wrote up the report. It's in a file on my desk. But I need more time."

"Why?"

"It gives you a clear and compelling motive."

"But I'm not the only one, surely?" she asked.

Gabe took his time answering. He swivelled his desk chair around so that it faced her then lowered himself into it. It was like watching a heron settle. His knees touched hers. He leaned forward, as though the walls might have ears. "Do you know a good lawyer?"

She felt a chill as Gabe explained the toxicology results. "There's not much of a chance that it was an accident. There was no reason for her to have cimetidine and no record of a prescription."

"I'm not afraid, Gabe," she said, but it made her sad to hear that Peg's death, in all likelihood, was murder. That warm, animated woman, with her joyful dark eyes, had made her feel welcome in Madden. It was Peg's invitation that had reconnected her to her past. She also knew that her murder would resonate beyond the Wong family and the local community. Joan had misjudged the scope of Peg's world. The nurse, mother, and friend, comfortable in her hometown, had devoted months of time and her own funds to bring all of their class together for one short weekend. Peg had touched so many.

"She did this for all of us and it may have been what killed her."

"The status change to suspicious death isn't public yet," said Gabe."I wanted you to look at this." He placed the photocopy of the class picture into her hands.

In Hazel's hotel room, she hadn't paid it much attention. Seventy-some kids, some of the worst hair she'd ever seen, all standing on the stairs of the old school. On either end of the back row were the twelfth grade homeroom teachers: Mrs. Bednarski, who was old then and had long since passed on, prudish Miss Lange, and Mr. Fowler, staring proudly at the camera. The photo had been taken just prior to the spring grad celebration. "May 1979" was written on the lower border, five months after Joan had moved to Vancouver.

Gabe asked, "Does anything jump out at you?"

"Besides the fact that I'm not in it?"

"Look again. Concentrate on the rip."

She studied the vertical tear that divided the image in two just to the right of centre. The clear tape, yellowed with age, blurred some of the detail. As Joan's eye reached the second row from the top she saw that the photo hadn't been randomly destroyed. It had been carefully torn around Roger, separating him from the students on the other side of the page. Below Roger was petite and perky Marlena. Instead of facing the camera, she was coyly looking up at the dreamboat rock 'n' roll star of Madden High. To the left of Roger, directly on the other side of the jagged rip, but distanced by the barbed-wire effect of the torn photo, was Daphne. The years had treated her more kindly than all the others but she had definitely changed. My God, thought Joan, how they had all changed.

"So, what does this mean?"

"You tell me."

"Well, I'm surprised that Daphne is in the picture. Hadn't she left?"

"She left just before the end of the school year," said Gabe. "Anyway, I need you to help me find out what this means. People will talk to you, Joannie, in a way that they won't talk to me. I'm the law."

She glanced up at him. "Don't remind me." Gabe was easy to spot in the picture, standing slightly apart from the others. His long hair fell over his shoulders and he wore a shirt with billowing sleeves. Then she realized that the "guy" standing next to him was Hazel, decked out in a full tux. They wore matching bow ties. "You look happy," she said. "You and Hazel."

Gabe moved behind her. "Yeah. We danced the last dance together. We were happy to get out alive. We took off from Madden so fast." He shook his head. "Our shadows didn't know we were gone for two days. It was bad after you left, Joannie. We were so lonely for you. Somehow, with three of us, there was protection." His hand moved to her shoulder.

"How was I supposed to know? Why didn't you tell me that when we connected in Vancouver, when we were at university?"

"You'd become superwoman by then, kicking ass at school, cleaning up with the academic awards, plus taking care of your mom and working. What, I was going to whine about how hard it was for me?"

She had no response. In truth, she'd been too busy getting on with life. She turned her attention back to the photo and something caught her eye. "Do you have a magnifying glass?"

Gabe rummaged over the surface of his desk and handed her his reading glasses. "Next best thing."

"Thanks." Joan tilted the glasses over the rip in the photo until the image of the tape repair came into focus. It hit Joan like a bullet. "Are Roger and Daphne holding hands?" She had thought that beautiful, elegant Daphne had been somehow beyond Roger's reach.

Gabe shared what Ray had told him, that Roger and Daphne had dated, then he grasped *her* hands. "Joan, you're twice as sharp as the officers on my team. Don't get me wrong, they're good men, all of them but I need your help with this. I thought I could do it without you, but nobody on my squad has the history to solve a murder that was motivated by events that happened thirty years ago."

"I wasn't there either," she reminded him.

"But you know the players. Besides, you've always had an uncanny ability to get inside someone else's head. Call it empathy."

"Or dangerous curiosity." She smiled, but couldn't admit that she'd started her own sleuthing twenty-four hours earlier.

He remained serious. "I have to resolve this before anyone else gets killed."

"Okay, I'll help, but there's one condition."

"Tell me."

"You have to share everything about the case, even the details that don't seem important. That's what it would take," she said. He was nodding in agreement, without hesitation, and it made her uncomfortable. "Except that's not ethical, Gabe. I'm a suspect."

"Nobody has to know. Not Des, definitely not Smartt. Just you and me, Joan." He was holding her gaze.

Why should she be taken aback by his disregard of the rules? In truth, he hadn't changed much. When he placed his hand on her knee and gently squeezed, she looked at him. His eyes were glistening. The business part of the meeting was over. He leaned over and kissed her. He moved his lips to her ears and neck, letting his kisses slide farther down.

"Not here," she said.

"Then where? When?" He brushed the hair from her face and, again, she tingled, tiny electric currents beneath her skin reminding her that she was alive, so alive. "What if you leave and I never see you again?" he asked.

He could be right. She knew herself too well. Once she left Madden, when would she make the trip again? Could these be the last moments of their own private reunion? She shyly entwined her fingers in his, kissed the back of his hand. He led her to the sofa then pulled her down on top of him. The taste of his lips was becoming so familiar. She felt his fingers fumbling with the buttons on her blouse. Working downward, she unbuttoned his shirt, then reached for his heavy belt buckle. Suddenly she thought of Betty. She could now conjure the image of Gabe's wife from the photograph in the living room. But despite a distant voice urging her to stop, she couldn't.

The Stanfield family van slowly rounded the corner into the crescent, idled briefly beside Joan's Honda then sped away.

Chapter Sixteen

The sun had shifted so that late morning light cut across the den. Joan inhaled Gabe's scent. She could chart his day from the bath soap and toothpaste mixed with oranges, to the coffee and gasoline. His quiet snores rumbled. Barely moving, she stretched her fingers toward her bra on the floor, praying that she wouldn't wake him. The first time that they had slept together it had been gracefully dark in her motel room. No man, besides Mort, had seen her naked in a very long time. Even her gynecologist allowed her the Victorian dignity of a blue paper jacket. She was in relatively good shape, not great, but good for her age. It was, however, all relative. At forty-eight, some of the blush had definitely come off the peach. As a matter of fact, she reflected, the fruit had fallen from the tree, bounced a few times, and started to compost.

Gabe stirred and she froze. When his breathing settled again she fastened her bra and was just slipping into her panties when he opened his eyes.

"You're beautiful." He smiled at her.

She was so glad that she'd spent the extra cash on good underwear.

The day had turned chilly so Laura Rimmer threw a cardigan over her shoulders before answering the door. A pretty, dark-haired girl stood on the steps. Something about her seemed instantly familiar, but Laura couldn't put her finger on it. The girl appeared nervous, or maybe she was just cold.

"Hello. My name is Daphne Pyle. I went to school with your son."

Laura let her in then busied herself in the kitchen making tea and setting out sandwiches for an early lunch. Their freezer and fridge were jammed with the generous offerings of the funeral brigade. She'd done her own years in service, providing freezer cakes to households in mourning. Cherry walnut squares were her specialty. Tom had locked himself in his basement office after breakfast to review patient files. The stream of people coming to pay respects had slowed, and this morning had been quiet until now. There was some confusion about when they'd be able to hold Roger's funeral since the police hadn't yet identified the person who had taken his life. When she returned to the living room the young woman had one of the family photo albums on her lap. It was opened to the pages of Roger as a baby. He had been such a beautiful child.

"I hope you don't mind me saying so, dear, but you don't look old enough to have graduated with Roger."

"Roger had it rough, Laura. You know that." Her husband stood in the doorway. He kindly took the tray and held it out to Daphne. "Our son had aged beyond his years."

Laura smoothed her skirt as she sat and smiled. "I'm not daft, Tom. I know that the drugs were hard on him."

They'd always skated around the topic of Roger's addiction. Tom looked at her aghast now that the elephant in the room was doing back flips on the carpet. She turned her attention back to Daphne.

"No, you definitely look younger than the other girls. What's your secret?"

Tom interrupted to say that he knew Harold Pyle, who lived at the lodge and asked if she was related.

The younger woman muttered, "My dad," then made abrupt excuses to leave, abandoning a half-eaten egg salad sandwich on her plate. The etiquette of mourning is acquired, Laura thought, but nobody had taught this girl.

Gabe placed a steaming cup of coffee in front of Joan, who was perched on a stool at the kitchen island. Although the front of the house was stereotypical suburbia, the view from the back more than made up for it. The expansive lawn sloped down to a ridge of trees and wild grasses on the edge of a fast-moving creek. Strains of Bach played from an IPod dock. Gabe had given her his robe. His clean-soapy smell, she knew, would transfer to her body and she welcomed the thought of wearing his scent. The adolescent idea that she wouldn't bathe for days caused her to smile. Gabe had slightly eased her discomfort of being in Betty's house when he showed her that the sofa was a hide-a-bed and the closet in his den contained his clothes. He'd been sleeping there since before Christmas. As she sipped her coffee she wondered how many marriages devolved in that direction, couples maintaining the illusion of togetherness long past the expiry date. Then there were those, like Mort and her, who appeared to have made a clean break but continued the conjugal visits.

She pondered the copy of the grad photo in front of her, picking out all the characters from their lives: Steve with his huge hair; Candy as hard as steel in a slinky dress; Peg with her straight black hair falling over her faux ermine collar. Only Daphne didn't appear to be dressed for the prom. She wore what looked like a man's shirt and Joan couldn't help but wonder if it had been Roger's. She guessed that the Pyles hadn't allowed her to attend the prom, concerned that Satan was the event coordinator.

Laura Rimmer tidied the living room after the Pyle girl left. When she went to put away the photo album, she smiled down at her three-year-old son, his sweet face surrounded by golden curls of angel hair. Those were the days when he brought them nothing but joy. Had they been too indulgent? Is that what brought him down? They send you home from hospital with those precious bundles and no instructions. Even a coffee maker comes with instructions nowadays. She had always blamed herself for what had happened to her son. Flipping back to earlier photos, she was met by a blank square in the middle of the baby pictures. The picture must have fallen out in the past few days, with everyone admiring her baby. She got on her knees and began to search for it under the furniture.

Joan and Gabe finished their coffee as they shared information on the case. Gabe let her know that there was no clear indication, yet, of exactly how the deadly medication had been administered to Peg or when it had been ingested. He intended to talk to Daphne and Candy again, since they had both been at Peg's house and may have noticed something unusual. He mentioned that Daphne and Ray had been at the Elgar motel on Sunday morning when Peg had had her attack.

"Popular spot," said Joan.

"You been there?"

"No. I mean because that's where Hazel and Lila stayed last Friday night."

"What?"

It turned out that this was new information to Gabe, which confirmed the value of them sharing the fine details. When Hazel had sketched out her Friday evening to him, he, like Joan, had concluded that Hazel and Lila had stopped for the night because they were too tired to drive any farther. With the deluxe suite at the Twin Pines waiting for them only fifteen minutes away, the rundown motel was an unexpected choice. They decided to put this in the "coincidence" column, but not at the top of their list for follow up.

At that moment Gabe's phone rang. He glanced at the call display and started walking down the hallway as he answered. Joan instantly knew that it was Betty calling. The warmth in his voice made her uneasy. She was taken aback when she heard him laugh.

As she drove back to Madden, she angrily demanded the tears to go away, but couldn't control them as they slid down the side of her nose. She had sunk so low that she wished ill feelings between Gabe and his wife. This transgression had gone farther than she ever could have imagined, after a lifetime spent mastering control over her emotions. How stupid, to let her feelings for him go this far.

When she arrived at her cabin, the phone was ringing. She heard her mom's voice and knew that she'd probably been calling every ten minutes trying to reach her. "Joan, you'll never guessed who called me," gushed Vi.

"Mr. Fowler?"

"How did you know? You didn't put him up to it?" Her mother sounded disappointed.

"He didn't need any encouragement. He has the hots for you," she teased.

"Oh, shame on you. We don't get that way at our age." Joan could tell that she was smiling.

"Oh, I know. It's more 'warm and fuzzy' isn't it?" There was still that piece of Vi's puzzle that was missing. "Mom, how did you find out about Marlena's dad and Suzy Fowler?"

The line went silent for several seconds then her mother sighed. "I don't like to think of unhappy times."

Joan kept prodding. It turned out that Vi remembered the exact moment and could describe it as though it was yesterday. It happened on the same day that she'd received her first pay cheque from Twin Pines, the first pay cheque she'd ever received in her life.

"It was the middle of the afternoon and I was pushing my cleaning cart across the parking lot." Joan couldn't imagine how her little mom had moved that cart a foot across the gravel, let alone drag it back and forth day after day. "That Prychenko girl was leaning against her dad's truck in the parking lot."

"Marlena?" asked Joan.

"That's right. That's what got my attention. It was like she was waiting for him. I thought it seemed odd, her there in the middle of the school day but," she sighed, "none of my beeswax. I was unlocking a room, a long-term rental, when the door to the next room opened. There was all this yelling. I was worried that someone was hurt. Well, there was that girl pounding her father and grabbing at Suzy Fowler. When they recognized me they were all embarrassed. They were used to cleaning people being faceless, nameless robots. I learned that soon enough on that job. They didn't expect to see their neighbour in a motel uniform. They were the most gawd-awful pale orange colour."

"I remember." Joan conjured the memory of the cheap cotton dresses with attached white aprons, grey from a thousand washings.

"Well, that poor girl turned pale and ran toward the river. Suzy Fowler went and sat in Dan's car with her head down. Dan started after his daughter but must have known he'd never catch her. He never looked at me once, but Suzy saw me as they were driving off. She told Ed as soon as he got home after school, probably afraid he'd hear it from someone else first. You know what I wish?" asked Vi.

"That you hadn't come out of the room?" ventured Joan.

"That's what I used to wish, for years. But now," she lowered her voice, as though sharing a conspiracy. "I wish I'd gone and married Ed Fowler when he'd asked, even if he was years younger than me." She hooted. "Wouldn't have that have sent a shiver of scandal through that old town?"

"That it would have," agreed Joan.

Then her mother went quiet and became serious again. "But there were his kids to think of, and Suzy. Ed should never have blamed her. I told him that. He wasn't good at hiding how he felt about me. It never went beyond him looking goo-goo eyes at me and I never encouraged him, but I knew it was hard on poor Suzy." Another silence. "She wasn't in love with Dan. He was a just a convenient weapon to use against Ed. Any woman who wanted to have sex could have had it with Dan Prychenko. There's always one of those around."

The comment opened Joan's eyes. Roger had fallen into that category in their youth. They had all thought their generation had invented illicit sex, possibly sex period. She listened as her mom continued.

"At first I thought Marlena had caught her dad by accident, seeing his truck, thinking he was at some meeting. But what kind of business do you have at a motel, besides monkey business? No, I think she knew her dad was in that room. Who was with him almost didn't matter. There were women before Suzy and there'd be more to come."

Joan promised her mom that she'd come home as soon as she could then she hung up. Gazing out the window, she realized that she was staring at the same parking lot where Marlena had sat waiting for her dad thirty years before. No wonder Marlena had attacked her at the gas bar. Joan had believed it was because she wasn't cool enough, was inferior. In reality, Marlena was probably trying to retaliate against Vi, who had witnessed her shame. It would have burned Marlena to know that Joan never mentioned the attacks to Vi. Up until this trip to Madden, Joan hadn't shared any bad news with her mother, fearing that she was too delicate.

Appearances meant everything to Marlena, then and now. She'd still do anything to protect herself. Joan thought of Daphne. If Daph was fooling around with Ray, it could explode like a grenade. She decided again to warn Daphne to watch her back.

When the band arrived at the cultural centre to set up for the much-anticipated Rank performance, Ed Fowler was enjoying a game of hearts with Daphne. He had a bad feeling that Ray was being overly friendly to her, that she wasn't comfortable at the Stanfield house. She hadn't said so, but she was spending a lot of time at the Couch. Daphne was a pretty girl. Today she had rushed in with her hair still wet. Instead of the stiff up-do that she'd worn since she arrived, her hair hung in soft ringlets. What would Marlena do if she picked up the scent of Ray tom-catting? He'd told Daphne that she could stay at the centre as long as she wanted. He'd even bring in a sleeping bag from home if she wanted to sleep on the sofa. She had declined but he'd brought it anyway in case she changed her mind. He swore to himself that he'd do whatever he could to protect her. It wouldn't be the first time.

Ray entered the room carrying a small amp. When he spotted Daphne he made a beeline for her and grabbed her by the belt loop of her jeans.

Ed was shocked. "Ray Stanfield, unhand that girl!"

Ray just smiled. But Daphne turned and said something to him that Ed couldn't hear. Ray blanched and stepped away. Ed couldn't contain a grin. It was good to see that Daphne had learned to take care of herself. For the next hour Ray concentrated on setting up the sound system, darting the occasional glance toward the pretty woman.

Poor little Daphne Pyle. She'd almost sunk before she learned how to swim. Ed realized that he was probably one of the only people left who knew what had happened to her. The sexual revolution of the sixties had hit Madden early and hung around long after AIDS was making headlines in the eighties. In the late seventies Ed was doubling as the school counsellor at Madden High. One afternoon Daphne came into his office and burst into tears. It was only two months from the end of the year, but she already had a significant bump. Her situation was complicated by the threat of her father. Ed Fowler knew that Harold Pyle beat both his wife and daughter. According to the old man, the Bible demanded that he keep them in line. In their fundamentalist church pre-marital sex bought you a one-way ticket to eternal damnation. Daphne was scared to death of her father and knew that her mother couldn't risk a hand in her defence. Ed, for once, agreed that it was better not to tell her folks. He'd always been able to reason with parents in the past when it came to pregnancies and other life-altering events, but this time the risk was too great. He offered to help her find someone who could do an abortion, but she said it was too late and was adamant about keeping the child. She never said who the father was but Ed thought he knew. He could've been fired for helping her leave town. Now she was back again, he was curious about the outcome of her pregnancy. Part of him wondered if she'd like to talk about it, but he didn't want to raise unhappy memories. Poor girl. She'd suffered enough. Now she'd pulled herself up and made something of herself. Good for her, he thought. Good for her.

Marlena opened her door wearing yoga gear that outlined her muscular body in detail. She was warm and chatty, which caught Joan off guard. Daphne wasn't there and Marlena had no clue where she'd gone.

"It's been fun having another woman in the house. The girls adore her. When she told them that she'd kept a diary as a kid, the girls actually read her their latest entries. Can you imagine that? God, they won't even tell me what they want for breakfast."

It appeared that Marlena hadn't figured out what was going on between Ray and Daphne. Maybe it had been a one-time fling and Daphne had come to her senses. Regardless, with Marlena's history with her philandering father, who knew what she'd do if she discovered that her husband was fooling around.

After the Stanfield's, Joan stopped at Jacques. The waiter remembered Daphne, but she hadn't been there either. Joan wound her way to the Madden Cultural Centre, peering down side streets for a glimpse of Daphne's champagne-coloured rental car.

When she parked at the Couch, Steve and Rudy were carrying music gear in from Steve's roofing truck. It gave Joan a twinge to see all the tools of her father's trade tidily stacked against the back. The unmistakable odor of tar permeated everything.

She was relieved to find Daphne with Mr. Fowler and waited until they finished a hand of hearts before suggesting to Daphne that they get a breath of air. Mr. Fowler had his jacket on in an instant. It would have been awkward to leave him behind. Thankfully, Steve interrupted with a question about the power supply. The two men headed to the basement to check out the electrical panel, and Joan quickly led Daphne out of the building.

The playground behind the school blended new with old; a climbing wall with bright plastic holds next to remnants of the playground that had been there when they were kids: the old metal swing set, a spiral slide, and monkey bars. The women sat side by side on the swings. Joan wasn't sure how to warn Daphne about Marlena without admitting that Gabe had told her about the Elgar Motel. She started by mentioning the class picture, saying that she'd seen it at Hazel's.

"You and Roger were holding hands. You were dating?"

Daphne gave her a startled look, then turned her head away. "I'm not sure. Kind of."

Joan waited while Daphne pulled a vivid image from her fractured memory.

"The whole time he was effin' around on me. And I was stupid enough to keep seeing him. All he could think about, besides sex and girls, was splitting from here so he could be some big rock star."

Joan considered. Roger had been a drug addict and alcoholic but had he also struggled with sex addiction? It was a problem without a name thirty years earlier.

"He held your hand in front of other people. That may not seem like much, but for him that was a huge deal, a public declaration."

"Really?" Daphne looked bemused.

"According to other girls, he'd resolved to appear single. He was afraid that his career would bomb if he were attached." Then Joan warned her. "He was crazy about you, Daph, and that may have been enough to make someone else angry. People carry grudges." She stopped her swing and looked at Daphne. The other woman was staring down at her feet as she dug her heels into the sand. She was listening intently and looked so sad, so much more fragile than Joan had yet seen her. "Promise me that you'll be really careful."

"You're talking about Marlena, aren't you?" Joan nodded. Daphne's tone became cold. "I can handle her. Don't you worry." She brightened. "I'm really glad you came to the reunion, Joan. You were kind. It's been a dream of mine to say 'thank you' one day."

"You mean because I agreed to split the lemon gin?" laughed Joan.

But Daphne was serious. "You loaned me books and gave me a sweater."

"You remember that?" asked Joan.

"I still have the sweater, a mauve pullover."

Both women shoved off on their swings at the same time, heads back, looking up at the clouds, the squeaking sound of the chains transporting them back in time.

CHAPTER SEVENTEEN

JOAN SAT IN HER ACCORD IN the parking lot of the Couch, drew the copy of the grad photo from its folder, and studied it. Rank band members Steve and Rudy wore sunglasses. Possibly to hide dilated pupils, but more likely a tribute to the Blues Brothers, whose shtick and music was smoking hot at the time. They stood shoulder to shoulder in matching jackets and ties. The one band member missing from the photo was Ray. He'd graduated a year earlier and was well on his way to earning his plumber's ticket by the spring of 1979. Although Sarah and he were officially engaged, Ray's evenings and weekends had apparently been devoted to Roger and the boys. Rank had played together from junior high school until Roger left town. Their dedication to their music, and to one another, propelled them to the top of the local touring scene. They'd even had a hit single. "Love Stop" made it to the top ten on local radio stations and stayed there for two months. Roger had used the song as a springboard for his career, claiming international fame. On a clear night, CXGO could be picked up on radios in the Northwestern United States and anywhere on the planet with shortwave.

Joan tucked the photo away and pulled out her small spiral notebook. She'd convinced Gabe that she should speak to Rudy and Steve before he made his official visit about Peg's death. There was a chance they would reveal more to her in a candid discussion. He had filled her in on the interview he had conducted with the band members on Saturday morning, hours after Roger had been stabbed to death. It all seemed routine, straightforward. After the gig on Friday night, they'd rehearsed until Roger got so drunk he was falling down. He'd gone to his cabin. Steve and Rudy continued without him until Marlena's scream sounded the alarm that something was horribly wrong. Just over half an hour between those two events. Rudy had been very precise about the time. Somewhere in there Roger had knocked on Joan's door. She estimated that he'd been there for no more than five minutes. At the time it had seemed an eternity. It was probable, according to Gabe, that someone had waited in Roger's room and stayed hidden while he undressed. This, combined with the fact that nothing appeared to have been stolen, posed various possibilities. His attacker hadn't planned to harm him. Or the killer needed to work up the nerve to commit the crime. Or the killer waited until Roger was in bed so that he was at his most vulnerable. Was the killer uncertain of his strength to overpower Roger? When he'd been at Joan's door he couldn't stay on his feet. It wouldn't have taken much to get the better of him. Did this point to a woman, or possibly someone older?

Steve's first response when Marlena had screamed hadn't been to call the police. He had immediately called Ray and reached him on his home phone line. Why was that? Had Marlena really been waiting *outside* Roger's motel unit?

Joan found Rudy on a tall ladder in the former gym, adjusting lights on the grid. It surprised her to see the large accountant move so nimbly. He climbed down when he saw her.

"Man, I'll need another shower before we go on tonight. I hope I have enough time." He wiped his forehead with a paper towel. "So what's up, Joan?"

"I'm tired of sitting in my motel room all by myself. I thought I'd come help." She smiled innocently. Soon Rudy had her wrapping the bright electrical cable that he'd unhooked from the grid. "It's so horrible about Peg. I still can't believe it," she said.

Rudy nodded in agreement. "I bet most of us plan to die of old age, then something like this happens. It's creepy. Monica won't let me out of her sight." He nodded toward the wall and there she was, reading *Chatelaine* and drinking take-out coffee. "Ever since Roger was, you know, she doesn't want to be left alone." He went on to describe the rest of their weekend. The previous morning, when Peggy had died, they'd ordered breakfast to the room and read the newspaper. "Whoever would have thought that's where we'd get our kicks, eh Joan? An exciting morning in bed with the *Globe and Mail*? By the time we got downstairs, the wine-and-cheese thing was happening. We planned on heading back to Prince George, but Ray called." Rudy seemed embarrassed. "He begged us to stay to play this gig." He shrugged. "What the heck, eh?"

"I didn't get to see Peggy at all last week. Did you?" asked Joan.

Rudy nodded. "She dropped by our tech rehearsal on Wednesday. Just like the old days. Peg was always there with Marlena and Candy, watching us rehearse in the garage."

Joan asked him if he knew how her name got on the invitation list and explained that the RCMP staff sergeant from Kamloops was asking questions about it. Rudy said that he knew nothing about the list and seemed genuinely surprised that anyone would object to Daphne and her being there. "We all grew up together. Why would it make a difference?" He gave her a squeeze. "We're all glad you're here."

"Thanks." She knew that not everyone was glad. "You know where I can find Steve?"

"In the truck. We're having a hell of a time with the sound system. He's Mr. Fix-It, you know? When we played on Friday we used the built-in system at the hotel. These speakers at the Couch are candy-assed. Our old ones are kick-ass."

"You still have them?"

Rudy smiled and nodded in response. "You bet. Steve dragged them out of his uncle's barn on the old family farm. With a little tweaking, they should work great." Then he added, "We hope. They've been in storage for thirty years."

Joan approached the Madden Roofing company five-ton that was doubling as the band's equipment truck. She and Steve Howard hadn't done much more than nod hello over the past few days. Her relationship with him was awkward. They had a history that went so far back that neither of them could remember life without the other.

Chuck Howard, Steve's father, had been Leo Parker's first employee in the roofing business. Chuck and Leo were like brothers. As a toddler, she'd stayed at the Howard's house when her mom went into the hospital to have her brothers. Steve and his three sisters stayed with them when his parents went on their one and only vacation without kids. He had called Joan's mom and dad Auntie Vi and Uncle Leo; she'd called his parents Uncle Chuck and Aunt Alma. It had all changed, like an iceberg abruptly surfacing on the open seas, after her dad died. It came to light that Leo owed Chuck more than just back salary. Her dad had convinced Uncle Chuck to invest in the company. For years Chuck had believed the illusion of success that Leo had conjured and had turned large portions of his salary back into the company. One cloudy afternoon, shortly after Leo's funeral, he'd come to see Joan. Nobody wanted to upset Vi, and since Joan behaved like an adult compared to her peers, she was the obvious Parker to approach. She remembered Chuck Howard avoiding her eyes as he stood in their front hall. He pulled files from a musky, old-style accordion briefcase, then handed her a wad of papers. They were reports that her dad had given him, estimating the company to be worth hundreds of thousands of dollars. The reports were fantasy. When she was younger, Joan believed that her dad had made an unintentional mistake. Now she knew too much about business to swallow the lie. When she thought about it now, with thirty more years of living behind her, she understood why the Howard family had cut them off. It may not have been the kindest reaction, but her father had shattered their world. They'd been betrayed. She hadn't had a conversation with Steve since.

When she reached the truck, Steve was deep in the shadows, surrounded by wires and sound gear. At first she thought he was working with fine tools. As she got closer, though, she realized that he was frowning at something in his hands. Was it a document? When the gravel crunched beneath her shoes, he shoved the paper under a stack of pale green forms that she recognized as purchase orders.

"Joan!" His smile came slowly and was more grimace than grin. She smiled back tentatively, but knew that Steve was spooked. Whatever he'd hidden, he didn't want her to see.

"Something the matter, Steve?" she asked.

Steven fumbled and mumbled. "These old speakers, I just opened them up. I expected to find mice turds and spider webs, but they're pristine inside, after all these years." The back panel had been removed from both speakers. Screws lay in a neat pile.

"So they'll work for you?" asked Joan.

Steve nodded as he began to put the speakers back together. "Oh, yeah. Yeah. Once we get them hooked up, we'll see if they're as good as we remember. Would you mind getting Rudy to give me a hand? We need to get them inside."

"I'm stronger than I look, Steve. I don't mind helping," said Joan. She saw his eyes shift to the roofing supplies in the corner. The motion was almost imperceptible, but she was used to watching for just this kind of reaction among her food test subjects.

"Just get Rudy." He finally looked up at her. "Please, Joan." Clearly, he wasn't going to budge.

Joan watched Steve and Rudy secure the large speakers onto a dolly and move them into the gym. To avoid suspicion, she followed them inside, then slipped out to the parking lot once they were preoccupied with the sound system. She climbed into the truck, staining her jeans with grease as she shimmied onto the tailgate, then she shuffled through the pile of work orders. Whatever Steve had been looking at had been moved. Creeping to the very back of the five-ton, where the roofing supplies were neatly stored, she shifted heavy buckets of black sealant. Nothing underneath. Rolls of thick tarpaper caught her eye. One was standing askew from the others. She leaned it over, looked through the long, dark tube, and saw something stuffed in the end. Reaching in, she felt cloth, soft and velvety. She pulled out a purple Crown Royal bag. Inside there were large-format photographs rolled up and secured with a rubber band. Aware that Steve would be back at any moment, she hid the sack in her jacket and walked briskly around the corner of the building.

Joan wasn't used to taking things that didn't belong to her. Her fingers shook as she reached into the bag and pulled out the photographs. There were four. She turned the first over and gasped. It was a grainy photograph of a girl lying on the grass, between ragged trees. She'd caught Steve with porn, a picture faded with age. The teenager was obviously passed out and her body had been positioned so that she was spread-eagled. She was wearing panties. Her bra had been pulled up to expose her breasts. Joan knew in an instant that she was the girl in the photo. Her stomach churned at the sight. The image of her own corpse couldn't have shocked her more. She shuffled through the other three pictures; different angles of the same incident. Her first thought was, who took the photographs? Her next was, who would have processed them?

Her mind was racing. The only time she'd ever been drunk enough to pass out was the Night of the Lemon Gin. Recollecting the bush party was like trying to focus through a vague and fractured kaleidoscope. Anything could have happened. As much as she was sickened and embarrassed by the photographs, fury propelled her forward. She needed to address this head on.

People were beginning to drift into the gymnasium for the Rank performance. Long tables had been decorated with paper covers and topped with centerpieces made from gold-sprayed branches that had been stuffed into blue detergent bottles; the colours of Madden High. Stacks of chairs waited to be dispersed. The centre of the room had been left clear, an invitation for dancers once the music started. With the Crown Royal bag clutched to her chest, Joan made her way to the stage and slid behind the closed theatre curtains. Rudy was on the ladder, tweaking the lights on the grid. When Steve saw her and the velvet sack, he put down the bass that he'd been tuning. He was embarrassed to look at her. She watched him chew his lower lip.

"Did you shoot these?" She whispered harshly and waved the roll of photos under his nose.

Steve blanched and his eyes widened. "God, no Joan. I'd never do something like that."

She wanted to believe him, but years ago she hadn't thought he'd draw a penis on Hazel. By now, Rudy was straining to hear their conversation.

"Where did you get them?" she asked.

"From the inside of a speaker." He glanced up at Rudy, who was starting to climb down the ladder.

"Before that?" As Joan shook the roll at him for emphasis, the rubber band, brittle with age, popped and the photos floated to the floor. When she fell to her knees to retrieve them, Steven was immediately at her side to help collect the damning images.

He shifted his gaze toward her. "I had nothing to do with it, I swear." She felt as though she was with a fumbling teenager. As they stood up, Steve turned to Rudy, who was unabashedly eavesdropping. "Could you give us a minute, man?"

Rudy shrugged and reluctantly lumbered away.

"Okay, so you didn't shoot them, Steve." She stuffed the photos in the Crown Royal bag. "These were taken before my dad died. You had no reason to be mad at me then. Did you?"

"No, not then." He thought for a moment. "Not you, ever."

"You know I'm sorry about what happened." It was out of her mouth before she thought about what she was saying. It felt good. She'd spent so many years feeling as though the town had shunned her unfairly. Now, through adult eyes, she understood the extent of the damage her father had caused. She was truly sorry.

He met her gaze. "I missed you, kiddo. We all did." He squeezed her shoulder. It was uncanny how much he looked like his father. It was like getting a hug from Uncle Chuck.

"Do you know anything more about the pictures?" she asked.

"After Roger left town to become a rock star, we moved a bunch of stuff to an old barn my uncle used for storage. That speaker has been there for years, since Rank broke up."

"Your uncle?"

"Uncle Dan." And Joan remembered. Dan Prychenko was Steve's maternal uncle. Marlena was his first cousin.

Try as she might Joan couldn't imagine Dan Prychenko taking the pictures. If he'd showed up at the bush party, it would have been to shut it down. He may have been a philandering husband, but nobody could have been a better boss when she worked for him at the gas bar. Aware of her family's financial downfall, he'd paid her more than he had the other young employees, and he'd done it without apology. On December 24, he'd gruffly shoved a hundred-dollar bill into her hand, calling it a "little bonus". It meant they'd had Christmas that terrible year, the first without her father. When he drove her home on dark, sub-zero winter nights, after her shift was done, he'd never once touched her or made an off-colour remark. Sure, Dan Prychenko had been a known ladies' man, but she had no reason to believe he'd been a camera-toting pedophile. Chances were that those photos had been placed in the speaker before they went into storage. She knew, though, that her investigation would be incomplete if she left any stone unturned.

"I should talk to Dan," she said flatly.

Steven looked stunned. "But, Joan, he died years ago, in the early nineties. He was coming home from the Legion, blind drunk. He hit a tree."

She remembered that Dan Prychenko, a barrel of a man, had been a champion drinker. He'd left many a fellow Maddenonian under the table on a Saturday night. It wasn't a surprise that alcohol had painted his final canvas. "Steve, you're sure that nobody else saw the pictures?"

"You mean since I found them today?" he asked.

"Yeah."

"Positive. And if I get my hands on the bonehead who took them, I'll take care of him myself." He pounded his fist into his hand. "You know, Joan, I was going to rip them up and get rid of them, if you hadn't got to them first. And frankly," he spoke shyly now. "I don't know that anyone would recognize you. I mean," he smiled meekly, "you do know that you've changed?"

The shock of discovering the photographs had exhausted Joan. She'd rather have gone back to the motel, but if anyone else was killed, and she didn't have witnesses, she'd probably end up as Smartt's prime suspect in another death. She stood on the front steps of the Couch, where she had a strong cell signal and called the RCMP detachment. When she told Gabe about the photographs of her lying half-naked in the grass, he offered to come immediately. He was in the middle of reading the reports from his officers, comparing notes from witnesses, and verifying statements, but he'd drop all that. Joan reminded him that nothing would get solved if she kept pulling him away. He lowered his voice to discreetly share one more piece of information. The toxicology report on Peg Chalmers had arrived by email.

"She took the cimetidine with her breakfast along with her regular medications, yet there is no record anywhere of a prescription in her name."

"Maybe she has another doctor who prescribed it," suggested Joan.

"Not likely. It's for ulcers or severe heartburn, and she didn't suffer from any ailment of that type. It gets stranger. They found medications in her system used for a host of disorders that she didn't have."

"Do you think she was trying to commit suicide?"

"Most of the drugs wouldn't do anything to her in the doses she'd taken, except make her feel drowsy and nauseous. It's only the cimetidine, mixed with the warfarin for her heart condition that was so dangerous. It makes no sense. There's no telling where she got the pills."

"Did you ask Daphne? Maybe they belonged to her," asked Joan.

"First thing we did was interview Daphne again, but she says she's healthy as a horse, only takes herbal remedies. She has no idea where the medications came from, swears that she just gave Peg the pills from her cupboard as she'd been asked. Peg had fallen back to sleep by the time Daphne brought her tray yesterday morning, so she just left it on her night table."

"What else was found in her system? What other pills?" asked Joan.

"Primarily chemotherapy medication, and Peg didn't have cancer." There was silence as they both considered the same question. Why would someone randomly swallow medication for illnesses they didn't have? Did she ingest them knowingly? Gabe promised that he'd get to the Couch as soon as possible, although he couldn't stay for long. He had a lot of work to do.

The bathroom sinks had originally been installed for grade school children, so Joan had to bend to see her reflection. Bracing herself to face the crowded room, she felt as exposed as the grainy images in those old photos. Then she reminded herself that the horrific pictures in the Crown Royal bag had been snapped thirty years ago. Although it was fresh in her mind, nobody else would be thinking about those images when she entered the room — except for Steve and, possibly, whoever had taken them. While taking one last look in the mirror, looking for the girl in the photographs, she heard voices coming down the hall.

" . . . fancy-assed home in France, thinking she's so much better than the rest of us." Marlena's voice was instantly recognizable. "Sarah's husband looks like he's ready to drop. I'd never marry a man that much older than me. Years ago I told Ray that Sarah better not expect us to support those kids if the old guy croaked." Marlena entered the bathroom, yapping like a chihuahua, with Candy in tow, "Thank God they're all grown up now so I don't have to worry."

Candy stopped abruptly. "You mean that your cheap bastard husband didn't support his own kids?"

"Of course not! Why should he? He never saw them."

"You wouldn't let him." Candy was looking at Marlena as though seeing her for the first time. "You know, Marlena, I've been thinking lately, sometimes you hold onto people out of habit. You think there's some sort of value to a friendship because it's been there so long. Then you stop and look at it and wonder 'What am I getting out of this?' I think it's time I cleaned house." She turned around and went into a cubicle.

Marlena shouted at the grey steel door. "Oh, it's all about what you get out of it? That's pretty selfish if you ask me. What about what I get out of our friendship? Huh, Candy?"

Joan slipped out of the washroom, before she got caught in the crossfire.

Chapter Eighteen

A CIRCLE OF WOMEN, INCLUDING LINDA Howard, Monica Weiss and Daphne Pyle, danced in the middle of the room, something that wouldn't have happened in Madden thirty years ago. Joan watched from the sidelines until she felt a tug at her arm. It was Hazel and Lila, beaming at her. She followed obediently. Hazel, in yet another ankle-length hand-painted silk gown, danced with unexpected grace for someone her size. She managed to get the entire circle of women, as well as Gerald Gillespie, coordinated into synchronized movement that reminded Joan of water flowing and winds swirling. She couldn't help but smile at Gerald, who moved with his eyes closed, as though in a trance. Couples danced on the edges of the small auditorium.

Candy had temporarily been lifted from the doldrums and was performing a robust version of "the bump" with a barrel-shaped man who looked vaguely familiar. Each time Candy rammed him in the hip, he rammed her back as though it was a competition to see who could bounce the other farther. Mr. Fowler watched everyone, keeping time to the music with his tapping foot.

Marlena had dragged Gabe to the dance floor. She seemed oblivious of her husband on the stage, his drums keeping beat for Rudy and Steve. A shy grin betrayed Ray's nerves at his imminent debut as solo vocalist. Joan felt sorry for him. Wasn't he like the rest of them, just a big kid hiding wounds and weaknesses? The sores begin accumulating when you're young. Some you deal with and they become strengths and person- ality. Others get pushed into dark corners where they fester into fears, chronic sorrow, and anger, sometimes even physical pain. Had those seeds, sown in one of these former classmates, been responsible for the deaths of Roger Rimmer and Peg Wong?

Ray timidly pulled the microphone toward his mouth. His voice caught on the first couple of notes, but he steadied himself and was soon belting out a version of a Mog Campbell hit, "The Mountain". Joan was floored. Ray sang with powerful, sweet clarity. People around the room gradually stopped dancing to marvel at the captivating sound coming from the stage. With each bar Ray gained confidence.

This road is heading home. I'm longing for your arms.

Wanted to do more, didn't happen as we planned.

His eyes scanned the room, passing over the heads of the crowd, looking for one person. His gaze finally settled and he smiled warmly.

Tried to stand alone, a tree that's lost its roots.

I fell and washed away. You're the rock and I'm the sand.

Curious, Joan craned her head to follow his gaze and was surprised to see that, in a roomful of swooning women, Ray was singing to his wife. Marlena looked as though she might die of embarrassment. Rank finished the song then segued directly into CCR's "Stuck In Lodi". Dancers once again began writhing. All Joan could do was wonder why Roger had been the headliner all of those years rather than Ray. She caught Gabe's eye across the room and suspected he was chewing on the same question. Ray was halfway through the Credence tune when, without any warning, the room went dark and the sound system died abruptly.

Rudy's voice bellowed, "Oh, crap!"

A murmur rose and the crowd froze. Joan knew this uniform response. When people are cast into sudden darkness, deprived of their sense of sight, their instinct is to stay still. The only illumination now was the red glow of the exit sign. From the corner of her eye, Joan saw the door swing open. A figure rushed out. She hadn't time to get a good look, but she had the impression that it was a woman or perhaps a slight man. A few people started flicking lighters on, and the crowd started to move.

A scream cut through the shadows. Joan rushed to the source of the cry: the doors at the side of the auditorium leading to the basement. Gabe darted ahead of her, taking the stairs two at a time. Over his shoulder she could see a figure crumpled at the bottom of the stairs.

"Are you okay?" Gabe was asking. "Can you hear me?" He looked up at her. "It's Ed Fowler. He's hurt."

Heart racing, Joan felt her way to the bottom of the stairs. It was easy to see how someone could fall down this dark, narrow passageway. The dank smell transported her to her childhood and the rare occasion she had gone to the eerie basement of the old school. Mr. Fowler lay unmoving, his body crumpled in an awkward contortion. Then a low moan rose, and the pile of fabric took the shape of shirt and trousers, arms and legs. To her relief, Mr. Fowler started to unfold into a sitting position.

"Stay still. We'll get a stretcher," said Gabe.

Mr. Fowler brushed Gabe's arm away. "Nonsense. It's nothing. I'm cool. I'm cool." As he awkwardly got to his feet, Joan could tell that he was in considerable pain. "I might be a bit stiff tomorrow, but I'll be fine. Went downstairs to put the breaker on. Must've tripped."

"I can see how easy it would be to slip," Joan consoled him, but Mr. Fowler was quick to correct her.

"Man, I'm up and down these stairs at least a half-dozen times a day. I didn't slip. I tripped. There was something on the stairs."

"Maybe you dropped something when you were setting up for the concert," she offered.

"But I'm the one always telling people how dangerous it is. All day I've been after everyone. Hell, now I feel foolish." He tried to make light of it and smiled. "Ghosts." He pushed his hip out against his hand. "Ow, I'll have one giant bruise tomorrow. You know what surprises me? That the electrical system couldn't take the drain on power."

"All those amps and speakers?" she guessed.

Ed insisted that it had often dealt with more than the simple sound system and a few lights. "It can handle a far bigger load." He added, with a sad smile, "When Peg was around, every concert included some sort of spiffy light show. She'd put them together using the old lighting board from drama class productions." He went on to explain that the building had been completely rewired when the restoration was done eight years ago. It had to be brought up to code. "As a matter of fact, Ray's company did the plumbing."

Gabe went with Mr. Fowler to find the electrical panel, and Joan, using the LED light on her keychain, scoured the stairs for the object that had tripped him. If there had been something, it had been removed.

She returned to the main floor to assure the grad class that everything was fine, then stepped outside to get a breath of air. Apparently, half the crowd had decided to do the same thing.

People stood in small clutches, shivering without their coats. Most looked worried. Ray stood with Candy Dirkson and Linda Howard, both making a fuss over his debut as lead singer. Sarah came over to him with her husband. She took the hand of her childhood sweetheart and ex-husband, patting it between hers, saying something that made him smile shyly. Joan mused that it was something a grandmother might do. Their children had been born when Sarah and Ray were very young, barely out of high school. Did Ray have grandchildren that he'd never seen? The entire time that he was in conversation with Sarah, he was straining to stare over their heads, obviously looking for Marlena.

Candy waved at Joan, then made a bee line for her. "You seen Gabe, Joannie?"

"He's still inside."

"There's something I've been meaning to tell him. Early menopause. It's not just the hot flashes. Half the time I have sieve-brain. I'll just have to start writing everything down," she rattled on, "if I can remember to put a pen and notepad in my purse."

Before Joan could offer to take a message, Candy had flitted away.

As the lights in the building flickered on, Joan saw Mr. Fowler emerge from the old school to herd everyone inside. Worried that he may have bumped his head in the fall, she asked him if there was anyone he could call if he needed help. "Do your girls live nearby?"

"Hell no," he chuckled. "You teach kids to be free spirits, to have minds of their own, and what do they do? They question everything you say, then they sprout wings." He rubbed his shoulder as he reflected. "Though I guess all kids do that. No, Sky and Summer, they flew to the city as soon as they could.

Sky landed in Brussels, works as an environmental consultant. Summer roams. She still hasn't found herself."

"Do they stay in touch?"

"Every week." He smiled proudly. "We Skype. I won't tell them about this little tumble. How lame is that, to fall over like an old man?"

She gently touched his arm. "You get that shoulder looked at," she advised.

"Oh sure, I will," he said dismissively, then led the class back inside, giant students obediently following their teacher.

Joan moved to the far side of the building where it would be quieter, where she could concentrate on assembling information. She sat on the low, horizontal steel tubing that served as a fence. Covered in thick coats of forest-green paint, it seemed unchanged since her school days. She was quietly pondering Mr. Fowler's bizarre accident when, without any forewarning, Marlena came out of the shadows, weaving slightly.

"Why, if it isn't Dr. Smell. That's what you do, isn't it? Create a big stink?" She didn't give Joan a chance to respond, diving into her attack with vehemence. "Why did you come back? You know you don't belong here," she hissed. "You never did."

Before Joan could control herself she raised her hand and slapped Marlena hard.

The other woman laughed. "Oh, smooth, Parker." Then, with Joan off guard, Marlena grabbed her hair and tried to tug her to the ground.

She could feel the strength in Marlena's arms and knew that she'd have to take drastic measures. With her head being forced toward the gravel, Joan turned and clamped her teeth on Marlena's thigh, biting through size A Evening Shade pantyhose. It felt strangely methodical, the whole process. How odd, she mused, to be in a cat fight.

Marlena let go of Joan's hair and grabbed her own leg. "You bitch, look what you've done to my pantyhose!"

Joan stumbled and fell on her butt. She cowered, covering her head with her arms, afraid that Marlena would go after another mitt-full of her hair.

"You had enough?" sneered Marlena, her foot poised to kick.

"Yes," mumbled Joan, then yanked the other woman's leg and sent her sprawling to the ground. "And so have you."

Neither spoke for a moment, then Joan asked, "Why do you hate me so much? I've never done anything to you."

"Oh, you haven't, eh?"

Joan shook her head. She only knew that Marlena had hated her a long time. It went back to their teens; everything about this woman reminded her of a wounded teenager.

Marlena crawled into a sitting position. "Do you know how many times I sat through dinner listening to my dad talk about how smart you were? How you worked so hard? In his whole life he never once talked about me like that." She continued in an angry whisper. "And I know that your mom probably told the whole world about my dad using the motel like a brothel."

Joan listened to the litany of sorrows and realized that she hadn't had to do anything to hurt Marlena. That intimidating strength and confidence, in reality, had been a smoke screen. Marlena had been a wounded girl. Nothing had changed. Standing over Joan again, her wounds were still evident. The fight wasn't finished.

"You think you can come here and do whatever you want and maybe you don't care what us people in Madden think, that we're just a bunch of hicks, but I can make life miserable for that boyfriend of yours. Real miserable."

"What are you talking about?" asked Joan but she already knew.

"It won't just be his marriage that's over. I can't imagine the RCMP will be thrilled about one of their cops sleeping with his murder suspects." Marlena smiled with satisfaction, turned and sashayed back to the party just as Rudy's wife Monica came around the corner.

Joan slowly rose and brushed the dust from her pants.

"Are you all right?" asked Monica.

Joan contemplated answering that Madden was becoming increasingly dangerous. "I'm about ready to get home," she answered simply.

"Hallelujah, me too." Monica Weiss sighed as she sat beside Joan on the fence.

They'd shared pleasantries over the past few days but hadn't had anything you could call a conversation. Monica, though, was either comfortable with Joan or desperate to talk to someone, or both. She fumbled through her bag, pulled out a crushed cigarette and disposable lighter, then smiled conspiratorially.

"Rudy doesn't like it when I smoke in public, especially here, in Madden. He says I look trashy."

Trashy was the last term Joan would use for this matronly woman who used minimal makeup and dressed in the conservative manner of a bygone era.

"Rudy recites stats on smoking like some guys do baseball." Monica paused and took a long drag. The smoke lazily drift from her mouth. "And not just the health outcomes. He can name the dates of the studies that prove that smokers have less education and lower IQs, all that stuff."

Joan thought of Mort. He wouldn't do that to her in a million years, no matter what her bad habits. There were aspects of Mort's personality that she had taken for granted. His socks always matched his pants, but he'd never raise an eyebrow if hers didn't. When she blurted an awkward comment, he somehow made her social gaff disappear. Did it matter that their relationship had settled into a cushion of comfort rather than a bed of passion?

Monica hid her cigarette as a couple walked by, and then she spoke in a tone of conspiracy: "I hate coming here, to Madden. Rudy changes. He never worries about his hairline or his waistline at home. In Prince George he's proud of himself. Here it never seems to be enough. I'm never enough." She stubbed out her cigarette. "Now it's just creepy with people dying all over the place. I can't wait to leave." With that she tucked her purse under her arm and headed back into the school.

Left on her own, Joan thought about what Marlena had said about her dad. Had Dan Prychenko had some sort of obsession with her? Had she too easily dismissed that married Romeo as harmless? He'd been a drinker and one of the few people in town who could have afforded to stock his booze cabinet with Crown Royal. Could he have been the pervert who had taken those photos of her? But the appearance of any parent at that Labour Day weekend kegger would have been noticed by the teenagers and sent everyone scrambling. Besides, if he really did respect Joan in the way Marlena described, it didn't make sense that he'd have taken pornographic snapshots of her. The only other obvious candidate in her mind, was Roger, the photos possibly representing a victory trophy of the damage he'd done. And he also had access to the speakers. Now both men were dead. She might never know the truth.

CHAPTER NINETEEN

WHEN JOAN WENT INTO THE GYM to bid goodnight, the party was again in full swing. Marlena was actually standing with her husband, laughing, as though the altercation in the schoolyard had never happened. With a girlish inflection, she was feeding Ray chips and salsa, giggling as the tomato dropped onto his shirt and wiping it off with her finger. Had his stake been raised because of his skilled performance on stage or because of the attention that the other women, including his ex-wife, were heaping upon him? Joan suspected it was the latter.

Hazel, encircled by a gaggle of dancers, was demonstrating a complicated group routine. She held them in rapt attention. Lila watched from the sidelines, towering over them all in spiked heels and a sleek pantsuit that accentuated her height. She was obviously feeling ignored and twirled the glass of wine in her hand with an intensity that could ignite flames. In a far corner, Gabe spoke into his cell phone, looking very grave. Police business, thought Joan. Others had already departed: Steve, Daphne, Candy, Rudy and his wife. She decided to sneak out without saying goodnight. Her mind was preoccupied with the events of the evening and she doubted that her absence would be noticed.

As she unlocked her car door, a sedan across the street caught her attention. Staff Sergeant Smartt was slouched in the seat, eyes intent on her. She knew that Gabe was irked that the cop from Kamloops was on their heels, waiting for a misstep. Refusing to be cowed, she waved and smiled. He didn't respond.

The cabin felt chilly. Joan locked the door behind her, then fiddled with the unit that was a combination heater and air conditioner. Still it made no sound, as though it were simply an empty façade. By now she was shivering so she added a sweater to her sweats and pulled on a pair of thick socks. Rummaging through the mini-fridge, she came up with an apple and a handful of Edam cubes she'd smuggled from the wine-and-cheese function the previous afternoon. If I stay much longer, she thought, I'll have to go grocery shopping. It made her think of Mort. If he were there, he'd ensure that she ate properly and the fridge would be stocked. She glanced at the phone. If she called, she'd be sending mixed messages. Now she wasn't so sure of herself. Yes, she wanted to hold onto his friendship. But what was enough and what was too much?

Propped up in bed, she pulled the covers to her chin and flipped through the pages of the *Madden Gazette* that had been left in her room. Roger's death made the front page, but there was no mention of Peg. She checked the date. Sunday's paper, yesterday, the day that Peg had died.

She turned to the classified ads in the back, imagining that she was looking for a job and home in Madden. A luxurious two-bedroom condo overlooking the river, only five years old, cost a fraction of what the same place did in Vancouver. She noticed the name Stanfield Developments splashed over ads for high-end homes in a new subdivision. Smiling young couples with perfect teeth and one perfect child frolicked on the lawns of enormous houses — "mansions" by the standards of Joan's childhood. So many of the happy young couples from her previous life in Madden had become bitter and desperate or just plain sad. So many marriages, including her own, had fallen apart. Of those who remained together, many seemed disenchanted. Why did people demand so much out of their most intimate relationships? If they expected half as much from themselves, the world would be a much better place. Guiltily, she thought again of Mort but quickly shoved him to the compartment of her brain labelled "do not disturb".

She flipped to the employment section of the *Gazette*. Lakeview College, which the province had situated in Madden in return for local votes, was advertising for various positions, including a chemistry instructor. Joan had all the qualifications, and the salary was handsome for a job that wouldn't be nearly as draining as working for Constellation Inc. Or maybe she'd re-invent herself completely, find work in a greenhouse or transfer her skills to aromatherapy. But, in reality, was life in Madden what she wanted? How long before the novelty of Jacques Bistro wore thin? Once winter socked in, could she bear the deep-freeze temperatures? Would the romance of snowshoeing on starlit evenings be enough to fill the long, dark hours until spring? Surely she'd go bonkers. Already she was starting to miss her comfortable, modest condo in the city.

Joan was shocked out of her daydream by a sharp rapping. She stared at the door a moment before throwing back the blankets, exposing herself to the icy air, then crept silently forward as though sudden movement might send out an alarm. She looked through the peephole, but all she could see was a dark blur. The knock came again. Frantic, she grabbed her reading glasses, to see if they would help her detect the identity of her visitor. No luck. Whoever it was must be tall and standing right at the door, or else the peephole was filthy and clouding the image. She could either pretend she wasn't there or reveal that she was. In a voice just above a whisper, she asked, "Who's there?"

"Joan, Joan is that you. Are you okay?"

She slowly opened the door a crack to ensure that, indeed, it was Gabe.

He looked over his shoulder before sliding into her room. "You left without saying a word."

She was self-conscious about her bizarre appearance: baggy sweats, bright pink fuzzy socks, and hair standing on end.

Gabe didn't seem to notice. "You're shivering." He wrapped her in his arms and she relaxed into the warmth of his embrace. "It's like a fridge in here."

"The bloody heating system is a joke," she sighed from between chattering teeth.

"Come here." He led her to the bed and drew her down.

"No, Gabe."

"Shh. I'm just warming you up. I promise."

She could feel him unbuttoning his rough duffle coat, a cocoon of wool alive with his scent. He opened it and drew her to him. Conflicting thoughts rushed through her brain: Staff Sergeant Smartt keeping surveillance, Marlena's threat to expose Gabe, her own desire to be held, the fact that time was running out, how the large piece of cheese that she'd just eaten might affect her breath.

His strong hands turned her toward him. "Joan." He looked directly into her eyes. "I'm staying the night."

She buried her face in his chest, shaking her head "no", and trying to swallow the lump in her throat.

He tilted her head back. "Why not?"

"You have . . . a wife," was all she said. She'd given voice to the burden that was a rock in her gut.

"How do I make you believe that we're not living as a married couple anymore. Listen, I wouldn't have kissed you in public at Jacques. I wouldn't do that to you." He was still looking her squarely in the eye. "Or to her." His voice softened. "I wouldn't be here now."

She couldn't count the times she'd heard this story from her women friends, women facing menopause on their own, frantic that their only chance at love was passing. How many had insisted that their latest beau was only living with his wife out of convenience, that the wives were, themselves, done with the marriage? Like a skipping record, it always seemed to unfold that the wives were stunned to discover that their husbands were cheating on them. Although she hoped that Gabe was different, Marlena had made her doubt him. How could Gabe, *her* Gabe, whom she had known all of her life, how could he betray any woman?

When he brushed his lips against hers, she kissed him hard, then pushed him away so that she could read his reaction to her next question.

"Gabe?"

"Hmm?" he moaned the response softly.

"I need to know something. Why are you so sure that I didn't kill Roger? And Peg, for that matter?" He gently brushed the hair from her brow as she continued. "I was the last person to see Roger alive. I had plenty of time to go up to Peggy's on Sunday morning. How do you know it isn't like Smartt thinks, that I invited myself to this party so that I could kill Roger? What if I wanted Peg silenced? How do you know it wasn't me?"

"Because I know you. I always have."

And at that moment, Joan knew they were fooling themselves. One of the things that she remembered about Gabe was his ability to separate passion and logic, which was why his protests were so convincing. If she were the lead investigator in this murderous puzzle, she'd be on her own suspect list. Before she could question him further, before she could ask if he had a prime suspect that he wasn't telling her about, there was another knock at the door. This time, a not-so-subtle voice accompanied it.

"Hey Joannie, let me in!"

Gabe groaned. Joan shrugged and went to the door.

Hazel barged in with a hotel blanket, a pillow, and a large brown paper bag. "I knew you wouldn't have extra blankets. They keep this place so damned cold." She acknowledged Gabe as though it was perfectly normal that he should be in Joan's room late at night. She turned to Joan. "You mind if I spend the night?"

Joan and Gabe forced smiles.

Hazel complained that Lila had kicked her out of her own hotel room, angry that she hadn't paid her more attention at the dance.

Gabe made his excuses, kissed Hazel on the cheek, then kissed Joan on the mouth and whispered, "I'm not done with you," and left.

Joan could smell the hot ginger beef and broccoli with garlic through the brown bag and tinfoil containers. She realized just how hungry she was and tied into the Chinese takeout with gusto. The two stayed up far too late, finishing a bottle of wine before they pulled out the hide-a-bed. Hazel was still talking as Joan drifted into her own pre-dream thoughts. She was glad that Hazel had saved her from temptation. Something nagged at her. She had been so relieved to see Gabe when she arrived in Madden, so swept up in her feelings for him, that she hadn't questioned deeply who he had become. She had projected onto him the person she wanted him to be. Was Gabe keeping information from her? Did he know who had killed Roger? Was there another reason he was so sure that she didn't do it?

The streets of Elgar were dead quiet when Gabe turned off the highway. He knew that there would still be officers working at the detachment office, scratching their heads over clues that didn't seem to be leading them anywhere. It had only been seventy-two hours since Roger's death. The Elgar RCMP were accustomed to identifying homicide perps quickly. Barroom brawls and domestic disputes left grizzly evidence and a clear trail of blood and witnesses to the killers. A lot was riding on Gabe's association with the graduating class, but now he was beginning to worry that his pre-existing knowledge might, somehow, be blinding him.

Bypassing Centre Street and the office, he zig-zagged through the residential roads and finally turned into his crescent. At the far end of the street a dim light glowed in the second-storey window of the master bedroom. Betty was probably sitting up in bed with a bodice-ripper, the familiar cup of hot water and lemon by her elbow, one ear alert to his footsteps on the stairs. He parked as silently as if he were staging a surprise drug bust and quietly let himself into the house. Avoiding the two stairs that creaked, he made it to the top landing without making a sound.

He crept to his son's door, slowly turned the knob and pushed it open a crack. Teddy, now a lanky six-footer, was curled up like a little boy, clinging to the covers that threatened to fall to the floor. His shallow breaths didn't alter and Gabe pulled the door closed without disturbing him. It had only been three days that they'd been apart and Gabe had missed him. What kind of hole would it leave when Teddy headed to university in the fall? Facing the door at the end of the hall, he debated going in to say goodnight to his wife. As he shifted his weight, the floorboard beneath his feet cried out. Instantly the ribbon of light at the bottom of her door went dark. So much of their communication had become non-verbal over the past couple of years. This one said, "I have nothing to say to you." He turned and went down the stairs.

The den was chilly. He pulled out the hide-a-bed and stripped down to his shorts. Now wide awake, he draped a woollen blanket around his shoulders and sat at his computer. After checking his email, he began to Google people of interest, to see if he'd missed anything; Joan, Roger, and Ed Fowler were all on his list, each for different reasons. The ticking of his father's old wind-up mantle clock kept time from a scarred side table. Gabe knew it would be another sleepless night.

Chapter Twenty

Joan dreamt of bees and sweet wine-scented vineyards warmed by the sun. She was jarred awake when the soft buzzing was interrupted by a loud snort. She rolled over to see Hazel sprawled on the pullout, deeply asleep, gently smacking her lips over her last snore. Daylight streamed in the skylight and Joan lay still a moment to get her bearings. She reminded herself that it was Tuesday, and that May was slipping away. The message light was flashing on the phone. She actually hoped it was Tony or Ted calling, needing her at work, desperate for her to solve a puzzle. It had been five days since she had left the office. This was the longest break that she'd had in over a year.

She quietly dialed in for voicemail, watching Hazel to make sure the soft touch-tone beeping didn't wake her. Two messages had been left. The first was from Candy saying that since today would be everyone's last in Madden, she had organized a memorial ceremony. It would be at the school gym since there wasn't a church big enough to hold all the people likely to attend.

"It's in honour of Peg and Roger, a tribute, remembering the good things. It's what Peg would have wanted so . . . 6 PM. Be there or be square . . . " She sighed then added, "as Peggy would have said."

The reference to "everyone's last night" confused Joan until she played the second message, which was from Corporal Cardinal at the Elgar RCMP detachment. Soft-spoken and considerate, he said that many people had expressed a need to return to their homes and jobs. The attendees of the reunion were being requested to please leave their contact information at the office.

She rolled onto her back and stared out at the clear sky. If the weather held, it would be the perfect day for the service. In the few short days she'd been in Madden she'd witnessed the transition from spring to summer. The musky smell of leaves composting in the drizzling showers had given way to the scent of new lawns, and the river, swollen with continued snowmelt and the heavy rains of last week, kept the air moving, fresh and alive. It was only four weeks from the longest day of the year. At this latitude that meant they'd have light until well into the evening. When they were kids, they had tested the length of the days by how late they could read an *Archie* comic outside without the use of a flashlight. As she lay with her hands folded over her stomach, she solemnly admitted to herself that once she left Madden, there was a good chance that it would be years, even decades before she returned, if she ever came back. There were a few things she needed to tie up before tomorrow. She wasn't sure if there was a connection between the sordid photographs of her at the 1978 bush party and the reunion murders, but she was determined to resolve at least that mystery before leaving town. She dressed quietly, wrote Hazel a note about the memorial, and tiptoed out the door and into the daylight.

The first bell had rung and the teenagers slowly, reluctantly, gave up their freedom and filed into Madden Composite High School. With a little over a month until summer holidays, the upcoming weeks were the most challenging of the year for both students and staff. Exams conflicted with parties at the lake, droning teachers competed with spring fever and the hopes of summer romance. Joan became self-conscious as she followed a group of chattering girls through the double doors. She corrected her posture and added a purposeful spring to her step.

The students all looked so young. Did the farm kids still do a double shift, toiling in the fields at the end of the school day? At their age, Joan had been working full time in Vancouver and studying at night. David, her youngest brother, had paid for all his school clothes from his paper route, and Anthony had worked twenty hours a week washing dishes, covering his own expenses as well as handing a portion to Joan to help cover household costs. She'd made them show her their homework every night before they went to bed. Vi was a distant, frail figure in the shadows of Joan's memory. That first year the slightest reminder of Leo would send their mother into tears. She had loved him so much, despite the trail of ruin he had left. The kids had been left to manage their own lives and to mourn as orphans.

Joan found the glass-walled school office and waited in line to speak with the secretary. She introduced herself as one of the graduating class visiting Madden. Immediately, the young woman offered condolences for the reunion that had become such a fiasco. Others in the office, overhearing the conversation, peered at Joan as though she were a species from another paleontological period.

She listened patiently to the secretary, until it was her turn to speak. "There was a yearbook, a 1979 yearbook, on display in the gym the other day. Is it here? There was such a crowd, I didn't have much of a chance to look at it." She smiled, hoping her request sounded innocent enough that it didn't raise further questions.

The secretary answered proudly. "We have a copy from each year since 1953, when Madden started issuing yearbooks. I'm not sure it's been returned yet." Without waiting to hear more, the woman scurried into the principal's office, where a grim-faced man sat ploughing through a pile of paper. He looked at Joan fleetingly through the open door, then nodded to the secretary and dismissed her with a wave. Returning to the main office, she went to a tall cedar bookcase and ran an index finger along the book spines on the uppermost shelf. She frowned then studied the lower shelf, finally selecting a slim volume with navy and gold binding. "Misfiled." She smiled apologetically, cleared a space at the end of the counter, and placed the book there. "I'm sorry. We're short on office space. Will this do?"

"This is just fine, thank you."

"Can I get you a coffee?"

Joan looked at the coffee pot, a dark layer of brownish oil rising up the sides. It made her think of a badly kept chimney. "I've had way too much already this morning," she lied. "But thanks anyway."

She opened the yearbook at random and saw the photos of grade ten students. There was Anthony's photo at the top of the second page. She touched his image and smiled. He'd been so nervous about starting high school, to the point that he'd vomited that morning. Joan sometimes wondered if it had been some sort of premonition. She flipped to the grade twelve section at the end of the book. Roger Rimmer smiled crookedly from the page. His ringlets touched the high collar of his shirt. The details printed beside his picture read:

Favourite saying: Yo, man.

Ambition: Get my picture on the cover of Rolling Stone.

Likes: The sweetest chick in the county. You know who you are babe.

Dislikes: Canned peas and wet grass.

Joan figured there had to have been a dozen girls who hoped they were "the sweetest chick", but wondered who he meant on that particular day.

She continued flipping pages until she reached the sports photos. All the senior teams had been called Rockets, male and female, whether volleyball, basketball, or football. There was Hazel, beaming out from several of the team photographs, her broad grin lighting the page. Even on paper her personality stood out. Joan scoured the photos, searching for the most out-of-focus and poorly framed. Her suspicion was confirmed. Each fuzzy shot was identified by the credit, Marly. When she had seen it the other day, she had thought that this nickname was a misspelled tribute to Bob Marley. With the Wailers, he was at the height of stardom in 1979. His association with ganja had made him a particularly popular idol in Madden. Now, though, Joan had another theory. She flipped to the acknowledgement pages: coaches, special thanks to the grad committee, volunteers for the drama program. She searched until she came to the photo of the school newspaper committee. Slouching in the back corner, draped entirely in black, was Gabe, who had written a weekly column on activism, encouraging youth to question authority and take action for social change. Supervising teachers had scrutinized his rants for signs of sedition before publication. Occasionally, though, he'd snuck in wry analogies, to the delight of students thirsting for dissent. The credits printed above the photo included committee members who had not been present for the group photo. Joan's name was listed as former co-editor, even though she'd only worked on the *Madden Magpie* for a couple of months. Gabe would have insisted she be recognized. She couldn't suppress a smile. Then she found the image she'd been seeking. Posing in cheesecake fashion, with camera slung around her neck, was Marly: Marlena Prychenko. Joan stared for several moments until the secretary asked if there was something wrong. She mutely shook her head and the woman left her alone. As she lifted the book, a slip of faded pink paper fell out from between the pages. It was the original order form for this copy of the yearbook. " Joan Parker, 12A" was printed in capital letters. Thirty years this book had been waiting for her. She was torn. On the school shelf its job was to represent the collective history of the school, but it was her history too. The book belonged to her. Her parents had paid for it. She left the office with the yearbook under her arm. If nothing else, Vi and the boys would get a kick out of it.

When she arrived at the Stanfields' glamorous house on the hill, Marlena's luxury SUV was gliding into the triple-car garage. There was a gleaming powerboat in one bay and the last was empty. Daphne's champagne-coloured rental car was nowhere in sight. The Stanfields' houseguest must have left for the day, perhaps had already returned to Calgary. The entire street was eerily deserted, inhabitants either away at work or locked securely inside their suburban homes. Clutching the Crown Royal bag, she marched toward the garage. Marlena saw her coming and instinctively pointed the remote at the door. As the garage door was descending, Joan darted toward it and ducked inside, aborting the attempt to lock her out. The powerful combination of exhaust fumes, motor oil, and pine air freshener assaulted her as she planted her feet firmly on the concrete floor.

"So, what's up, Parker?" asked Marlena. She was trying to appear nonchalant but her body was tense.

Joan had caught her off guard and didn't want to lose the upper hand. She shoved the yearbook at the other woman. "Marly?"

Marlena retorted with a sneer. "Like that's news to you?"

"What do you mean?"

"You were on the committee that tried to boot me off the paper." Marlena grabbed her gym bag from the front seat and slammed the vehicle door for emphasis. "But I was the one who stuck it out in the end." Joan's throat tightened. Her greatest regret in leaving Madden High had been abandoning the *Magpie*. Marlena tossed the remote through the open SUV window onto the seat then took a step toward her. Light filtered through a small window high on the wall. "Do you know what's even funnier?" Joan looked at her blankly. "The only reason I joined the school newspaper was because you were on it."

Joan was stunned. "But you hated me."

"Oh, don't get me wrong," Marlena said with a laugh. "I loathed." The laughter deserted her voice as she continued. "But my daddy didn't. I thought it would impress him. He didn't even notice."

Then she remembered. At the beginning of grade twelve, Marlena had shown up with a brand-new camera. It had lenses that had the true photographers drooling, and her equipment bag, rich with new leather smell, was more valuable than their cameras. Marlena had decided that she wanted to be one of the photographers. She had expected to jump in to cover the high profile events single-handed, the hockey games, drama productions, and the Halloween dance, but she came with no experience and unbearable attitude.

"You told me that I wasn't good enough," said Marlena.

The memory fell together like a slowly forming jigsaw puzzle, faint recollections randomly filling the gaps. The student paper had operated out of an oversized storage closet on the second floor of the school, filled with the damp odour of mimeograph ink. The meeting? Yes, she vaguely remembered it.

She'd attended all the school paper meetings without Gabe. All he cared about was his column. At one meeting in the fall of 1978, the rest of the committee had voted to kick Marlena out. Her imperious air made the rest of them mental. Besides, she didn't know the lens from the viewfinder or what it meant to keep a shot in focus. As the others complained bitterly about Marlena's personality, it became clear to Joan that the newspaper, by and large, was just another clique. Although Marlena hadn't been anything but rude to her, Joan objected on principle when the others wanted to exclude her. Everyone should be given a chance, and she convinced the others to give Marlena the benefit of the doubt and time to show that she could improve. Grudgingly, the committee agreed, but on one condition. Joan had to be the messenger. She must tell Marlena that, henceforth, she would be assigned the lowest profile shoots, including the team photos, and would be given the boot if she didn't smarten up.

She couldn't remember how Marlena had dealt with the news because soon after Joan had dropped out of school. She turned to Marlena now.

"Did you take those pictures of me?"

"What pictures? I took a lot of pictures."

"The ones that were hidden in the speaker." She didn't take her eyes off Marlena.

Marlena glanced down at the Crown Royal bag, the reality slowly dawning on her. Frightened, she replied, "I don't know what you're talking about."

Joan just continued to stare. They both knew the truth. Marlena was being defensive in the way that a teenager tries to justify errant actions.

"It'll only be worse if I have to go public with this," Joan said. "If I have to go to the police."

"Worse for who?" blurted Marlena, but she immediately seemed to realize that her words were as good as a confession. "You were so drunk," she said, "lying there like a little slut, half-naked. Everyone at the paper thought I was such a loser but they had no idea what I was capable of. I wasn't the ditz they thought I was. I processed those photos all by myself when nobody was around. I was going to show my dad that you weren't so great." There were tears flowing now.

"But I never did anything to you," said Joan.

"I was mad. And I was pissed on rye and ginger." Marlena dropped her gaze to the garage floor and added quietly, "Afterwards I realized that my dad would have killed me if he ever found out."

"So you put the photos in the speaker?" asked Joan.

"Yeah," said Marlena.

She'd have had ample opportunity. She had hung around rehearsals, flanked by Peg and Candy. Their connection to Rank, especially Roger, had become their own claim to fame.

Marlena looked up. "I never showed them to anybody."

"Then why did you keep them?"

"I dunno! In case I changed my mind? After a while I forgot about them, at least where I'd put them." She sneered. "Just be thankful there was no internet back then. You'd be famous."

Marlena turned and fumbled with her house key in the door, trying to escape. Joan was struck by the irony. She had so easily forgotten the newspaper incident, it meant so little to her — but to Marlena it had been life altering. Probation on the paper had been humiliating to the popular teen. She had become bitter.

Before she could get away, Joan caught her with another question. "What about the grad photo, the one with the rip across it? Were you responsible for that?"

"What photo?"

Joan pulled the photocopy from her purse, unfolded it, and held it out.

Marlena took it gingerly and studied it. Moments passed before she glanced up. "I was pretty, wasn't I?"

Her remark caught Joan off guard, not because it seemed entirely self-centred, but because of her uncertainty. Marlena had always been attractive and seemed so sure of it. A wave of pity swept over Joan. The Marlena of her memory was a thin veneer over the real Marlena, who had been as fragile as a gawking, featherless sparrow.

"Did you rip it?" asked Joan. "Roger's print?"

"It was his?" There was a sorrow in her voice as she scanned the blurred faces. "I've never seen this before. How come I never got one?" She released it reluctantly when Joan reached for it. "Are you trying to pin something on me, Parker?"

"Don't worry," said Joan as she slid the copy back in her handbag.

"You're trying to get fingerprints or something? You think I'm stupid?"

The heat in the closed garage accentuated the scent of Marlena's flowery skin products. Expensive. European. They blended with the odors of paint, acetone, and motor oil. "No, Marlena. It's just a copy of the original."

"I was done with him by the time that was taken, you know," Marlena said. "Daphne never knew that I was sleeping with good ol' Rog at the same time he was hustling her. You think those Pyles were religious? He was the one that was religious. The church of Daphne. He totally worshipped her. I never stood one damn chance."

Despite the years of bullying, Joan couldn't help but feel sorry for her. The way she looked at Roger in the photo, her willingness to sneak into his room last Friday night — Joan realized that the singer had really meant something to her. "You really were the queen of the school," she said, trying to console her. "You had everyone eating out of your hand."

"Oh, shut up. I was a bitch. Now even Candy has dumped me. " She pulled herself up. "But, I've got my girls. They're the best thing that ever happened to me. Not like you, Joannie. You'll grow old alone."

Joan shook her head. All this and the mix of smells was becoming overwhelming. She was desperate to leave. She wanted to say, "You're still a bitch." Instead, she asked one more question. "Marlena, what made you stop accusing me of killing Roger?"

"For one thing, you weren't interested in him. Gabe's your type." She spoke with the air of authority that comes from reading stacks of *Cosmo* magazine. "Besides, you're not a good faker." Her eyes were stone cold. "Not like some ass-kissers."

Back in her car, Joan studied the photocopy. At seventeen we want people to be good or bad, nice or mean. There's no room in between. As she drove off, she decided that Marlena hadn't moved from that paradigm.

Marlena locked the door behind her and hurled her gym bag onto the floor. She'd been left looking like the bad guy again. But she wasn't the only one. How about Daphne? Cute little Daphne Pyle, the biggest faker of them all, pretending to be her friend. She could read Ray like a thermometer. The way he'd been drooling over Daphne. He'd had a piece of that juicy ass. He'd gone all mushy. Those hens hanging all over him last night. How could she admit to anyone that she was the one who'd been made a cuckold?

She found two large Holt Renfrew shopping bags in the broom closet and filled them with Daphne's things. She didn't want that whore back in her house.

CHAPTER TWENTY-ONE

SPICY CHAI STEAM DRIFTED UP JOAN's nose as she stirred cream into her teacup. She nestled into the high-back leatherette seat. Jacques back booth gave her privacy to flip through the pages of the yearbook, trying to detect a killer. Marlena certainly had motive and she was plenty bitter. Ray? He'd had reasons as well. He'd been overshadowed in the band; his wife had lusted after Roger for decades. Did he know Marlena had slept with Roger when they were teenagers? The more she thought about Ray and Marlena, though, the more she thought that Ray had more reasons to kill his wife than to kill Roger. The other band members? The army of women that Roger had screwed and dumped? And were Peg's and Roger's deaths linked? Daphne, Candy, even Marlena could easily have given their classmate the drugs that killed her. Any of the men from their class? Who would have the assortment of drugs? And what about Lila, or even Hazel? Joan knew she was spinning in circles. It was frustrating. A shadow blocked her light.

"I've been looking for you." Gabe slid in across from her and shook his head when the owner came over to take his order.

"So, Sergeant Theissen, we're free to go?" asked Joan.

"Yup."

"Have you figured out who did it?"

"Nope," he said.

"Wasn't there any DNA left behind?" she asked.

"Here we go again," Gabe said. "I wish CSI would go to hell."

"Sorry. I should know better. I've spend my life in a well-funded lab. Even with a budget, science doesn't happen overnight."

"We're no closer to an answer, but we can't ask people to hang around."

"Even me? I know Smartt has his suspicions."

"But not enough to lay charges. You should go before he changes his mind." He placed his hand over hers on her teacup. "Don't get me wrong. I want you to stay."

"To help with the investigation," finished Joan.

"The thought of you leaving again," said Gabe. "It's the worst kind of déjà vu."

"C'mon, Gabe. We both knew that all we had was a weekend." Making light of it, she was trying to convince herself as well as Gabe that they could simply say goodbye and walk away. He had her hand in both of his now and wasn't letting go.

"We'll get this wrapped up. Then I'll come to Vancouver." He responded to her look of astonishment. "We'll move in together."

"You can't do that," she gasped.

"You don't want me too?"

"It's crazy," she said. "You have a life, a home, a job." But she knew that he meant it. The old Gabe — the idealistic, intelligent, passionate youth — had completely meshed with the strong, honourable public servant. She felt a deep and overwhelming sorrow. No matter how much they both wanted it to be, he wasn't hers. Not now, maybe not ever.

At that moment, as though another dimension had opened, a young man walked through the door of the cafe. Joan recognized him immediately, not just from the family photos but also from his striking resemblance to the man across from her. He was Gabe, right down to the irritated acne. She withdrew her hand and whispered. "Gabe, your son."

Gabe turned and smiled as Teddy approached, then stood and hugged his son warmly.

Teddy grinned at her. "You must be Joan. Dad's been talking about you ever since we got back from Kamloops."

"Nice to meet you, Teddy." Confused, she stole a glance at Gabe but got nothing.

"It's cool that the three of you can hang out," he said. He responded to her shocked stare. "You know, you, Dad, and Hazel."

"Oh, yeah, cool," replied Joan. "Very cool."

The boy turned to his father. "I saw your truck out front. Can I get forty bucks? I didn't pay for my yearbook yet and they won't let me pick it up until I do."

As Gabe dug out his wallet, she examined them in profile. It truly was Gabe all over again, although Teddy had his mother's redder brunette hair and green eyes.

Before leaving, Teddy asked, "Will you be coming to the house for dinner? Mom told Dad to ask you."

Joan looked at Gabe then back to Teddy. "No. I'm not sure. I'll be leaving soon, right away probably."

Teddy nodded as though adults and their schedules were out of his realm. After he bounded out of Jacques, she looked at Gabe questioningly.

"I told Betty this morning."

"Told her what?"

"That I'd fallen in love with you, that maybe I always have been," said Gabe.

"Oh, no!" But he was serious and she knew it. Gabe always said what he meant. He didn't beat around the bush. She glanced toward the door.

"No, Teddy doesn't know," he said. "It can't end here. Not again. I'm coming with you."

She tried to reason with him. "You can't leave your job, your son."

"I might get fired before the day is out. Teddy will be in university in the fall."

For all of her blaming Madden for not wanting her, Joan suddenly realized that it wasn't the fault of this town or the people or her family's past. It was her fault and hers alone. She had left it all behind and made a clean break years ago. This was too fast, too complicated. That familiar feeling of being trapped was creeping up on her. If Gabe lost his job, it would be because of her. She became curt, officious, as though she truly was a member of the investigation team.

"Gabe, I can't think of anything else until we know what happened to Roger and Peg. Don't you think you should be focusing on that? It's your job, not mine."

It was her escape route, again, and they both knew it. Shaken, she gathered up her things, paid for her tea at the cashier, and left. As she stepped out onto Main Street, the wind started to whip up, sending leaves and debris into swirling gusts. She pulled up her hood and held her collar closed as she made her way to her Accord.

On the outskirts of Madden, the Greyhound Bus sign attached to the pole outside the Redi-Gas station swayed in the wind. Ed Fowler pulled his ear buds from the side pocket of his suitcase, stuffed them into the pocket of the jacket he was wearing, then handed the bag to the bus driver to put in the cargo compartment. It was a large suitcase. He didn't expect to be back in Madden anytime soon.

Laura Rimmer braced herself for the chilly air as she opened her front door. The flow of visitors had slowed since the weekend. With a little help from their well-stocked medicine chest, she had finally slept through the night. Thank goodness the pharmacy still honoured Tom's prescriptions. That beautiful girl stood on the step again, this time looking lost. As Laura ushered her into the front hallway, she tried hard to remember her name. She knew that she'd been there before. She was having such trouble with names lately. Daffodil. Davina. Daphne. Yes, Daphne.

Once inside, the girl looked over her shoulder, then to Laura's surprise turned the deadbolt on the door behind her. "For privacy," she said, before heading directly to the living room. "The RCMP told us that we can leave anytime, all of us from the reunion." She was shivering but the room wasn't cold.

Laura smiled. "I'm sure you'll be glad to get home. Where did you say you live now?"

"You need to know something before I head out."

Tom entered the room. He stood in the doorway, blocking the exit.

"I had Roger's baby," the girl blurted out. "Your grandchild."

Laura simply nodded, but she stole a glance at Tom. His face had flushed red.

"What right have you . . . barging in here, making up stories," Tom sputtered. Laura went over and put a hand on his arm, but he continued, "Get out. Get out of our house." He grabbed the girl's arm. Her reaction was to shake him off. In doing so, she caught his cheek with her forearm. His hand flew to his face.

"Don't touch me," she hissed.

A bright red welt grew where her bracelet had scratched him. "I'm calling the police," he shouted.

"Sit down," Laura said. "Right now. Both of you." Neither sat. She looked at the girl. "It's Daphne, am I right?" The girl nodded "A boy or a girl?"

"A girl."

"And where is she, this girl, my granddaughter?" she asked.

"She's grown up now," came the response and then, in a whisper, "Patti."

Laura tested the name on her lips, "Patti. Patti. Short for Patricia?" The girl nodded. "Patricia is my middle name." She glanced at her husband. His mouth was agape. It was the last thing that either had imagined. "And where is she, Daphne?"

"I can't tell you."

Laura made her voice firmer. "You do know where she is?"

Another nod, then, "But I can't tell you. I just wanted you to know."

"This is about money, isn't it?" Tom had gone pale. Faltering, he made his way to a dining chair that had been placed in the living room to accommodate the trail of visitors over the past few days.

"I don't want anybody's money. And if you tell anyone . . . "

"Then why did you come to tell us, dear?" asked Laura.

"I wanted someone to know that she has been loved more than anything, more than life, even, and because you're her family." Then she looked up through those long, dark lashes. "And in case something happens." She corrected herself. "Something is going to happen." Then she was gone.

A KILLER SCENT

Chapter Twenty-Two

THE THOUGHT OF ENTERING THE CABIN where Roger had been murdered terrified Joan. It wasn't just the violent, hideous crime that had taken place within those walls, but the threat of being arrested if she was caught. It would look as though she were there to make sure her tracks were covered or for whatever other psychopathic reasons a criminal returned to the scene of a crime. For the past hour, she had been sitting in her room, adding up the facts. She was the number one suspect in Staff Sergeant Smartt's mind and that wasn't going to change unless new evidence emerged. Also, so far she'd focused on her own generation, gathering clues from former classmates about the two deaths. Yet one of the most startling revelations that she'd had since arriving was about her own mother. Vi had been much more on the ball than she had ever imagined and was still. Had she missed a valuable information source, hiding behind bifocals and grey hair? Or perhaps she'd overlooked the killer? A father whose daughter had been dumped by Roger, holding a grudge for forty years? If Dan were alive, he'd be on that list.

As the layers of the investigation began to emerge, so did an impediment. Gabe's proposal that they move in together should have made her leap with joy. Instead it worried her. His reputation and job were on the line. His refusal to hide his feelings for her was getting in the way. She couldn't ask his permission to enter the crime scene or even let him know her intention. That would implicate him even more. But maybe something had been missed, something that she could detect. It was worth the risk.

There were fewer cops at the scene today than yesterday. Joan waited until they had left for lunch before she sauntered toward the cabin, crossed the fluttering yellow ribbon. The door opened easily. As she stepped over the threshold, she was assaulted by the stench of harsh cleaners. She could tell by the ultra-clean scrub trails around the bed, that it had been a blood bath. A new mattress, delivered prematurely and still wrapped in plastic, leaned against the wall, waiting for the next unsuspecting guest, who wouldn't know the grisly history of this room. She pulled her leather gloves onto her hands and glanced around the cabin. What would remain after such a thorough scouring? First, she knelt on her hands and knees, using her keychain flashlight to look under the bed. Then she went through the closet, the dressers, and every inch of the dinette area. In the bathroom the aroma of cheap jasmine motel soap lingered slightly despite the strong scent of glass cleaner and bleach. The assault on her olfactory system would soon diminish her ability to smell anything. Within a minute, maybe two, her nose would shut down. She removed her shoes, and climbed into the bathtub, then looked out to see the murder room from that perspective. Suddenly she felt foolish. Why did she think that she, a civilian, could do a better job than the cops? She heard voices and slipped back into her shoes. The officers must have finished their break. The voices were coming toward the door. Damn. Now she'd risked it all for nothing.

In a panic, she decided to exit through the glass patio door. As she pulled the drapes aside a wave of scent took her breath away. Lifting her palate slightly to help expand her nostrils, she breathed in rapid, shallow sniffs. She knew the smell that had been trapped between the patio door and the drapes or, more accurately, that combination of smells, but couldn't immediately pinpoint where she'd come across it. She sniffed again. Yes, it was among the myriad of scents she'd experienced since arriving in Madden. Holding her breath, desperate to memorize this clue, she slid the door open and slipped out. Now hidden by the drapes, she slowly, silently eased the door closed behind her as the police officers entered the cabin.

Once she was safely in her car, Joan debated calling Gabe. She had little to offer him. How seriously would the Elgar RCMP take her when she explained how a few million molecules wafting through the air could give her information very few others would be aware of? The simple action of moving the drapes would have dispersed the scent to a level where even she might have trouble identifying it again. No normal nose could possibly detect the smell. Besides, she had a clue, but didn't know where it led yet. She wouldn't be doing Gabe any favours by sending him on a wild goose chase. She needed to figure this out on her own.

The day had started to warm as Joan drove into the parking lot of the Mountain View Lodge. She veered to avoid a pair of elderly women pushing walkers, both of whom stopped and stared before they continued on their way, shaking their heads. Joan admitted to herself that she was distracted and had been driving too quickly. Time and space were collapsing on her.

Mountain View Lodge was a three-storey brick-and-siding structure built in the Sixties. There had been expansions since then. A glassed-in dining room and lounge protruded from the front; this gave the place a more contemporary feel, yet the fragrance of the traditional flower garden, of its geraniums and hollyhocks and lily of the valley, transported Joan back to her grandmother's welcoming cottage.

The resident manager, Theresa Milton, was a tall, warm-mannered woman in a pale yellow business suit. She led Joan past the front desk and into her office, leaving the door open so that she could keep one eye on the reception area.

"We usually have more volunteers than we can schedule. People enjoy coming here." Then she added with a smile, "And we feed them well in exchange for their time."

Joan got right to her question. "Was Roger Rimmer a volunteer here?"

The happy glow deserted Ms. Milton's face. She shook her head slowly. "No."

"But he did come here?"

"If you're referring to the theft, I was the one who caught him. The jar was full of bills and coins in the morning that he was here, then gone right after he left."

"So you didn't actually see him do it?" asked Joan.

"One of our residents did. He denied it, of course. Tried to charm his way out of it, which was, to say the least, unappealing."

Joan imagined time-ravaged Roger playing the lady's man with this centred, much younger woman. "There was nobody else who could have done it?" she inquired.

Theresa went on to explain that everyone else who had been at Mountain View that day had a clear reason.

"He wasn't visiting anyone?"

"Can I ask why you're interested? I do have to protect patient confidentiality."

"Was it Mr. Pyle?" continued Joan, "Harold Pyle?"

Theresa Milton hesitated then nodded. "Mr. Rimmer came a couple of times the week before he died. Tragic, just tragic," she added.

Joan explained that she had known Mr. Pyle when she was a girl. "How's he doing?"

Ms. Milton said that life at the lodge agreed with Harold Pyle. Since moving here he'd transformed. When he first arrived he wouldn't play cards or dance and he criticized most of their movie choices, but after getting over his wife's death, his religious fervor died. "Now he teaches the two-step class. But," she warned, "he still has outbursts. When you're a control freak all of your life, it doesn't desert you completely. But, a good brisk walk and he returns a new man." She wrote a room number on a slip of paper and slid it across the desk to Joan.

"He goes out on his own?" asked Joan.

Theresa Morton smiled kindly. "It's their home, not a prison."

It was past lunch and the sunroom was crowded with residents playing cards and socializing. Joan continued down the hall until she came to room 107. The door was partly open but she knocked anyway.

A voice called out, "Hold your horses, hold your horses. I'm just getting my specs. Deal me out of this hand if you're so impatient." He came around the corner from his closet and saw Joan.

She pointed above his brow. "There, on your head, your glasses," she said.

He patted his head, looking confused. Mr. Pyle's clothing was faded. His pants were threadbare. When his hand touched his glasses, his eyes lit up. "Thank you, dear. You're new here. You'll like it. All the volunteers do."

"Oh, I'm not a volunteer." She held out her hand. "My name is Joan Parker and I'm a friend of your daughter's."

Harold Pyle glowered at her. "Daphne?" he asked. She nodded. "What d'ya' mean 'are a friend'? She's dead. My girl is dead." He whispered the last part then looked at her with a flint-hard gaze.

She wasn't sure what he meant. Was he confused? Most likely, she thought, he had disowned Daphne and she was dead in his books. She apologized for upsetting him, but he just waved her away.

After a moment he eased himself onto the bed then sat looking at the ground. "I'm tired now," he said gruffly. "Go. Just go."

As Joan pulled the door closed, he made one last comment for her benefit. "She had a baby, you know, a little girl. Cute little thing. Head full of curls."

On the way out of the building, Joan stopped by to see Theresa Milton. She wrote a cheque as a donation to Mountain View Lodge and asked that it be contributed to the fund for clothing and incidentals. As she handed it over, she asked one more question.

"Did Mr. Pyle's daughter ever come to visit?"

Ms. Milton looked surprised. "I didn't know he had a daughter."

Staff Sergeant Smartt didn't, or couldn't, hide his contempt. "Why don't we just put the entire town under house arrest, eh Theissen?" He sneered from behind the desk reserved for visiting officers.

Gabe turned his back on Smartt and did a slow count to five. The spacious office had been vacant since cutbacks had reduced the detachment by three personnel. When their Commander,

Lou Takahashi, had retired, he hadn't been replaced. Once the reshuffling was complete, though, everyone knew that Gabe would be offered the title, and he was currently the de facto head of the unit. Until it was official, though, Gabe had decided to keep his old office. It was smaller than this one but it had a better view, taking in a sharp bend in the river and a copse of elms. This visitors' office, Smartt's temporary digs, doubled as a storage room. File boxes were stacked against two walls.

Gabe turned around again. "All I'm suggesting is that we ask some of the key witnesses to stay a few more days if it's convenient. Once they're gone from here, we have no choice but to open the investigation nationally." Then he corrected himself, thinking of Sarah Markle and her husband. "Internationally. Time's running out."

Des Cardinal, standing in the open doorway, added, "They're packing now. Most of them I talked to are leaving in the morning. We can thank Candy Dirkson for holding them here for the memorial this evening"

Smartt ignored Des and addressed Gabe. "Have you got anywhere on this case? Do you even have any suspects?"

Gabe produced a list and placed it on the desk in front of him. "Right here."

Smarrt responded curtly. "This is one long list."

"They're all people who have had some sort of conflict with Roger. None stands out more than another."

"And Mrs. Chalmers death, are there suspects?' asked Smartt.

"We're working on Peg's case," confirmed Gabe.

"And you've got nothing else?" Smartt was pointing to the folder Gabe was clutching. Reluctantly, Gabe withdrew another sheet from the folder and handed it to Smartt. Writing the report about Roger's two attempts to rape Joan had stung him deeply. If she hadn't made him promise, he wasn't sure he would have submitted it. Smartt's brow furrowed as he studied the report. Halfway through, he glanced sharply at Gabe then continued reading. When he finished, he spoke at a low boil. "How long have you known this?"

"I just found out," answered Gabe.

Smartt's eyes bore through him. "You're aware that if you knew any of this prior to Rimmer's homicide it makes you a suspect as well?" Smartt's tone was official.

"You have no grounds to make that statement," Gabe protested.

Smartt just sniffed and Gabe stifled further argument, knowing that the cop from Kamloops held the upper hand. Smartt looked down at the page, contemplating his options. "Theissen, you may think you're irreplaceable, but we have good men in the Major Crimes Unit in Kamloops; men I've worked with in the past and trust. I'm making some calls. In the meantime we're faced with time pressures that give me little choice but to keep you on this case. It might be one day, maybe two, before I can get more men here, but if you step one foot, one inch out of line, you'll be pulled off the case immediately."

"Parker volunteered the information." Gabe knew that he sounded defensive.

"We've never resolved the issue that she might have connived to have her name added to the invitation list," said Smartt. "I've been doing a bit of digging. Turns out that this is the first time she's come back to this town in thirty years. Don't you ask yourself, 'why now'?"

Before they could get into that argument again, Des meekly interrupted. He addressed Smartt but kept glancing at Gabe. "I'm sorry, sir. When Candy Dirkson called this morning and

I told her that we were advising the reunion guests that they could go home . . . " Des left it hanging.

Smartt grew impatient. "Yes?" he growled.

Des looked at Gabe. "She was calling, Gabe, to tell you that she'd remembered something. Peg Chalmers told her that Daphne Pyle had contacted her. She had called out of the blue about a month ago when word started getting out about the reunion. Ed Fowler had created a Facebook page for the reunion and posted it on craigslist and Ms. Dirkson thought it might have been Daphne Pyle who put the idea in Peg's brain to add her and Ms. Parker to the invitation list."

"For God's sake," Smartt interrupted. "That's not proof of anything." But Gabe knew that Des had just bought Joan a "get out of jail" card. Smartt lifted his large frame from the chair. "I'll go talk to Candace Dirkson myself. Enough of this touchy-feely, old-home-week style of investigation." He pulled his jacket from the back of his chair. "And you may not request anyone to stay in Madden any longer. Once they're gone, I'm moving the case to Kamloops. I don't believe you're focused on this case. "

"What do you mean?" Gabe felt the hair rising on his neck.

"Joan Parker. Has anyone told you that it's inappropriate for a cop to chase after a suspect? Not to mention plain bad taste." Smartt strapped on his gun and left the office.

Des piped up. "I never told him, Gabe, about, you know."

Gabe knew that Des was embarrassed about the incident before the Stanfield party, when he'd seen his boss making out with a woman who was not his wife.

"I didn't realize I was under investigation," Gabe said wearily. Then he left the building.

Joan knew that something was seriously wrong as soon as she heard Hazel's voice on her cell phone. She raced from

Mountain View Lodge directly to the hotel and pulled into the parking spot reserved for check in. She watched the elevator numbers slowly light up in descending order. When it stopped on the third floor for what seemed like an eternity, she decided to take the stairs up the six flights. She was out of breath by the time she reached room 610. Hazel opened the door at the first knock. Her grey hair stood on end and she wore the long, tent-like dress that she'd been wearing when she arrived at Joan's motel room the previous night. Her eyes were red.

"Her purse and coat are gone and that's it. I just got off the phone from housekeeping. They haven't been to this room yet. That means the bed hasn't been slept in."

The last time Joan could remember seeing Hazel this distraught was when she'd told her and Gabe that she was moving to the city with her mom and brothers.

"Who does Lila know in town?" she asked.

"Nobody. Not really. She's been here with me a couple of times but usually keeps to herself. She's met Roger's parents and had dinner over there, and I've introduced her to folks this weekend, but that's it. Except for Gabe, and you've seen how she reacts to him." She looked at Joan dolefully. "What if something's happened to her?"

The only comfort Joan could provide was reminding her that Lila was seriously pissed at her the previous night. Hazel admitted that it had been bad judgment, abandoning her and staying at Joan's, but then pointed out that Lila hadn't taken the rental car. Joan began to worry too. What if Hazel's partner had become a third victim? Unlike the others, he wasn't a member of the graduating class of 1979. Did Lila have something else in common with Roger and Peg? She didn't have a cache of bad blood going back three decades. Could they be dealing with a psychopath who didn't need a logical excuse to kill? Joan convinced Hazel to phone Gabe, but the call went directly to voicemail.

While Hazel waited for Gabe to call back on the landline, Joan went out to look for Lila. A woman with a big purse and a bagful of resentment had the means and motivation to disappear. Death was only one possibility.

CHAPTER TWENTY-THREE

MADDEN WAS SMALL ENOUGH THAT ONE could cover the streets by car in a half hour. When Joan found herself on the outer edge of town, she kept driving down the highway, whizzing past the sign indicating that Elgar was sixteen kilometers further on. Perhaps Lila had returned to the motel where she had spent Friday night arguing with Hazel. The hefty wind was sending clouds sailing across the sky, and occasionally a fierce gust forced Joan to hold tightly to the steering wheel. Aside from her visit with Gabe yesterday, she couldn't remember the last time she'd been to Elgar. As a kid, she hadn't had much reason to come down the road to the neighbouring town. Back then it had been considered Madden's rougher sister. None of her miniscule circle of friends had lived there, and the only school was elementary so there'd been no exchange in extramural activities.

Since those days, Elgar had grown from a farm community into an upscale extension of Madden. Subdivisions, such as the one in which Gabe and Betty lived, were sprouting up in a semi-circle around the older streets that bordered the highway. In addition to the RCMP detachment, Elgar boasted a Subway and a new PetroCan station. A Tim Hortons was going up where the Burger Baron had been. There was still, though, a row of dilapidated businesses that gave the town a shabby appearance from the highway.

The Elgar Motel qualified as an eyesore. The white-sided complex fell into a category somewhere between retro and nondescript. Joan didn't understand why Lila and Hazel would have stopped here on Friday. Lila struck her as a woman who enjoyed her comforts. Her clothing, perfume, and hairstyle were all high-end. Why stay here when their far classier destination was fifteen minutes up the highway?

When she entered the motel office, the heavy smell of bacon rose on the breeze. She rang the bell twice before the manager came shuffling toward her in slippers and sweats. He blew his nose before he addressed her. She explained that she was part of the high school reunion in Madden and that she was looking for Lila Wozny who had been a guest here the previous Friday. When she described the lanky redhead, the manager gave a lecherous smile and nodded.

"Oh yeah, she's here, this time without her mom. She's in Room 10."

So much for security. With a killer on the loose, this guy wasn't helping keep his customers safe. He may as well have handed her the key. She thanked him and turned to the door but he stopped her.

"Oh, and hey, there was another chick here. I think she was from that reunion too." His voice fell into a whisper, "From who she was with, the guy, you know?" He gave Joan a couple of seconds to figure it out then he added, "A babe, blackish hair and..." He motioned to indicate large breasts. Ray and Daphne. "She left a bag of stuff in the room. I was thinking she'd come back for it, but she never did."

"A bag?"

"There's nothing worth much, really," he sighed.

So, he'd already rifled through it. "Do you mind if I have a look?" she asked.

The clerk pulled a paper shopping bag from beneath the counter. Joan grabbed it.

"I'll see that she gets it."

The clerk started to protest then shrugged his heavy shoulders.

Alone in her car, she opened the bag and was greeted by a cornucopia of scents, overpowered by the aroma of rotting banana and apple core. She tossed the offending fruit out of the window into an overgrown ditch, then inspected the remaining items one at a time. There were several pieces of poorly constructed jewellery, the kind of thing a dollar store would stock. The bright blue necklace and bracelet set may have been what Daphne had been wearing last Friday night. In dim light it would have had a convincing sparkle as long as nobody looked too closely. The bag also contained paper trash and a half-eaten granola bar. At the very bottom was the folder for the rental-car form. Joan flipped it open. It was a carbon copy and the print was faint. The car had been rented in Calgary ten days ago and had been due back on Sunday. Before she had a chance to read further, the door to Room 10 opened and Lila emerged, alive and robust. Joan sank down in her seat, but Lila strode directly to the car and swung open the driver's door.

"Are you stalking me?" Lila demanded.

Cowed by her Amazonian height, Joan dumbly shook her head, thinking that anyone, psycho or not, would have second thoughts before attacking Hazel's partner. "We were worried about you." She detected the tiniest glint of satisfaction in Lila's expression, the kind of reaction she'd expect in a test subject who was savouring the finest chocolate or champagne.

"Fine. Then you can give me a ride back to the hotel. The cabbies around here are robbers. This place is a dump and I don't have any clean clothes. You can't even buy a pair of panties in this town."

Joan could only imagine the attention she would have attracted trying to purchase lingerie in Elgar.

While Lila went to the motel office to check out, Joan flipped open Daphne's car rental agreement again, quickly scanning the document. The handwriting on the carbon copy was smudged. She could barely discern the surname "Pyle." It was impossible to make out the first name, but it seemed to start with a "P" rather than a "D," and filled eight spaces rather than six. The two letters, written sloppily, could easily be confused. Joan remembered her walk with Daphne on Saturday morning, Daphne speaking with a mother's pride of her daughter Patti, Patricia. She could see Lila concluding her business in the office and quickly dialed Gabe's cell phone. Her words came rapidly.

"I can't talk now, but I need you to do something. I have the rental form from Daphne's car. Call A-1 Rentals in Calgary. We need to know who rented the car. It's not clear on the form but I think it might be Patricia."

"A middle name? Or you think she changed it?" Gabe asked.

"No. I think her daughter rented it." She gave Gabe the phone number of the rental car company and the contract number as Lila approached the car.

"What's the connection to the case?" asked Gabe.

"I'm not sure yet," answered Joan.

"Thank you for the information. I'll check into it." Gabe was suddenly all business. He didn't even ask her how she was.

Once Lila was safely buckled into the passenger seat, Joan was tempted to drive the two blocks to the detachment, just to see if she could catch a glimpse of Gabe. Instead, she turned the car toward Madden.

Gabe hung up the phone and turned to Betty.

She repeated herself. "We should put the house on the market right away, before summer hits and the slump comes with it." She barely looked at him as she scrubbed the invisible stains on the kitchen counter. "The timing could be a lot worse. With Teddy going off to college, it won't impact him that much."

"What do you mean? His first year of university and his parents are splitting up." Gabe stared at his wife, shaking his head.

"C'mon, Gabe. Do you think this will be news?"

He had gotten used to her emotionless smile. Was this the same hollow, calculated look that she gave her welfare clients? "Do you hate me?" he asked quietly.

"Hate you? That's a strong word." She contemplated a moment. "But I guess it fits. Yes, I'm sure you left no doubt in Madden this weekend. I've made one hell of an effort not to draw attention to our situation." Her jaw tightened. "But you've never been diplomatic. Did you leave us any thread of dignity?" She studied his face. "But I'm grateful, too, Gabe. It's saved me from pulling the plug."

"You mean it saved you from being seen to be pulling the plug," corrected Gabe. "When were you planning on telling Teddy that you've been looking for a job in Kamloops?"

"You're an asshole, Gabe. That's all there is to it. But good genes, I'll always be thankful for that."

He suddenly felt sorry for Betty. It must be exhausting trying to organize the world. He wrapped his arms around her. She didn't struggle but didn't soften into his embrace as she would have twenty years ago.

"Okay then," he said, letting go. He put on his ball cap and left the house.

Joan suggested that Lila call Hazel to let her know that she was still alive, but the auburn bombshell refused. Joan placed the call herself before they left the parking lot. When Hazel heard the news she began to sob loud tears of relief. As Joan steered the car through high winds, Lila reclined the seat right back and stretched out like a cat.

Joan glanced over at her. "You put Hazel through an ordeal. She really loves you, you know."

Lila shrugged impatiently, but kept her eyes on Joan as they continued down the highway. Eventually she spoke. "She loves the entire world, our Hazel does. I'm just convenient."

The description surprised Joan. From everything she'd observed, she thought "high maintenance" fit better than "convenient".

Lila read her mind. "I'm not imagining it or feeling sorry for myself. You see Hazel's public side. At home she'll mope over some problem in the community. I live for days in her self-imposed silence. If I'd had half the attention that she paid Roger or a small fraction of the praise she afforded you . . . "

"Me?"

Lila chuckled. "Yeah, you. Your struggles thirty years ago motivated Hazel. Too bad you never bothered to call." She yawned and complained again about the uncomfortable bed at the motel. She continued drowsily. "For years I've asked her to get help."

"For what?"

"Depression. I'm pretty sure she's clinically depressed."

"Why did you just up and leave this time?"

Lila frowned. "Everyone has a breaking point." It was almost a whisper.

By the time they reached Madden, Lila was sound asleep and the sun had started to break through the clouds.

Gabe hung up from the Calgary rental car office, leaned back in his office chair, and looked up toward the florescent box above his desk. The two youngest officers were laughing in the corner, hanging out by the coffee pot and stirring sticky, vanilla-flavoured phony cream into their mugs. Gabe was glad to see them in high spirits. Long hours affect men in different ways. He'd take this giddy energy over dragging resentment any day. He'd miss this place when he moved to the city.

The faxed copy of the car rental form was centred on his desk. The car had been reported stolen when it hadn't been returned and the company hadn't been able to reach the renter. The cell phone number provided wasn't assigned. It wasn't just the name on the form that leapt out at Gabe, but also the date of birth from the Alberta driver's license: May 29, 1979. Patricia had been born the month before they graduated from Madden High School. After jotting quick notes to be included in the file, he pushed away from the desk and called over to Laurel at the reception counter. "I'm heading back to Madden." One of the junior constables offered to accompany him, but he declined. He was normally enthusiastic about mentoring the young officers, but lately he preferred to operate on his own, especially when he expected — hoped — to see Joan.

Before Hazel had called in a panic, Joan had been headed to Marlena's to track the scent she had detected in Roger's cabin. Now she drove through the alley behind the Stanfields' house and parked around the corner, trying to figure how she could convince them to let her into the house to have a sniff around. They'd think she was a lunatic. Marlena probably wouldn't let her through the door. Ray's and Daphne's cars weren't in sight. She considered trying the windows, but her credibility with the police in town, except for Gabe, was shot. If she was caught attempting to break in, she'd land in jail. No, the only way to get in the house to snoop around would be to march up the front steps and face Marlena again.

"What the hell do you want now!" Marlena screamed at her. She was loaded down with two large shopping bags filled with clothing.

"I'm here," Joan stammered, "to apologize."

Marlena looked paralyzed. "Apologize?"

"I should have given you more support on the newspaper. I realize that now," said Joan. A satisfied smile appeared on Marlena's lips until Joan continued. "I was hoping I could come in so we could talk about it."

"You're up to something, Parker. What is it?"

"Nothing!" Her voice went high and she felt herself blush.

"You need to take some bullshitting lessons from Daphne. Except she's not as smart as she thinks either." Marlena nodded down at the bags. "She's not getting back in here, thank you very much. You can't prove I took those pictures. I have nothing more to say to you. Get out or I'll call the cops." She stood her ground until Joan walked away.

As Joan turned the corner she glanced over her shoulder and saw Marlena stuff the bags into the trash cans beside the house. She'd wait in her car until the coast was clear.

When she reached the Accord, her voicemail beeped. The message was from Gabe, insisting on meeting with her alone. She was curious but knew that they'd end up in the sack if he came to her room. Their affair was on Smartt's radar. She'd avoid another compromising encounter for both their sakes. When she called and got Gabe's voicemail, she left word for him to meet her in an hour in the parking lot at the head of the riverside trails. It was public enough to ensure chastity and private enough to share information vital to the case.

As she waited, she played Gabe's voicemail message again; the slow and considered words, so protective and warm. Until two days ago she'd never questioned Mort's skill as a lover. He knew which buttons to press, and he performed with studied timing and consideration to her needs. She had believed that the metamorphosis from their original raging, fiery passion to the more recent hot-water-bottle comfort was due to the natural progression of age. It was fine, good, perfectly adequate. After she and Mort separated, she had rationalized that she had been lucky to have any sex at all, thus the "friends-with-benefits" relationship. Now, however, she had a new barometer against which to measure. Her experience with Gabe had led her to an erotic place that she had never known existed. It caught her off guard, and she knew that the only way that she could resist him was to avoid being alone.

The air inside the Accord was getting nippy, so she pulled her jacket from the backseat and wrestled into it. Fifteen minutes passed before she felt secure enough to enter the Stanfields' yard again. Keeping one eye on the door, she crept to the trashcans. It was the second time today she'd pawed through garbage. She grabbed the Holt Renfrew bags, ran to her car, then pulled away from the curb as quietly as possible.

Back at the Twin Pines, she dumped the first shopping bag onto her bed. A familiar scent rose from the crumpled clothing. She felt a surge of confidence that she was on the right track. She emptied the second bag, eagerly pawing at the makeup case that sat on top of the pile. There it was, a tiny sample bottle of

Angel, a Thierry Mugler fragrance. She held the bottle at arm's length, to avoid being overwhelmed by the top notes — the bright mandarin, coconut, and cotton candy. The heart note of honey worked its way to her nostrils, and then the warm base note of amber and caramel. This combination, almost edible, was one that very few women over the age of thirty-five ever wore. Buried beneath the perfume bottle and other toiletries was the foundation, a thick paste bearing a scent found in less expensive products. Blended together, the perfume and foundation — here was the fingerprint. It was the scent wrapped in the curtains at the scene of Roger's murder. She started to shove the articles back into the shopping bags, and touched something hard at the bottom of one. She pulled out a pink spiral notebook, and glanced at the clock. Only twenty minutes before Gabe expected her. Rubbing her hand over the cover, she felt the down of aged paper and smelled a faint odor of mildew. The notebook was in a style that had been popular when she'd been in high school. She settled on the bed and opened the book. There it was, right there on the page, circled in red, "Joan P. laid a mauve sweater on me today plus a copy of Siddhartha by Herman Hesse. I'll have to hide them from Mother and Father. They'd freak if they found any of it." She flipped randomly through the pages and found another passage circled in red. "Talked to Joan today. We're going to split a bottle of LG for the party this weekend."

Chapter Twenty-Four

Nestled in his bed, Harold Pyle could feel a presence in his room. Staff usually didn't disturb a nap, and if they came into the room for something, they didn't linger. Too busy; all of them, all the time, were too busy. He opened his eyes. The lined drapes made it as dark as night in the room and there was no movement. He shut his eyes again and started to drift, wondering if the presence was imagined – or divine. Maybe the angels were coming for him. Or maybe his departed wife was watching over him. He often wondered what she'd think about him now, dancing and flirting. When the faint sound came again, he opened his eyes and saw a figure. "Daphne?" He shook the wool from his head. It couldn't be his daughter. His eyes adjusted. "Oh, so it's you."

"Yes, it's me," she said as she took a step closer.

"I didn't reckon you'd come back."

"But I have to know one more thing," she said as she stood over him. "Why did you hate me so much? You didn't even know me."

"We were foolish." A knot of guilt twisted his stomach when he remembered how unkind he'd been. It had been a blistering hot day when his daughter had shown up at the door with her little girl. He tried to sit up and got as far as propping on his elbow then stretched his arm toward her. "Forgive a stupid old codger."

The dark-haired girl pulled away. "Forgive! You didn't forgive us! You didn't forgive my mother. That's what gave her the ulcers, and the cancer. That's what killed her." Now she was shouting. In a burst of anger, she turned and swept the framed photos from his bureau. Harold cowered back as she paced around the room, jerking her head, hunting for something else to destroy or to use as a weapon to destroy him. "Stupid is no excuse. You're mean and hateful." Before she could continue, the door abruptly opened and Theresa Milton's tall frame filled the doorway. The girl fled.

He called out, "We loved you. Even if we didn't know you. " Then the damn burst with a lifetime of restrained tears.

Ms. Milton tried to comfort him. He continued to call out, but the words were caught in his throat and came out as a croak. "So did your father. He loved you. He asked about you." But it was too late. She was gone.

Although the sun was shining, the spring breeze was cold, chilling the sensitive hairs inside Joan's nostrils. She perched on the picnic table with her scarf looped over her hair and the long end wrapped twice around her neck. Daphne Pyle's journal was tucked securely in her purse. Gabe was late. While she waited, a couple of women came back from a hike, got in their car, and drove off. That left only one other car in the parking lot. A large man in a business suit was behind the wheel, enjoying a late bag lunch, sipping pop from a can as he gazed at the river. Joan often thought about leaving her office at lunch and driving to eat at a spot like this, with a water view. She was going to make some changes when she got back to Vancouver. The gravel crackled beneath Gabe's tires as he pulled up in his truck. He rolled down the window.

"Hop in," he said with a casual smile.

"Why don't we sit out here?" Joan patted the picnic table.

"It's freezing. C'mon, you're not dressed for this weather."

Joan glanced at the man in the car eating his lunch. How much trouble could they get into with that guy sitting right there? Gabe opened the door from the inside and she climbed in, pulling off her scarf. The Eagles played softly on the stereo. It was warm inside and permeated with Gabe's clean scent. At the sight of his slightly drooping eyes she softened like milk chocolate under the hot sun. He reached up and wove his hand through her hair to cup her head.

"Gabe," she warned as she glanced at the other car. He just smiled and bent into her, kissing her long and gently. She pulled back. "We have to discuss the case." Her willpower was evaporating under the warmth of his hand.

"Of course we do," he smiled. "That's why we're here." But he didn't take his eyes off her. He kissed her again and this time started unbuttoning her coat.

"We're not alone." Her voice quivered. She heard an engine start. Coincidence or telepathy? Gabe grinned and she knew that they were now alone. He slipped his hand under her T-shirt and she put her hand on top of his, at first to stop him, then to encourage him. "We shouldn't," she murmured.

"Life is too short for shouldn'ts," he said as he flipped the armrest out of the way.

Tomorrow she would be gone. This could be the last time she was with Gabe for a very long time, maybe forever. She wanted to make love right here, right now. She wanted to say to hell with Smartt, the investigation, or men eating lunch. But who was she kidding? They weren't a couple of adolescents, and they had serious matters to discuss that couldn't wait.

"Not now, Gabe." Her sudden shift in body language sent a clear message.

"Okay." He shifted to business. "Daphne's daughter rented the car for her mother. There's no question in my mind."

"I don't think so, Gabe," she said.

"But it was Patricia Pyle's credit card, her driver's license, used for ID . . . Maybe Daphne doesn't have a credit card."

Joan interrupted. "No, Patricia didn't rent the car for Daphne. She rented it for herself. Daphne is Patti. Patti is Daphne," she said.

"What do you mean?" But she could tell the answer was dawning on him.

She rummaged on the floor for her purse and pulled out the pink notebook. "I couldn't figure out why she cringed at the memory of lemon gin but not at the strawberries. The woman who we've been calling 'Daphne' was chowing down on strawberries like there's no tomorrow. She remembered hardly any details about Roger, but she remembered the mauve sweater I gave her." Joan opened the notebook on her lap, found the page dated Labour Day weekend, 1978, where there was a detailed account of the bush party written in the telltale blotted scratching of a light-blue cartridge pen. The LG — lemon gin - incident was circled in red. She handed it to Gabe.

He read quickly. "Maybe Daphne wanted to remember those times specifically. Maybe she's been using the notebook to try to recover her memory."

Joan shook her head. "It's not just that the diary entries are similar to what she remembers. They're identical, word for word, as though she's memorized them, including the lemon gin fiasco."

"But we all do it to a degree," reasoned Gabe, "depend on the record of events to reinforce what we remember. I recall exactly what you and I looked like trying to get up on water skies for the first time, what you were wearing, that red-striped bathing suit, how you wore you hair. Then I look at the photo album and it's all there. But I can't remember what you wore earlier that day or an hour later."

Joan shook her head. "It's more than that. Even if Daphne had brain damage it seems off that she would eat strawberries. When I was working on my Ph.D. I investigated the relationship between memory and scent. We fed rats oranges injected with lithium, so they'd get nauseous. You couldn't get them to eat oranges after that, ever. A single bad olfactory memory will stay all your life. It's coded into one of the most primitive parts of the brain. Daphne had a near-death experience when she ate strawberries as a kid. That's going to make one hell of an imprint. It doesn't make sense that she'd remember lemon gin but not strawberries. It's the same part of the brain."

"Couldn't it be some sort of anomaly?" asked Gabe.

"Highly unlikely." She tapped the open book. "Daphne wrote vividly about the lemon gin. There's no mention about her allergic reaction to strawberries. No record. Not much in here about Roger either. Maybe Daph was honouring his demand for secrecy. It's definitely not something she would have wanted her parents to know. Gabe, this book *is* her memory. Earlier today Marlena said something that's stuck in my brain. She said that not everyone is who they seem to be. In Daphne's case, it's literal. She's not Daphne. She's Patti."

"So where is Daph?" asked Gabe. "The real Daphne?"

Joan looked at him sadly. "I'm pretty sure she's dead."

"Why?"

"All sorts of reasons, but the main one? Her dad told me she was."

"Daphne . . . Patricia — she may be a liar but it doesn't mean she's a killer. And, if she is, why Roger? Why Peg?"

"Daphne didn't write much about Roger. Doesn't mean she didn't talk about him to her daughter. And there's this." She read from the telltale diary. "'If I drink the gin all at once, maybe my problem will go away'."

"Her problem?" Gabe shook his head.

"Yeah. Daphne wasn't drinking to cut loose. It was a teenager's attempt to induce a miscarriage. That first time it must have worked. But it didn't when she got pregnant again. Remember the man's shirt she was wearing in the picture?" Joan sighed. "Roger was Patti's father. I'm almost certain."

"You think she came here to kill him?"

"You're the cop." Joan shrugged. It was starting to drizzle again, "Maybe it was simply too much baggage for one young woman." She stared at the rain on the window, one rivulet blending into another, then another, and another until they flowed as one steady trickle down the windshield.

He gave her shoulder a squeeze. "What's the matter? Something else is bothering you."

"Can you find out how Daphne died?" she asked.

"I'll put somebody on it." He looked at his watch. "Although I don't know if we'll get the answer today. You're wondering if the answer will be cancer?" She nodded. "A lot of people die of cancer, Joan."

"Then check to see if she suffered from ulcers. Can you do that?"

"Yeah, but it will take longer," answered Gabe.

"While you're at it, can you find out the side effects of all the medications that were found in Peg's system?" She went on to explain. "When I'm designing a flavour I sometimes include a fragrance, not for its dominant characteristic, but for its lesser characteristic."

"I don't get it."

"Marmalade. It's made from the bitter peel, but the real target is the more delicate underlying orange flavour. It's more subtle. It's possible that the drugs weren't intended to kill Peg, that they were given to her for another reason."

"To put her out of commission?" asked Gabe.

Joan nodded, then asked, "Did Peg give Daphne an alibi for the night that Roger died?"

"She confirmed that Daphne was staying with her and told Des that she had come in quite early on Friday night."

As Gabe spoke Joan remembered seeing her in the lobby chatting with Ed Fowler. "But, once she got to Peggy's, did she leave again?"

"Peg was on Des's list to do a second interview," he paused then finished slowly, "on Sunday morning."

"If Patti had seen her mother doped up on a cocktail of medications," said Joan, "incapable of moving, too drugged to reveal secrets . . . "

The pieces were falling into place like blocks in a game of Tetris.

"But why would she be carrying her mother's pills around?" Gabe asked doubtfully.

Joan thought of the eclectic assortment of junk that had been in Patti's bags and was now lying on Joan's bed at the motel. Besides the diary there were faded concert tickets, letters, and makeup products that hadn't been manufactured in years.

"It's her way of holding onto her mother. She's not operating in the same reality as the rest of us. There's no telling what she's thinking." She paused. "Or what she'll do."

Before Joan had a chance to say another word, a vehicle squealed into the parking lot, sending stone chips flying. The contorted grimace on Staff Sergeant Smartt's mug bordered on glee as he approached the truck. He'd finally caught them. Gabe climbed out and faced him.

"You're off the case Theissen. Report to the detachment, now! You can be damned sure that disciplinary action will start immediately."

"On what grounds?" Gabe's voice was quiet and controlled. So controlled, in fact, that it made Joan shudder. She slid out of the truck and stood by his side. There was no time to lose and this pissing contest between Gabe and Smartt wasn't solving anything.

"Listen to me," she stated sharply. "There's a murderer out there and we have to stop her before anyone else dies."

"We? Her?" asked Smartt sardonically.

Joan ignored his tone. "Every suspicion that you've hurled at me applies to someone else as well." She had his attention. "Daphne Pyle. Both our names were added to the invitation list after the fact. Both of us returned to Madden after a long absence. Neither of us graduated from Madden High."

Smartt interrupted. "But he was seen outside of your cabin. And, by your own admission, he attacked you thirty years ago."

"But there's another way our circumstances differ. My father's death forced my family to leave town. Daphne left because she was pregnant." She glanced at both men. "And the baby's father was Roger Rimmer."

Joan had felt like an imposter when she'd arrived in Madden. She hadn't noticed that someone in their midst was wearing a much more elaborate disguise. Patti had found a life in her mother's stories, and then used the information to create an illusion. "And that child is here posing as Daphne Pyle."

"Oh, that's ripe," guffawed Smartt. "You're not serious?" he asked, looking from Joan to Gabe. "You think I can't tell the difference between a woman in her late forties and a thirty year old?"

Joan was surprised to see Gabe looking uncomfortable. She protested. "Our brains are driven to fill in the blanks. In my lab we trick people into thinking one thing is something completely different. Label kitchen compost as ripe blue cheese and testers will insist that they're smelling Roquefort. "

"Okay, so you fool a few housewives with cheese," said Smartt.

Gabe was shuffling his feet. He wasn't coming to her defence. It was clear that she was losing both of them. "Listen. Once I had to create a flavour for a cake mix. Subjects were asked to discern between artificial and natural flavours. Believe me, not one of them, not one, could tell the difference between the scent of a real orange and the one we created in a lab. Patti's done the same thing, fooled us all. She's not the real thing."

Smartt looked at her as though she was crazy. Gabe appeared increasingly uncomfortable. She suddenly realized that she wasn't the only imposter in Madden, celebrating a high school graduation she'd never experienced. They were all faking something: Marlena posing as a happy wife, Hazel as an unflappable pillar of stability, and Gabe as a satisfied cop and husband. So much had changed since those yearbook photos were shot. Smartt was probably hiding something too, beneath the slick veneer. Feeling panicked, Joan knew that she couldn't risk playing her final card. If she explained that she had smelled Patti at the crime scene, it would be confessing that she had gone into Roger's room.

Smartt turned to Gabe. "I'll see you at the detachment." The cop from Kamloops didn't budge until Gabe was in his truck and driving away. Then he looked at Joan, shook his head, and walked off without a word, leaving her shivering in the cold spring air.

As she walked back to the motel, a twinge of panic needled her gut. If Patti was guilty of both murders, was Marlena also in danger? She'd dumped Patti's belongings in the garbage. Joan had overheard her blabbing to Patti about her lust for Roger. Who knew what else she had done or said to her house guest. Daphne had seemed patient with Marlena, but maybe she was just biding her time. Maybe sleeping with Ray hadn't been revenge enough. When Joan reached the Twin Pines, she used the reliable landline to call Marlena. It rang several times then went to voicemail. Joan threw on an extra sweater and raced to her car.

Driving through town at breakneck speed, she drew stares along Main Street. Only testosterone-pumped teenagers and emergency vehicles drove this fast in Madden. Swerving into a parking spot at the Stanfields' curb, she dialed Gabe as she unclasped her seatbelt. He didn't answer. Her message was simple. "I'm at Marlena's. Call me."

The garage was closed and there was no sign of either Daphne's rental or Marlena's SUV on the street. Joan dashed up the wide stone steps and pounded on the heavy wooden door. Minutes passed with no response. She tried the door. It opened easily. She stepped into the front hallway and called tentatively, "Marlena? Marlena, are you here?"

Another step into the ornate hallway and she saw a flash of movement as someone fled from the kitchen and down the hallway. Joan gasped, and took a step backwards, She heard shuffling from the kitchen and Marlena appeared, tying her robe to cover her naked body.

"Is that what people do in the city, just walk into someone's house? God, you're nervy."

A toilet flushed down the hall.

"I'm sorry, Marlena," she said. "I was worried that something might have happened to you."

Ray came out of the bathroom with a towel wrapped around his waist. It didn't take a genius to realize what they'd been cooking up in the kitchen. Joan wouldn't have been more shocked if it had been Marlena with any other man in town. Every time she'd seen them together her old high school nemesis had treated her husband as though he was dirt under her toenails.

"What d'ya' mean?" asked Marlena.

Joan didn't want to get laughed at again or give Marlena fuel for her poisonous tongue, so she kept quiet. There was no proof that Patti had done anything besides posing as her own mother.

"If you're here because of that thieving little bitch Daphne," Marlena said, "you're right. First she tries to steal Ray, and then she stole my cash stash. And I know how to hide cash in the house. I have two daughters, after all."

Ray awkwardly looked at his feet.

Joan realized that she had a better understanding of life on Mars than of anything that went on in this household. No, farther than Mars. Neptune, at least Neptune. "Sorry to intrude," she apologized as she backed out of the house.

Ray called after her. "See you at the memorial tonight?"

She gave a wave and an apologetic, lopsided smile as she headed to her car.

CHAPTER TWENTY-FIVE

THE ONLY OTHER PERSON LIKELY TO know the whereabouts of Patti Pyle was Ed Fowler. Joan suspected that his fall was no accident. Had the person fleeing through the gym door last night been Patti? Was she worried that she had said too much to Fowler? Would she make another attempt to silence him?

Joan took a left-hand turn off Main Street and wove her way through the quiet streets to the Couch, then pulled into the waiting zone behind an idling minivan. The front door of the old school was locked, but rehearsal had just ended and a stream of babbling young thespians trickled out the back. Joan caught the door as the teens made their way down the steps and into the mom-mobile waiting at the curb.

The dark hallway was illuminated by red exit lights at each end. She knew from the dank stench that the colourful murals on the walls hid a sadly rotting foundation. Local support of culture was superficial. Give the artists an old building too expensive to repair and let them stay until it disintegrates beneath them. She trod quietly, stopping to glance inside the gymnasium where Ray had debuted as Rank's vocalist. It was empty. Farther down the hall, the door to the darkened lounge was open. There was no sign of Mr. Fowler. She took the three stairs into the sunken room.

Something rustled behind her. She turned abruptly. Patti Pyle was frantically searching through an open storage cupboard, emptying jars and cans. The young woman spun around and looked directly into Joan's eyes, then blocked her path to the door. Tall, dark, and with the ferocity of a wild animal caught in close quarters, she looked ready to run – or pounce.

"Where is Mr. Fowler?" asked Joan, feeling the strain in her voice.

"I don't know. I was wondering the same thing." Patti gave a stiff, forced smile, then followed Joan's glance to the cans and jars on the floor. "I need to borrow a few dollars." A strangled laugh came from her mouth but there was no real joy. "I have to get back to Calgary. I'm almost out of gas." Her words were infected with desperation. There was no warmth in her expression. "Can you help me?"

How carefully this thirty-year-old woman had laboured to perfect her masquerade to convince them all that she was their contemporary. The hair dyed a solid black and tightly coiffed, thick foundation, heavy eye makeup and penciled lips. As a trained esthetician, if indeed that part was true, Patti would have learned the standard tricks to try to hide age. She would also know that the same techniques, used on a younger woman, would make her appear harder, older. Joan couldn't let Patti get away from Madden. Who knew who would be her next victim? She played along. "I'd like to help, Daphne, but I left my wallet at the motel." She edged toward the door. "I'll get it and come right back."

"I'll come with you."

Joan felt her plan unraveling. She tried to hide the tension in her voice. "Then let's take your car." If Gabe spotted Patti's rental car he'd stop them. He may have already issued an alert on the vehicle.

Patti followed her closely, their brisk footsteps echoing down the dark hallway, as the painted caricatures in the murals mocked them with ill-proportioned grins. Joan considered bolting but knew she would be no match for Patti in a race. When they stepped outside, Patti broke the silence.

"Let's take your car instead," she said stonily.

Although Joan was shaking inside, she played it as though there was nothing wrong, no urgency. "But the motel is on the highway. You could leave from there."

"Mine's on empty. I've been driving on fumes all day."

"Sure. Hey, have you had dinner? We could stop at Jacques and . . ."

"There's no time. I have to go, now!" Patti's voice was rising and her eyes were darting along the street, as though she expected to be entrapped at any moment.

Joan fought to keep her voice calm, gentle. "Sure, okay."

Patti clambered into the passenger seat before Joan could make it to the other side of the car. The rental car form lay on the floor. She winced. Why hadn't she given it to Gabe? As they drove, she glanced involuntarily at the pink form, but Patti didn't seem to notice. When they arrived at the motel, Joan knew that she'd have to move quickly -- straight into her room to call Gabe. He'd be able to catch up with them when she drove Patti back to her rental car. She parked. Her hands were shaking as she opened the driver's door.

"I'll be right back," she said with a smile.

Again, she fumbled with her key in the worn lock. Just as she got it in and turned the handle, that scent wafted from behind her.

Patti reached over her shoulder and pushed the door open. The first thing they saw was the pile of Patti's belongings strewn on Joan's bed.

"My wallet is in the drawer," said Joan, although logic told her that the charade was over.

Patti pushed the door and it slammed closed. She pushed the lock in the handle, slid the security chain into place then turned. They stared at each other.

"What are you doing with my stuff?"

"I had to be sure."

"What, before you went to the cops?"

Joan answered with a slight nod and a whisper. "Yes." She hadn't imagined being trapped alone with Patricia Pyle. She had always managed her life with careful advance planning and research. She couldn't stop staring. Patti was such a clear blend of Daphne and Roger. Her mother's voluptuous build, with her father's long, lean legs. A black ringlet had escaped from her ponytail. Was her natural hair raven blue like her mother's or angel-blond like her dad's trademark mop?

"I had to know where I came from." Patti sounded sad and frightened.

"I get it," Joan whispered.

"You do?"

"Sure." She measured her next words carefully. "How did she die, your mom?"

"She was always sick, as long as I could remember. Emphysema, ulcers, but it was the cancer that killed her. She suffered such pain. It wasn't fast, and it wasn't fun watching."

"I'm sorry."

"She was so ashamed. She said God was punishing her. She came back here, just once, to ask forgiveness." Patti's mouth twisted bitterly. "My grandmother called her a whore, her dad slapped her while she stood there on their doorstep holding my hand."

Gabe stood in the Stanfields' doorway, keeping his heavy black shoes planted on the hand-painted doormat. Marlena repeated the conversation that she'd had with Joan. He asked her to contact him if Daphne came back or if they heard from her. As he walked to his truck, his cell phone rang. It was Hazel.

"Thanks for getting back to me," Gabe said.

"Sure, kiddo, what's up?"

Gabe revealed that Patti was allegedly the orphaned daughter of Daphne.

"Allegedly?"

"Joan thinks so."

"And you doubt her? Ms. Pragmatic?" Hazel gave a low whistle. "The daughter is the mother. Boy, that's what you call searching for yourself."

"I'm not a jury or a judge." He paused. "But the evidence Joan dug up is convincing. Have you seen her? Have you seen Patti?"

"We just drove by the Couch on the way back from dinner. Her car is parked in the back lot there, but it looks pretty quiet."

Gabe instructed her to call him if she saw Patti. "But don't approach her. She's dangerous. A report came in a few minutes ago. She's on probation. She punched another woman in a road rage incident. Knocked out a couple of teeth. This girl is ready to explode."

Joan took another step toward the door. "And our names on the invitation list, you did that?"

Patti nodded. "She'd do anything I asked. I told her to make sure Roger had his own room, him being the *star* of the show.

I had to talk to him alone. I didn't want to embarrass him. He wouldn't want anyone to know I was his daughter. No, that would never do."

Joan responded softly. "But why did you bring a knife?"

"You knew him! Would you go in a room alone with him without some way to protect yourself?" The colour rose in Patti's face. "I watched him that night."

"What d'you mean?"

Her lip was trembling. "I saw him try to pick up every woman he met. Sex meant nothing to him. I saw what he tried to do to you in the hallway. Once I got in his room I figured it was a stupid idea. I was going to sneak back out again. I waited until he was in bed. I thought he was asleep, but he wasn't. He had his hands all over me in a second."

Joan recalled the horrible smell of Roger's breath in the hotel hallway. "Did you tell him that you were his daughter?"

Tears welled in Patti's eyes. "I screamed it at him. He was drunk. He wouldn't stop. He wouldn't listen."

"And then you stabbed him?"

"The knife hit his arm first. He got so mad and tried to grab me. I stabbed his chest. I closed my eyes and just kept stabbing. I wanted him to stop." She looked up at Joan. "Quit blaming me! He deserved it! I was so sure my mom had exaggerated. She was mad about so many things. But she was right about Roger Rimmer. My father was the devil."

Joan held up her hands. "Shh. I know. I know. If you just tell the police what happened."

"There's not going to be any police." She snatched up the cheese knife that Hazel had left on the dresser and slashed at Joan's arm.

"Ahhh!" Joan felt a searing pain. She took a deep breath. "Then just go. There's money in my purse. Take it."

Patti waved the double-pronged knife in her face. "You're coming too. Nothing's going to stop me from getting out of this town."

As much as Joan wanted to leave Madden, this wasn't how she had imagined her exit.

"It doesn't matter what I do now," threatened Patti.

A loud knocking erupted at the door. "Joan? Joan, are you there?" called a man's voice.

Patti swung toward Joan. "Who's that?"

"It's Mort," said Joan.

"Your husband? What's he doing here?"

"I'll make him go away."

Patti grabbed her around the neck. "Shut up." She pressed the cold blade against her neck. "Don't say a word or I'll kill you. Lord forgive me, but I will."

Mort continued to bang on the front door. "Joan? Are you there? Is everything okay?"

Joan felt the taut, muscular arm pulling tighter around her neck as Patti pushed her toward the patio door. She stared through the glass into the dark woods by the river. In the reflection she could make out the glinting knife digging into her neck. Above, Patti's eyes glistened like steel. She had never before smelled this level of animal fear on a human being. The religion that Daphne had tried to escape had caught up with her daughter. Normally she would use words to calm someone who was in distress but she was too afraid to speak. If Patti got her outside, away from the motel, into the woods, her chance to escape unharmed would be lost.

"Slide it open," hissed Patti as she pushed Joan against the patio door.

Joan spoke with every bit of calm she could muster, intently watching the reflection of her captor's eyes in the glass. "My wallet. You need the money to get away."

In the split second that Patti's eyes shifted to the dresser, Joan grabbed the blade at her throat and kicked back with her boot, hitting Patti hard on the shin. The pain of the sharp serrated blade slicing into her palm sent a shock through her nervous system and she let go of the knife. Patti swiped it toward her face; Joan ducked. Patti had the speed and strength of youth on her side, so Joan relied upon the element of surprise. She butted her head into the younger woman's stomach and, before Patti could regain balance, heaved herself on top of her, toppling her to the floor. The twenty extra pounds she usually resented was now working in her favour. The banging at the door sounded like a battering ram trying to break through.

"Help! Help!" she screamed.

The doorframe gave way. First into the room was Gabe, followed by Des Cardinal and another burly young officer. Des pulled Joan out of harm's way, while Gabe and the other officer took control of Patti. Wide-eyed, Mort entered the cabin. The last Joan saw of Patti was Gabe and Des half carrying her kicking form toward the RCMP squad car. It looked strange for two strong guys to be holding onto a petite woman so forcefully. Joan was disappointed in Gabe, that he'd doubted her evidence against Patti. He'd betrayed her in front of Smartt. Once Gabe had put Patti in the back of the police car, he glanced back at her and looked puzzled. That's when Joan noticed the familiar weight of Mort's arm across her shoulders.

Chapter Twenty-Six

Joan vacated her motel cabin. It wasn't only that the cops wanted access to the scene of a crime. The place now gave her the creeps. Hazel made her comfortable in her top floor hotel room, magically producing the ingredients for hot rum toddies, along with ceramic mugs, from her bottomless bag of travel supplies. Nothing could have impressed Mort more. Hazel took to him as though he were a warm summer breeze wafting through the door and, surprisingly, Lila was nice to him, too. He obviously didn't pose any form of threat, at least not to Lila and Hazel.

"How did you end up here?" Joan asked.

He grinned at her. "Nothing as exciting as a premonition." He took her hand and squeezed. "I convinced you to come on your own, then all this crap happens. You were so aloof on the phone. I had to come and make it up to you."

Hazel, bless her heart, changed the subject, repeating that she was disappointed to have missed the drama of the arrest.

Joan described every detail and Mort picked up where she left off. He'd gone to her cabin and heard Patti yelling. As he had pulled out his phone to call 911, Gabe had swerved into the parking lot in his truck.

"He came without you calling him?" asked Joan.

"Just like Dirty Harry." Mort smiled.

"That's our Gabe," added Hazel.

"He's not what I expected from your description, Joan. I thought he'd be some scrawny guy with thick glasses." Joan and Hazel shared a glance. Mort went on to describe how Des Cardinal had arrived at the motel moments after Gabe. He'd been a few blocks away checking out Patti's abandoned rental car.

Hazel turned to Joan. "You'll come to the Rimmers' with me. I don't want some cop breaking the news, not even Gabe."

It wasn't a question, but Joan nodded anyway. How strange it was who ended up in a person's human orbit, and how lucky they all were to have Hazel. Joan took her rum toddy to the bath that Lila had drawn for her. As she laid back, the scent of cinnamon, butter and alcohol filled her nostrils. Her mind drifted to an early September afternoon almost thirty-one years ago: cinnamon buns, dry leaves, warm sun through blue jeans, crows cawing . . . Soon she was asleep.

As the two women approached the Rimmer's tidy split-level, Joan could see the doctor, pained and frail, peeking through the curtains. By the time they reached the top step, he'd opened the door. The sacks of flesh hanging beneath his red-rimmed eyes made him look like an aging hound. Mrs. Rimmer smelled of eucalyptus heat rub and wore an ivory silk dress with nylons, a cardigan, and gold broach, as though she was expecting company or preparing to leave for church. She sat quietly, understanding that they had brought news. When Hazel gently explained that they had captured Roger's killer, her hand flew to her mouth.

Dr. Rimmer collapsed onto the sofa beside her. "Who? When did they . . . ?"

"An hour ago," said Hazel.

Joan began, "We came from there –"

"Who? Who did this?!" It came as a cry from Dr. Rimmer.

Laura Rimmer didn't move.

Joan wondered if this elderly couple could take any more. "It was the girl with the dark hair who claimed to be Daphne Pyle."

"She came here." The old doctor was agitated. "She told us she'd given birth to Roger's child but she wouldn't tell us where she is. We have to call our lawyer, Laura."

His wife put a hand on his arm and stared at him firmly. He went silent. Calmly, strongly, she spoke to him. "That girl is not the mother. She's our granddaughter." She grasped her husband's hand. "We'll hear what she has to say, Tom." He looked stunned, but she reminded him, "She's our family. She'll need us."

Joan gently touched her bandaged hand where the knife had ripped her skin and wondered if she'd ever be able to make such a leap. Laura Rimmer was a saint to embrace her son's killer. Of course Patti hadn't tried to stab any of them. She made a mental note to get a tetanus shot.

Hazel had squeezed in between Roger's parents on the sofa, offering to do everything that she could to make it easier. The three of them began planning how they could help Patti.

When Joan got back to the Twin Pines, she had been assigned a different cabin, one of the newer ones. The upgrades were great. As she stripped down to her underwear and slipped the thick white robe over her shoulders, she thought how nice it would have been to have had these comforts earlier in the week. She was wondering where they'd put Mort, when the phone rang.

"It hasn't been hard to get information out of Patti," Gabe said. "We told her to wait until there was a lawyer present, but she wouldn't shut up. There's someone there now giving her advice, a friend of Marlena and Ray's."

"Did she confess to Peg's murder?" asked Joan.

"It's like you said. She claims that she just wanted to shut her up temporarily, so she gave her some of Daphne's medications. She didn't even know what the drugs were. She just knew that her mom fell asleep after she took them."

"The bag of Daphne's stuff that she carried around?" said Joan.

"Right," said Gabe. "The drugs were just one of the things, along with the Facebook page, that she couldn't let go."

"Two things I can't figure out is how she found out about the reunion," said Joan, "and why did she want me here?"

"She was her mother's caregiver most of her life, especially at the end. She set up a Facebook page for Daphne, before she died, to distract her from the pain. Poor kid was probably drowning under the responsibility. She was trying to give her mom happy memories. There weren't a lot. She'd completely disconnected from her past. After Daphne died, Patti didn't close down the Facebook account. It was like keeping her mother alive in cyberspace You know, Joan, I can understand it in a way." Joan heard his empathy. It was his best trait. He continued. "Ed Fowler posted the reunion announcement on Facebook in February. That's when Patti got the idea. Daphne died considering her life a failure. All the kid wanted to do was give her mom's life a makeover, wipe away her shame. And meet the friends who were so important to her. That's where you came in. She did want to meet you, but she also thought she'd stand out if she was the only one who showed up who hadn't actually graduated. You were camouflage."

"And she wanted to meet her father," added Joan.

Gabe nodded. "Mr. Fowler posted that Rank would be performing."

"Poor kid. No matter how hard she tried, she couldn't bring her mom back to life."

"About this evening, Joan. Can I come pick you up for the memorial?" He hesitated. "Or are you coming with Mort?"

She told him that she hadn't seen Mort since she had returned from the Rimmers. "But don't worry about coming to get me, Gabe."

"It's not a worry. I want to. Let me."

She winced at his pleading. He had asked her to stand by him professionally, but then had disregarded her expertise. No matter how hard she tried to rise above it, she felt dismissed as a scientist. Had he been humouring her all along to get into her pants? She'd already decided to leave for Vancouver in the morning. The memorial was her last chance to say goodbye to Madden.

"I'll meet you at the school, Gabe." She glanced at the clock. It was already after six.

"Sure," he said and she hung up before he could say more.

Immediately the phone rang again. It was Mort this time. He was disappointed when Joan said she had other plans for the evening. He tried to pry his way in. "I want to meet all these people you've gabbed about for the past month."

"I don't gab!" She hated to use this trick with Mort, pretending to be hurt by a minor offence, using it to distract him. However, it worked with him every time. He was so concerned about offending her or anyone else for that matter, even his enemies. What could a girl do? Time was what she needed now. Time to think. Time to sort out her feelings. She suggested that he try Jacques for dinner and give her a full report in the morning.

The idea of a culinary quest cheered him. "I could come by later and tell you all about it," he suggested.

She laughed. "Give it up, Mort. I'll see you in the morning."

After she hung up, she decided to call her mom before she heard about all the action on the news and panicked. The phone rang several times and Joan began to worry — maybe she should call Anthony or David — but when Vi answered on the fifth ring, there was laughter in her voice.

"Joan!"

She spoke quickly to fill her mother in on the discovery of Patti Pyle, to explain that she had to get going to a memorial, such an unexpected closing event to the reunion.

Vi listened patiently, making dramatic exclamations. "It was good for you to go to Madden, Joan," she said finally.

"Mom, do you ever regret the way things turned out?"

"Everybody has regrets, Joan, but I don't let mine last for more than a moment. There's too much good in life to dwell on the negative." Another of Vi's generalizations, but through this one Joan understood something important: it took grace not to let yourself get bitter. "Now, you give 'hellos' to everyone from me. And Joannie?"

"Yes?"

"Let them know that Ed Fowler won't be there tonight."

"What do you mean? How do you know?"

"He's here with me. We have a lot of catching up to do. And Joannie?"

"Yes?"

"I love you and I'm very, very proud of you."

When Joan heard this her eyes misted. "I'm proud of you too, Mom." And she was, more than she had ever expected to be.

CHAPTER TWENTY-SEVEN

JOAN ENTERED AT THE BACK OF the gym and stood for a moment beneath humming fluorescents, watching her peers mingle between rows of folding chairs. The atmosphere of the memorial resembled a subdued pie social more than it did a funeral. Despite the tragedy of the past few days, everyone was relieved to know the story behind the killings and that the danger was past.

Looking over the crowd, she was struck by the vast array of shapes, sizes, and hair colours. How amazing that this group of women and men in their late forties had been sold on the illusion that a thirty-year-old woman, even one so cleverly disguised, was their contemporary. Patti had used a physical makeover and a few well-chosen stories to play into mass wishful thinking. If she had paid a fraction of that attention to scent, she might have got away with murder.

Hazel and Lila were holding hands, smiling at something Steve was saying. Marlena was holding onto Ray as though he'd blow away in the first puff of wind if she let go. Gabe was nowhere in sight. Probably held up at the detachment.

Candy was behind a folding table covered in a holly-and-sleigh-bell vinyl cloth, handing out plastic glasses of wine, laughing flirtatiously with a large man in a plaid shirt. Although his back was to Joan, there was something very familiar about him. She wracked her brain, and unable to contain her curiosity sidled up to eavesdrop. When she was within three feet, Candy saw her and lunged with arms spread wide. The man turned, and she was face-to-chest with Staff Sergeant Smartt.

He bowed his head in acknowledgement. "Ms. Parker," he said in his most formal tone and waited to see which way her judgment would swing.

Candy took him by the arm. "Now everyone is here, I'm going to make a speech. I'm so nervous but somebody has to do it." The colour had risen in her cheeks. Smartt kept his eyes on Joan.

"Do you have a first name besides Staff Sergeant?" asked Joan.

"Stuart," he replied.

"Well, Stuart, I would've suspected me, too. I'd be top of my own list, as a matter of fact, very top. You were doing a job. Can't fault you for that."

He smiled, then looked over the heads of the revelers and turned to Candy. "Do you have a liquor licence for this event?"

For a moment Joan worried that she'd unleashed a madman.

Candy's response was to slap him hard on the back. "C'mon, Stu, give me a . . . " and, a buxom Tammy Wynette, she spelled out the last word, " . . . b-r-e-a-k," accentuating every letter with a poke in his belly. Candy had completely charmed Staff Sergeant Stuart Smartt.

He hesitated as she charged toward the stage, then turned to Joan and spoke in his official voice. "It was a good move for Theissen to request your assistance."

"He told you?"

"I even forgive him for his little ruse this afternoon. If I'd known the truth, that he trusted this business about you smelling the accused killer, I would have taken you both in then and there." He knew that. "Theissen's methods are unconventional. I would have said 'criminal' if this hadn't worked out." At that, he strode across the auditorium after Candy.

Joan smiled. So Gabe had been watching her back the entire time.

Candy was calling for attention in a booming voice. When that didn't work, she stuck two fingers in her mouth. A shrieking whistle exploded across the gym. Once the many conversations petered out, she spoke.

"Hello, everyone. I'm so glad you're all here." She looked around, making eye contact with many of the forty or so people in attendance. "And so would Peg have been. Like most of you, I left Madden not long after high school. I went country . . . " Hoots went up in the crowd from several other ranchers. Once they'd settled, Candy continued. "Most of you became citified. But Madden stayed in our blood. Peg Wong knew that, and she knew it was important that we all come together again. She wanted us to remember that our roots are always here, in my case showing a lot of grey these days. Peg knew that we may as well embrace where we come from, give our own selves a little bit of lovin' for who we are." Her voice became shaky. She stopped for a moment, then started again with full volume. "Coming back to Madden and having Peg as a friend gave me my life back. She taught me that I was okay, even if I thought I was broken, especially because I thought I was broken. And I know that she thought all of you were great too."

Joan looked around and could tell that they were all relating. At times during the past few days, they'd forgotten about all the things they hated about this town. They'd embraced the good times and found that the bits that had turned them into pearls and diamonds — the irritants, the crushing weights, the rough stuff — ultimately had made them stronger.

"So," Candy raised her wine glass, "here's to Peg." She looked up toward the heavens. "We know you're here with us, doll."

Joan felt a tap on her shoulder and jerked her head around. Hazel and Gabe, like giant, unscrupulous five-year-olds were holding fingers over their lips, warning her to be silent. Each grabbed an arm and marched her out of the auditorium. As soon as the double doors closed behind them, she asked where she was being taken.

"You'll see," responded Hazel.

Joan looked up at the word "welcome" from the front seat of Gabe's truck, where she was squeezed between her two friends. Her lavender bath scent blended with Hazel's eucalyptus cough drops and Gabe's wet wool, coffee, and soap. It was the aroma of friendship. The evening sun cast dazzling bronze and coral tones on the trees behind the sign. In the old days, this would have been Hazel's dad's old truck, and they'd be driving behind Steve's old Parisienne, charging ahead, packed to the doors with teenagers. A couple of older 149cc motorbikes would be puttering up to the Welcome sign, loaded down with drivers and passengers, barely making it up the hill. Tonight the gravel parking lot was deserted, just as they wanted it to be. This would be their own reunion and their private goodbye.

While Hazel was in the woods peeing, Gabe knelt by the makeshift fire pit to stack the split pine and lay the dry kindling that he'd brought from his woodpile at home. Joan handed him the matches and admired his weathered hands as he opened the package. When he struck a match, the smell of sulfur and fresh pine filled her nostrils. This was her Gabe. The man with magical hands that could make fire, turn her to butter in bed, capture criminals. Gabe, who still found a way to win right over wrong, even if it meant breaking the rules. She rested her hand on his back. It was comfortable there.

When Hazel returned, they ceremoniously opened a bottle of lemon gin, sipping the potion to prove that they had made peace with the past. Between mouthfuls of roasted hot dog, Hazel revealed that Joan's life wasn't the only one that had changed paths as the result of Labour Day weekend 1979.

"Gabe told me about your pact," she revealed. "That the two of you would lose your virginity together that night if you hadn't already. We were stoned out of our gourds, and he was so serious."

When Joan looked to Gabe for confirmation, he smiled meekly. The attack by Roger had dominated her memory of that night. She barely remembered the pact.

Hazel continued: "When he couldn't find you, and believe me we tried, I was your stand in."

Joan was stunned. "But you were already . . . "

"A confirmed lesbian?" She nodded. "Yeah, but I felt sorry for Gabe, and I needed to know for sure." She slapped Gabe on the back. "And you did that, thank you very much."

Gabe slunk into his jacket. At no time in the past few days had he reminded Joan of the teenager he'd been as much as he did at that moment.

"Hazel, you know I could turn you around now, you sexy broad."

"Sure, lover boy," replied Hazel.

"Yeah, well," he continued. "You made it so crystal clear that I wasn't up to snuff, I didn't try again until after I was engaged."

Both women looked at him.

"You're kidding?" said Hazel.

He shrugged sheepishly.

Joan couldn't take her eyes off him. Gabe, stalwart and sure. As she studied him, she admitted to herself that their weekend romance had been coloured by a sepia filter. The feelings that made her heart pound were partially based on the excitement of their youth. She loved Gabe, but they were so different. She lived by the rules that he only recognized if they served his vision of rightfulness. The truth was she didn't really know him.

Epilogue

Joan couldn't remember Madden ever coming close to the autumn colour and light on display this afternoon in Vancouver. The sidewalks looked as though a painter had splashed brilliant splotches as far as the eye could see. As she rolled into her underground driveway on this misty Friday, the sun was edging down toward the horizon forming a palette of gentle pinks and mauves beneath the slate-coloured clouds above. She'd made a commitment to herself to be home before dark, although when the clocks turned back at the beginning of next month, she'd have to adjust her schedule to the time change. Her promise had meant passing on a high-profile gig as lead designer on an intriguing project to enhance flavours in frozen seafood. And she knew deep down that this resolution to work shorter hours wouldn't last forever. But she also knew that she'd never completely go back to her old ways.

She unpacked the groceries onto the kitchen counter, excited to be cooking for her entire family. Tonight was an event none of them ever thought they'd see: her mother's engagement party. Vi's betrothal to Ed Fowler had sent a shock through the family, but the tsunami that followed was a wave of joy and approval. When she heard the front door, she quickly finished chopping the onions and wiped her hands. She was ready for the embrace when Mort folded his arms around her.

A step behind him was Hilda, his stunning German date. They'd met online and Joan hoped it would last this time.

"Hey, you didn't wait for me!" Mort announced as he looked down at the onions. "And those need to be diced a little finer."

She grinned at him and picked up the knife. "I'm holding a weapon," she threatened, but he took it as an invitation. Removing the knife from her hand, he shoved a handful of envelopes toward her.

"Here's your mail." As he chopped and shared the highlights of his week, she sifted through the envelopes and stopped at one bearing the familiar blue-and-gold crest of the University of British Columbia. The return address was "Alumni Association". Without a moment's hesitation, she tossed it unopened into the recycling bin, before Mort could see.

"Let me pour you both a glass of wine; then I'll make the salad." She placed the remaining mail on the sideboard. It could wait. Gabe would be hungry after his long drive from Madden. When he arrived the party would really start. Every time he came to visit they got to know each other a little bit better. Somehow, they would make this long-distance relationship work.

Glynis Whiting has been writing professionally for over thirty years. For the past twenty years her focus has been writing, directing, and producing documentary films, such as the award-winning *Weight of the World* and *Worst Case Scenerio*. Recently she has turned her pen to prose and, based on an early manuscript of her first novel, *A Nose for Death*, she received the Vancouver Mayor's Award for Emerging Literary Artist. She is now working on the second of the Nosey Parker Murder Mysteries. Glynis Whiting currently lives in Port Moody, British Columbia.